LOVE à la MODE

LOVE à la MODE

STEPHANIE KATE STROHM

HYPERION
Los Angeles   New York

First Hardcover Edition, November 2018
First Paperback Edition, October 2019
10 9 8 7 6 5 4 3 2 1
FAC-025438-19228
Printed in the United States of America

This book is set in Bembo MT Pro, Avenir LT Pro, Wingdings/Monotype; Bjarne Handwriting, Feltpen Pro, Mrs. Eaves OT, Parisian FS/Fontspring
Designed by Tyler Nevins
Title lettering by Andrew Brozyna

Library of Congress Control Number for Hardcover Edition: 2018002891
ISBN 978-1-368-02709-0
Visit www.hyperionteens.com

For Max. There's no one else I'd rather eat with.

CHAPTER ONE

Henry

The girl across the aisle was staring at him.

At first, Henry had thought it was an accident. Maybe she'd just looked his way randomly, or maybe he'd imagined it, but it wasn't an accident, and he hadn't imagined it. She was definitely staring at him. Well, maybe *at* him wasn't totally right, but definitely *near* him. Her eyes were fixed somewhere around his hands, which were holding the latest issue of *Lucky Peach* magazine. It was weird.

She hadn't been staring when he'd gotten on the plane. She'd been sitting there first, which made sense, because Henry had been one of the last people in boarding group four to file in. He'd decided that, yes, the mini Oreos *and* the Teddy Grahams were *both* good snack choices, so he'd circled back around to Hudson News to get the Grahams, too, and had almost missed his boarding group.

Henry hadn't noticed the girl because she was pretty—even though she was. At first he'd just seen a white girl around his age sitting across the aisle from him, but when he looked again, he'd noticed her crazy-big brown eyes and the thick toffee-colored braid resting on one shoulder. It was the exact same color as the peanut butter toffee Henry had gotten once at the Wicker Park Farmers Market and had never been able to find again. But he'd noticed her because she was just sitting. Calmly. Patiently. Like she was waiting for something. Not on her phone or on an iPad or flipping through a magazine like almost everyone else he'd passed, but just sitting there. She was still sitting, but now she was staring at him. Well, near him.

Henry tried to wedge himself farther into the aisle, trying to get away from the people next to him. Yes, his elbow had been bumped by the flight attendants twice already, but a bruised elbow was vastly preferable to what was going on next to him in 22A and 22B.

"We're on our honeymoon!" 22A and 22B had announced proudly, Mrs. 22B waving a giant diamond inches from Henry's nostrils. They had then proceeded to practically merge into one person, giggling and kissing, and now Henry was the unwilling third wheel in their relationship.

Man. Eight hours was a long flight no matter what the circumstances, but being stuck next to 22A and 22B was truly cruel and unusual. It wasn't the longest flight Henry had been on—that had been when his family had gone on vacation to Hawaii, and that had *also* been an excruciating trip. His little sister, Alice, had won "Halfway to Hawaii" and wouldn't stop gloating about the bag of chocolate-covered macadamia nuts she'd been awarded as a prize for correctly guessing the exact time their flight hit the halfway point. She hadn't let Henry eat any of them, and she'd eventually left them in the backseat of their rental car, where they fused into one giant melted nutty chocolate blob. Mom threw the bag out. On the flight back to Chicago, when Henry had fallen asleep on the plane, Alice had drawn purple zoo animals all over his arms. In marker.

But in eight hours, he'd presumably be purple marker–free—unless 22A and 22B had other tricks up their sleeves besides surviving without oxygen—and he'd be in Paris. *Paris.* Henry still couldn't believe he was really going to Paris. And not just going to Paris on vacation, but to study there. To live there. To *cook* there. For the next nine months, Henry wouldn't be just another random Chicago junior. He'd be a chef-in-training at the École Denis Laurent, the most prestigious cooking program for high school students on the planet. It still sounded unreal when he thought about it, like some place that couldn't possibly exist, but it *was* real, and he was going. Henry couldn't wait to trade the brown rice and bulgogi he served at his parents' restaurant for boeuf bourguignon and béchamel. There wasn't anything wrong with bulgogi—he was just ready for something different.

Henry wouldn't miss standing behind the register all weekend, every weekend, but he'd miss the kitchen. His earliest memories were of sitting on the counter, swinging his legs. *Taste*, Dad would say, and Henry would open his mouth for a meltingly rich mouthful of pork belly, or the sweet tang of pickled carrots, or the salty brine of a still-raw shrimp. It was Dad who taught Henry to eat, and then to cook. Because you have to know how to eat before you can know how to cook.

So Dad was the first person Henry told about the program in Paris, when he'd discovered that Chef Laurent took twenty high school juniors to live and train at his cooking school every year.

Henry had pulled up the website excitedly, heart hammering in his chest like he'd found a lottery ticket on the sidewalk. And in a way, he kind of had. The website was full of the accolades of graduates of the program, graduates who had James Beard nominations and featured spots at the Food & Wine Classic in Aspen and well-reviewed restaurants that Henry recognized by name alone, the kind of places you'd have to book a reservation for a year in advance. The kind of place that Henry dreamed of running someday. The kind of place Henry *could* run, once his year at the École guaranteed him a stage—kind of like an internship—in any kitchen he wanted, and ensured his future. Henry could still feel Dad's hand on his shoulder, almost an electric current running between them as they checked out the website together.

Dad loved Chef Laurent. Maybe even more than Henry did. "The only person on the Food Network who's still cooking," he'd say proudly, like Chef Laurent was his other son. Henry and Dad watched a lot of Food Network. Mom had no patience for it. "The last thing I'd ever want to watch is other people cooking," she liked to say, shaking her head in disbelief. "Don't we see enough of that every day?"

Mom liked crime procedurals. Henry didn't understand how watching people get chopped up and stashed in boxes was more relaxing than watching Chef Laurent sweat some onions in his bright French farmhouse kitchen, but sometimes Henry felt like there was a lot he didn't understand about his mom.

You don't have to go, you know. That's what she'd said. What she'd chosen to say after Henry had tried to hug Alice—she'd acquiesced half-heartedly—as his family stood on the sidewalk by the departures drop-off at O'Hare Airport, when they were supposed to be saying good-bye. Like Henry was just going to turn around and get back in the car. Like this wasn't everything he'd ever wanted.

She'd tried to backpedal, to say that even if he did go, it could just be a thing he did that looked great for college. That he didn't have to be a chef. She didn't want Henry *trapped in a restaurant for the rest of his life*—her words, not his. Henry didn't understand how someone who had knowingly married a chef could take such a dim view of running a restaurant, but as Mom liked to say, you didn't run a restaurant, it ran you. Mom wanted Henry to do something, anything, that didn't involve chopping vegetables. Henry was pretty sure Mom would prefer he cultivate a career cleaning up toxic waste—provided he had a degree from a four-year college. And preferably if he wore a suit while doing so.

This wasn't the first time they'd had this fight, and it wouldn't be the last. He knew it would come back over and over, like the refrain in that awful cello piece Alice wouldn't stop practicing. What would it take, he wondered, to get Mom on board? The École hadn't been enough. A stage at Alinea? A James Beard Award? A Food Network show of his own? Cookbooks with his face on them and kitchen utensils with his name on them and a fast-casual restaurant in O'Hare? Whatever it was, he'd do it. And then she'd see.

Henry flipped to the next page in his magazine, and the girl gasped, loud enough that he heard her over the drone of the engine and the sucking noises of 22A and 22B. He looked up, and they made eye contact, and the girl blushed the exact same color as the end-of-season raspberries he'd bought from Mick Klug Farms at the farmers market the Sunday before he left.

Why was everything about this girl making him think about food? He must not have bought enough plane snacks.

"I'm so sorry," she said, although her voice was so quiet, it was more of a whisper. "Oh my gosh. I'm so sorry."

Henry stifled a laugh at *Oh my gosh*. He couldn't remember the last time he'd heard someone say *gosh*.

"It's okay," he said.

"No. No it's not. Oh my gosh."

"Seriously. No worries."

"I was reading over your shoulder, and that was rude, and creepy, probably, and I definitely shouldn't have been. I really am sorry."

"It's fine. Really. Stop apologizing."

"Sorry," she said again. "I mean—not sorry. Sorry. Argh!" she exclaimed. "Saying sorry for saying sorry is like that snake eating its tail. You can't get out of it. It's linguistic quicksand."

They looked at each other, and Henry was struck again by her eyes—the exact color of tempered chocolate. Perfectly tempered chocolate. Again with the food? What was *wrong* with him? He must have been hungry. Too hungry. He reached into the open bag of mini Oreos in his seatback pocket, grabbed a fistful, and shoved them in his mouth.

Mistake. He started chewing madly, but the Oreo mass seemed unconquerable. The girl probably thought he was crazy. Why couldn't he swallow these Oreos? How were there so many of them? Henry chewed in panic as he contemplated the girl. What should he do now? He should offer her some. Right? Definitely. It was only the polite thing to do. Otherwise, he was being rude *and* gross.

He held the bag out across the aisle. He smiled, then realized there was almost no way his teeth *weren't* decorated by a fine coat of Oreo crumbs and quickly closed his lips. Henry was leering like the Grinch with chipmunk cheeks full of Oreos, and he had never felt more stupid. But he must not have looked entirely deranged, because, tentatively, the girl reached her hand in, and took out exactly three mini Oreos. Like a normal person.

Finally, Henry swallowed and cast about desperately for a new conversation topic. He jammed the Oreos back into his seat pocket—fat chance of him eating those again anytime soon—and looked down at his magazine. His magazine! That was a thing they could talk about.

"Wow." Henry whistled. "That's quite a cake. I would have gasped, too."

Henry had never seen a person literally light up before, but that's what this girl did. And now *he* was staring. Which he definitely needed to stop immediately. So Henry looked down at his magazine again. It *was* quite a cake. Three layers of cake interspersed with layers of jam and frosting—no, not frosting, lemon cheesecake, according to the caption—and topped with pickled strawberry icing and a ring of what looked like crumbled cookies. The sides were exposed so they could see every delicious layer.

"It—it's Christina Tosi, isn't it?" she asked shyly. "The exposed sides of the cake. That's her thing. And the milk crumbs on top. I recognize them, from the *Momofuku Milk Bar* cookbook."

Henry looked closer—she was right. They weren't cookies.

"Milk crumbs?" he asked, trying to imagine what a milk crumb could be.

"They're made with milk powder and white chocolate. Really good. You're not supposed to eat them on their own, I don't think, they mostly go in or on other things, but they're so good I always save a few to snack on. What flavor's the cake?"

"Strawberry lemon." Henry was staring at her again. He'd never seen someone's face look like that when talking about baked goods before. Not even his dad when he talked about the cinnamon buns at Ann Sather.

"Mmm. Strawberry lemon. That sounds good. That one's not in the cookbook. I've only made the apple pie cake and the birthday cake, of course. I make that one every year for Owen's birthday. My brother," she clarified. "Although . . ." She chewed her lip distractedly. "I'm not sure what he's gonna do this year. His birthday's in November. Maybe Mom will make him the Funfetti cake. You know, from the mix. Like I did. Before I knew about Christina Tosi."

She went back to chewing on her lip. Henry hadn't known that someone chewing on her lip could be quite so distracting.

"You can have it," he blurted out.

"What?" she asked.

"The magazine. You can have my magazine." Henry held it out across the aisle eagerly. Too eagerly.

"Oh, no, I couldn't—"

"Please—"

"No, I can't—"

"Take it." He shook it at her insistently. It was suddenly incredibly, vitally important that the girl take his magazine. "Take it. Please take it."

"I—I— When you're done reading it," she said firmly. "It's *Lucky Peach*, right? I've never seen a paper copy before. I've only read it online."

Henry nodded and put the magazine back on his tray table, wondering how he could possibly read it knowing she would have it after him. What if he left a sweat print? What if there were chocolate stains on the earlier pages? Had he *drooled* into his magazine, somehow? Who knew what horrors he'd left behind, lurking within those innocent pages? Was there an embarrassing way to read a magazine? Probably. And he'd probably been doing it the whole time.

"I just have one question—sorry."

Henry looked up, and the girl smiled at him apologetically. Henry smiled back, probably in a lame way. Why was everything he did so *lame*?

"Just one question before I let you finish reading. Sorry. I mean, I'm not sorry." She cleared her throat and shook her head. "I'm just curious. Does it say if she used an offset spatula to ice the top layer? Ateco, I'm assuming? Does it say what size the blade is?"

And that was the moment Henry started to worry that he might have fallen in love.

CHAPTER TWO

Rosie

Rosie couldn't remember the last time she'd talked to a boy she didn't know. She'd known every guy in her class since kindergarten, or earlier. And sure, it wasn't like East Liberty was so small that Rosie recognized every single person who browsed next to her in the aisles at Walmart, but she recognized a lot of them. Rosie couldn't run an errand or grab a pop somewhere or even walk down to the mailbox without being stopped for a *How's your mom?* or a *When's that brother of yours gonna stop playing soccer and start kicking for the football team?* Didn't matter which brother. They were convinced that any one of Rosie's four brothers was the missing piece that would guarantee East Liberty's long-awaited championship win. Even Owen, and he was still years away from high school.

Maybe that's why Rosie was so nervous talking to this boy. Maybe that was why she'd apologized so many times. And said *gosh* way too many times, just like her nana. Rosie was never nervous talking to any of the boys at school, not even when Brady Gill had asked her to homecoming last year, and he was a year older. But she'd known him because he played soccer with Cole and Ricky, her older brothers, and there was nothing particularly exciting or nerve-wracking about talking to him. The boys at school were taller than they'd been in kindergarten, sure, and some of them had developed muscles they definitely hadn't had when they were five, but other than that? They were pretty much the same.

But this boy was a surprise. The *Lucky Peach* magazine was intriguing, of course, but Rosie also found herself fascinated by *him*. He was so hot she almost couldn't look directly at him, but found herself staring at the most random things, like the short-trimmed dark hairs at the nape of his neck as he bent over to read. And the straight line of his forearms when he pushed up his sleeves. And his long, tapered fingers with cut-short nails, crisscrossed by faded burns and the scarred mementos of cuts long gone. Not unlike her fingers, actually.

His hands. The magazine. Rosie realized with a sudden jolt—a jolt that inexplicably caused her pulse to speed up and a distinctly uncomfortable, clammy feeling to start at her temples and spread toward her neck—that this boy was almost definitely heading to Paris for Chef Laurent's École. He had to be, right? She'd only seen hands like that on the guys who worked at Cracker Barrel with Mom. They were chef's hands.

The man sitting next to Rosie shifted as the baby in his arms stirred in his sleep. The baby, all fat, rosy cheeks and a soft blond crown of hair, drooled prolifically onto his dad's collar. Rosie thought, with a pang, of Owen, her youngest brother.

Most of her earliest memories were of Owen as a baby, how fascinated she'd been by this chubby pink creature with his endless supply of drool. Not unlike this baby.

The parents had apologized, profusely, as they'd filed into the seats next to Rosie, diaper bags and sippy cups swinging from every available appendage. "You're stuck with us!" the mom had chirped, as the dad announced, formally, "Congratulations. You've officially lost the airplane lottery. An international flight with an eleven-month-old." Rosie had waved off their apologies. She'd been babysitting for so long, she was pretty sure there was nothing this baby could do that would bother her. Honestly, she was *glad* to be sitting next to the baby. He'd distracted her.

Before the family had arrived, Rosie had been sitting in her seat almost paralyzed with fear. Not so much because she thought the plane would crash—not really—but because she just didn't know *what* would happen, what it would feel like when the plane took off, how *she* would feel, hurtling through the air thousands and thousands of feet into the sky. And it was that not knowing that Rosie hated. That was why she loved baking. Baking was all knowing. If you followed the recipe, you got exactly what you intended. An apple pie never surprisingly turned into lemon meringue halfway through the baking process.

Maybe it was that not knowing that had sent Rosie's stomach into a tailspin of anxiety on the five-hour drive to the airport in Chicago. What did she know about France, really? Aside from the food? Appallingly little. Maybe that was why she was having such a hard time imagining it, or believing that this was really happening, that she'd really be living in another country in a matter of hours. When she tried to picture herself in Paris, alone, all she could conjure up was a mental image of herself walking down foggy cobblestone alleyways, wearing a beret, even though Rosie was pretty sure she didn't have the kind of head shape to pull off hats.

It was funny—for almost as long as she could remember, Rosie had been desperate to get out of East Liberty. Desperate to be somewhere that things were different—somewhere where people didn't know everything about her. Or think that they knew everything about her.

But when it was actually time to go, it was a lot harder to leave than she'd thought it would be. Rosie had thought she'd be racing into the airport terminal, tearing straight toward an adventure that smelled like butter and sugar. But Rosie hadn't raced anywhere. Hugging Cole, then Ricky, then Reed, then Owen, and then Mom good-bye, she'd swallowed back the uncomfortable prickling of tears against the back of her throat. No crying. Not today. This was everything Rosie wanted.

When her mother had first told her about the École, Rosie had been lying on her stomach in bed, watching old clips of Chef Laurent's first TV show, *Laurent du Jour*, on YouTube. Mom had knocked on her bedroom door, and Rosie hadn't even looked up when she came in, hadn't looked up until her mother had dropped a packet of papers right next to her.

"Chef Laurent, Rosie," Mom had said.

Her mom knew all about Rosie's Chef Laurent obsession. Well, *Rosie* wouldn't call it an obsession—but everyone else did. She did own all of his cookbooks and read his blog religiously and watch all of his shows—the ones currently on the air and the ones she could only find online. So maybe she was a little obsessed. Which didn't even really make sense, because he wasn't even a pastry chef, like Rosie wanted to be. But there was something about him, the way he casually tossed off jokes in the kitchen as easily as he flipped a crêpe, something that made Rosie feel warm and safe, like she was sitting right there at the table with him, about to tuck into a perfect roast chicken or a salade Lyonnaise. But the idea that she could *actually* be in the same kitchen as Chef Laurent was something she didn't even know how to process.

Rosie had read the application six times right then, with her mom next to her, squeezing her hand excitedly. She'd read it again when she woke up in the morning. When she came home from school. Every night before she went to sleep. She read it so many times that she had all the questions memorized. Had all her theoretical answers memorized. She could have taken a quiz on it, could have recited that application as a dramatic monologue. But she hadn't applied. For weeks, she hadn't applied.

Rosie was more of a pastry chef than a chef, she argued with herself. They probably wouldn't want someone who was primarily interested in baking, since the program was mostly cooking. But Rosie *did* cook, all the time, and just because she wanted to be a pastry chef one day didn't mean she didn't want to learn how to cook from *Chef Laurent*, in *Paris*.

The idea of being so far away both terrified and thrilled her. But at least it made her feel *something*.

You miss one hundred percent of the shots you don't take.

Wayne Gretzky had said it first. But Cole said it all the time. And Dad had said it, too. Rosie heard it, then, in Dad's voice, as she sat in front of her computer in her darkened bedroom, staring at the application the night before it was due. And Rosie knew that she had taken very few shots in the sixteen years she'd been on this planet. And then she thought of Mom, finding the application, printing it out, probably hoping that Rosie would do something besides sit in her room, reading cookbooks and watching old cooking shows on YouTube. And Rosie wanted to do more than that, too. Almost as if Rosie's fingers were moving of their own accord, she filled out the application with the answers she'd had memorized for months, and she clicked SUBMIT.

The baby stirred in his sleep, bringing Rosie back to the plane. He fluttered his hand like a small pink starfish, opened his eyes briefly, looked at her, then closed them again, heavy.

Rosie was having a hard time imagining life without her brothers. What would it be like? Not to be *one of the Radeke kids* or *the Radeke girl*, but just to be Rosie? Her teachers at the École wouldn't call her Cole's sister or Ricky's sister. They'd just call her Rosie. This was uncharted territory, and Rosie was surprised to find herself feeling less excited and more unmoored by the prospect than she thought she'd be.

Hoping to ground herself, Rosie closed her eyes and thought of butter, the way other people probably pictured relaxing tropical idylls. Her favorite thing in the world was creaming butter and sugar, watching the way two disparate ingredients come together to form something new. She could picture it in her mind, back in the kitchen at home: the soft pale yellow of the butter, the old wooden spoon, and the cracked brown mixing bowl. Butter was magic. The starting point for cookies and cake and pie and muffins and everything good.

"I'm finished."

Rosie had been so lost in her thoughts she'd stopped staring at the boy and was almost surprised to see him there, holding the magazine across the aisle.

"I'm Rosie," she blurted out.

"Henry." He grinned. "Not, you know, finished."

"Ha." She'd spoken the word—*ha*—instead of actually laughing.

"Please, spare me the pity laugh."

"It wasn't a pity laugh. It was just . . . strange." *Just strange?!* What a weird thing to say. *She* was *just strange*.

"Do you, um, do you still want it?" The magazine sagged a bit in his hand.

"Yes. Please."

She took it from him and placed it carefully on her tray table, and then the lights went out, plunging the cabin into a soft darkness that Rosie guessed meant it was time to sleep.

"Crap," Henry muttered. "I guess you can, uh, turn the light on."

Rosie pressed the button above her head with the little light bulb icon. A beam of light that could have been used as a highway flare illuminated her seat. Embarrassed, she turned it off again.

"That's okay," Rosie said quickly. It seemed rude to have her light on, even if the family next to her had been sleeping since the flight attendants had announced they'd reached cruising altitude.

"They have the lights there for a reason. It's *your* light. You can turn it on."

"I should probably sleep anyway," Rosie said, hoping Henry

didn't hear any reluctance in her voice. "Here." She slid the magazine off her tray table. "You can have it back."

"Nah. Don't worry about it." Henry pressed a button, and his seat reclined. He stretched, his arms almost grazing the call button for the flight attendant. "Keep it. I read it already."

"I can't keep it." Rosie shook her head firmly.

"It's a gift. From one member of row twenty-two to another."

"I can't take a gift from you. I don't know you."

"Sure you do. I'm Henry."

He smiled, and Rosie felt an unfamiliar, swoony feeling, almost like when she flipped through the glossy pages of a brand-new cookbook, but better. He was even cuter when he smiled, and at that moment, Rosie would have done anything to keep him smiling—at *her*.

"I'm going to return this," Rosie said, but she tucked it into her seatback pocket all the same. "Once I've read it. Tomorrow morning. Or whenever they turn the lights on. I'm reading it, and then I'm giving it back to you."

"Boy, Christmas must be really rough in your house. Did you give Santa a hard time like this, too?"

"Santa's not real."

"NO." Henry catapulted his chair up to its full upright position, jaw open and eyes full of betrayal. "SANTA'S NOT REAL?!"

"Shhh!" Rosie admonished him, but she found, again, that she was smiling. She couldn't even remember the last time she'd smiled quite so much in such a short time. "You'll wake up the baby."

"Yeah, that baby's really about to lose it."

Rosie looked over. Baby and Dad were passed out with matching expressions, jaws hanging open as their heads lolled.

"And who's gonna traumatize that baby more?" Henry asked. "Me, waking him up? Or you, telling him Santa's not real?"

"I don't think he's verbal."

"When his first words are *Santa's not real,* you're really going to feel like a terrible human being."

"I'm going to sleep now," Rosie announced. Reaching down, she grabbed the small pillow—what an odd texture the pillowcase had—and pulled a fleece blanket and a sleep mask out of a plastic bag. "And then in the morning I'm reading your magazine, and then I'm giving it back to you."

"Oh you are, are you?" Henry wadded up his own pillow by his neck. "How will you even find me? What if I disappear into the streets of Paris and you never see me again? Kind of thwarts your magazine plans, huh?"

"Well, Henry," Rosie said, "I think I'll be able to find you. I'm going the same place you are."

CHAPTER THREE

Henry

"What?" Henry said.

"To the École."

Henry had no words.

"Chef Laurent's program," Rosie prompted.

Henry should definitely say something now. Respond. It was time to respond.

"I mean—I mean I think that's where you're going?" she added, more tentatively.

Of course she was going. *Of course she was.* He should have known from the way she was looking at the cake, from the fact that she knew what an Ateco blade was, from the shiny new burn on the inside of her right thumb, from the fact that maybe it wasn't surprising that two students traveling to the program—admittedly, a small program—would be on the same flight that departed from America's third-largest travel hub.

"Well, Rosie," Henry said, the same way she had said *Well,*

Henry, and was rewarded with a small smile, "I'm glad to hear that."

"Me too," Rosie said. Henry watched as she blinked once, then again, slowly, the prelude to falling asleep.

Henry had a million questions. Like where in Chicago she was from. Why she decided to apply to the program. When she fell in love with food. But the great thing, the beautiful thing, was now Henry had time. So he didn't need to ask her any questions now. He could just let her fall asleep. He *should* just let her fall asleep. And he definitely shouldn't say, *Hey, there's a chance I maybe might love you. Because of cakes.* No, that was not the thing to do. That was a thing a crazy person would do. And Henry was determined not to be a crazy person. Both in general and in this specific situation.

Henry didn't remember falling asleep—which was a stupid thing to think, because nobody remembers falling asleep—but it was the first thought he had when the cabin lights flickered on, flooding the plane with light and awaking him with a jolt. His cheek was damp, and Henry was dismayed to see he'd drooled a vastly impressive puddle onto his pillow and the back of his seat. Sneaking a quick glance at Rosie, who was, thankfully, curled away from him, he rubbed his hand on his cheek, trying to dry it, then quickly stuffed the damp pillow under the seat in front of him.

First, Henry heard a whole mess of French he didn't understand. Then an announcement that they'd be landing in Paris in thirty minutes. He craned his neck into the aisle to see the flight attendants wheeling a cart his way, hopefully containing breakfast and something to drink. His mouth was dry and sour-tasting. Probably because he'd drooled all the liquid from his body.

Henry grabbed the box the flight attendant proffered and opened it to reveal a plastic bottle of water, a yogurt, and a flattened croissant. Real exciting stuff for his first meal in France. He tore off one end of the croissant and stuffed it in his mouth. Not great, but definitely not bad. But when that much butter was crammed into just a couple square inches of pastry, it was hard to go wrong.

Henry wished Mr. and Mrs. 22A and 22B would open the window shade so he could see something of the descent into Paris, but it was firmly closed, and Mr. 22A snored contentedly against the shade. If the two of them hadn't been so annoying, they'd almost be cute, sleeping curled up together.

Henry turned to find Rosie blinking at him, sleep mask pushed up, a small halo of static hair sticking out from beneath it.

"I think you missed breakfast. You want some?" Henry held the croissant toward Rosie. With the end that looked like he'd bitten off facing her. Way to go, man. Gross.

"No thanks." Rosie shook her head, then peered at the croissant. "Look at the lamination. It's nonexistent."

"Lamination?" For someone who had been asleep not thirty seconds ago, that was an impressively multisyllabic word.

"Look." Rosie leaned out into the aisle, hoisting herself up by balancing an elbow on the armrest. "Do you see how it sort of looks like there's layers? But they're all doughy and squashed together?"

"Yeah."

"That's the lamination. It's what makes croissants flaky. The layers should be distinct, separate, and never doughy. You should be able to see way more layers than this. That's how you can tell this is not a very good croissant."

"Huh." Henry took another bite, chewed, and swallowed. Very good or not, he was still hungry. "Lamination. Learning already. And classes haven't even started yet."

"Not much of a pastry guy, then?"

"I have no problem *eating* pastries—"

"You'd just rather not bake them," Rosie finished for him.

"Exactly. Unlike you, I'm guessing."

"You guessed right. I like cooking, but for me, baking is, well . . . it's everything."

Rosie looked down the aisle. The flight attendant was long gone.

"Want my yogurt?" Henry asked.

"Sure," Rosie said, only the slightest pause of hesitation before she spoke. Henry handed her the box with the yogurt and the spoon in it.

"You know a lot about croissants," he said.

"I made my own, once," Rosie said as she pushed the plastic wrapper off the spoon. Henry realized he was staring at her mouth as she took a bite of yogurt and quickly refocused on her eyes. "Wasn't worth it. Took all day and everyone in my family said they'd rather have a Pillsbury Crescent."

"Ouch." Henry winced. "Sounds like something my little sister would say. She thinks all the food I make is too 'weird.' Won't even try it."

Rosie laughed, setting her spoon down in her yogurt cup. "At least with pastry everyone's pretty much guaranteed to try it. Half the time they'll say I shouldn't have bothered, that whatever I made tastes just as good coming out of a boxed mix, but at least they'll try it. It's hard to say no to butter, sugar, and flour."

"I think that's the national motto of France."

"I guess I'm going to the right place, then."

The flight attendant announced that they were approaching their final descent. Henry polished off his croissant, noticing that Rosie followed the instructions like she was worried she might be tested on them later. Seat upright. Tray locked. Gaze straight ahead. And a grip on the armrest that suggested maybe she wasn't the most comfortable flier. Henry wanted to reach across the aisle, to take her hand in his, but that seemed like a bold move for someone who was running on a lot less sleep than normal. And he wasn't sure he'd be able to pry Rosie's arm away anyway. That looked like a pretty viselike grip.

The plane bumped to the ground with a minimum of disturbance, and there was a smattering of polite applause for the pilot. Henry pulled out his phone and switched it off airplane mode—the only notification that popped up was a text from Verizon reminding him how astronomically expensive it would be to send and receive texts. He felt around in his seatback pocket in case he'd forgotten something, but there was nothing in there except for empty snack wrappers. This was it. Henry zipped up his hoodie like that might make him more ready, somehow.

Henry looked over, and Rosie was bent over her phone, smiling to herself. "Ridiculous," she muttered. "I don't usually talk to myself, promise," she said, when she noticed Henry looking at her. "It's just— I mean, look at this."

She held her phone across the aisle, and Henry leaned across to read it. It was a series of texts on the Skype app:

Ricky

Hey, Rosie, have you seen my sweatshirt?

Ricky

The gray one

Ricky

The dark gray one

Ricky

With the hood?

Ricky

The one I wore at your going-away thing

Ricky

Nevermind, it's in Brady's car

Ricky

And actually do you know where my gym shoes are?

Ricky

The gray ones

"Who's Ricky?" Henry asked, casually, like there wasn't a coil of jealousy curdling in his stomach.

"My brother," she answered, and his stomach uncurdled. "I love him, but he's completely helpless. Ricky loses everything, but nobody can ever stay mad at him. He misplaced the trophy after state finals last year and didn't even get in trouble. The trophy turned up two weeks later in an Arby's bathroom and the coach said, *No harm, no foul*, and that was that." Rosie rolled her eyes as Henry laughed. "He's a year older than me, but you'd think he's the baby. Owen, the actual baby, managed to remember I was on a plane and don't know where anyone's gym shoes are. See?"

She held up her phone again:

Owen

> Are you too old to get those wings from the pilot?
> YES OR NO.

"He's never been on a plane before, either," Rosie said, shrugging. "He had a lot of airplane questions."

"This was your first flight?" Henry asked.

"Yeah," she said, coloring slightly. "We're more of a driving family, I guess."

"Then we gotta get those wings."

The fasten seat belt sign switched off, and Henry was out of his seat in an instant, trying to unfold his body from the position it had been cramped in for so long. He grabbed his backpack and slung it on. Who cared if there were twenty-one rows in front of him? He was ready to go. With Rosie. And he was going to get her those wings.

"Henry." She was standing now, too, a beat-up navy backpack with the initials CJR stitched onto the front resting on her seat. Rosie was shorter than he thought she'd be, her eyes about level with his chin. "We are not getting the wings. They are for *kids*. Little kids."

"Or kids at heart," he argued. "Just say they're for the baby!" Henry pointed to the baby carried by the guy standing in front of the seat next to Rosie.

"I'm not scamming the baby out of his wings." The baby chose that moment to spit up all over his dad's shoulder. Henry grimaced sympathetically.

"That baby doesn't even know what wings are. He'd probably try to eat them! Honestly, we're saving him from a choking hazard."

"I'm too old for wings, Henry," Rosie said as she stepped out into the aisle, the line finally moving toward the doors of the plane. Toward Paris and everything that meant.

Henry waited until they got to the front of the plane and approached the flight attendant in her navy suit and printed scarf, and he said, "Excuse me, ma'am?"

"You are not seriously doing this," Rosie muttered.

"My friend here has just successfully completed her first aviation experience." He gestured to Rosie proudly. Rosie looked like she was trying to turtle into her sweatshirt and disappear.

"Congratulations," the flight attendant said warmly.

"Thanks," Rosie said, a lot less warmly.

"And we were hoping she could get a pair of wings to mark this momentous occasion."

"They're normally just for kids—"

"I *told* you, Henry—"

"But it sounds like this was a big day." The flight attendant winked and pulled a pair of plastic wings out of her pocket. "Enjoy Paris, you two."

"Well, that was completely mortifying," Rosie said as they walked onto the jet bridge, but she was laughing.

"That was not completely mortifying. That was barely even mildly embarrassing," Henry scoffed. "And you're glad you have them now, aren't you?"

"Maybe."

Henry thought her smile meant more than just maybe. And as she looked down at the plastic pin in her hand, he felt something within him soar.

"Come on." Out into the airport, he moved to the side, stepping out of the way of the tide of people streaming off the plane. "Pin them on."

"It's silly." She hesitated, turning the wings over in her palm.

"Yeah," he agreed. "It is."

Those chocolate-colored eyes met his, and they crinkled with a smile. She pinned the wings onto her hoodie. Henry saluted her, and she laughed.

"I guess this is it, then," she said.

"This is what?" he asked.

"The beginning."

CHAPTER FOUR

Rosie

Rosie touched the wings on her sweatshirt like they might keep her safe somehow, like the little plastic angel that had swung from the rearview mirror of Nana's car before Mom had said she shouldn't drive anymore. Cole had driven that car off to college in Akron, but Rosie doubted Cole still had the angel swinging from the rearview mirror.

It was silly to place any amount of faith in a piece of plastic. But Rosie found her hands migrating to the wings again, tapping them surreptitiously. She snuck a glance at Henry as he walked confidently through the terminal. *He* was silly. That whole thing with the wings was ridiculous. And yet . . . she was glad she had them. Maybe silly wasn't the worst thing to be.

It was certainly better than *overwhelmed*, which was how Rosie was currently feeling. If Rosie hadn't met Henry on the plane there was a definite chance she might have barfed in the middle of Charles de Gaulle airport. A representative from the program had told Rosie and her mom that someone from the École would meet her and any other students flying in that day at the airport, but the airport was enormous—full of places to get lost in.

"Come on." Henry walked decisively to the left like he knew where he was going, threading through the crowds of people, backpack slung casually over one shoulder. Rosie struggled to keep up, making sure never to lose sight of the dark hair and black hoodie. "*Bagages,*" he said.

"What?"

"Bagages," he repeated. "That's gotta be baggage claim. Yeah?"

"Yeah," Rosie agreed. Obviously. But she could barely process anything, she was so distracted by the burble of French around her, the women making *click-click-click* sounds as they trod down the walkway in heels, wheeling smart roller bags behind them, casually tossing their elegant scarves around their necks. There were other Americans, too, mostly wearing sweatpants, and Asian tourists talking in languages Rosie didn't know well enough to identify, and a group of rowdy Brits who shouted, "Sorry, love!" when Rosie walked into them accidentally, distracted by the food kiosk with the stand-up poster of a pop that read COCA LIGHT instead of DIET COKE.

It was such a little thing—a stupid thing, really—a pop ad, almost identical to one she'd seen at home. Except there was that difference, that one small difference, that meant Rosie was in a different country. It took almost every ounce of willpower she had not to abandon Henry and run into the Relay store so she could dive into the candy bars and study their labels, or peruse the pops in the big refrigerated case or see who was on the covers of the magazines here.

"What?" Henry asked. She'd slowed in front of the Relay enough that he'd noticed. "French candy!" he shouted joyously, and barreled past her into the store.

How had he known what she was thinking? He was rifling through the candy bars near the register, grabbing great big handfuls, wrappers crinkling as he tried to stuff them into his grip. "Rosie! Look at this."

"It's a Kit Kat," she said, somewhat disappointed that up close, French candy looked pretty much the same.

"A Kit Kat *Chunky*," he said, like that made all the difference. She watched as he piled all of the chocolate onto the register, the Kit Kat and a Lion bar and a Bounty with coconuts on the wrapper and lots of different things with red-and-white Kinder labels. Kinder. Wasn't that German? Like kindergarten?

"What are you going to try first?" Rosie asked as they left the store, Henry clutching a bulging plastic bag.

"*We* are trying the Lion bar. Because it has the best wrapper."

Henry unwrapped the chocolate, splitting the cartoon lion's face in two. He broke off half the bar and handed it to her. She took a bite.

"It's so sweet!" Rosie covered her mouth as she talked through her food.

"*You* think it's too sweet? I thought you were all about dessert."

"I don't eat a lot of candy. I like baked goods."

"Well, I like *this*." Henry finished the rest of the bar in one bite. She offered her half-eaten half to him, and he tossed that in his mouth, too. "It tastes like a Twix."

"With Rice Krispies in it."

"*That's* what the crunch is." Henry nodded, and Rosie found herself pleased by his approval. "Nice."

Henry tossed the wrapper into a trash can and they filed onto the escalator, descending under a sign with a helpful arrow pointing them toward bagages. Carefully, Rosie jumped off the last step—she'd never really trusted escalators—and right away she spotted a woman holding a clipboard, standing next to an East Asian teenage girl who sat on top of a giant suitcase. Rosie would have recognized the logo on the back of the woman's clipboard from a million miles away.

"Look." Rosie tugged on Henry's sleeve and pointed, like she was a kid at the state fair who had just spotted the fried Buckeyes stand. "She's from the École."

"Then I guess that's where we're going."

Henry readjusted his backpack and loped toward the woman. Rosie followed, her heart hammering in her chest.

"Bonjour," the woman said, and Rosie panicked, for a moment, thinking that maybe she'd misunderstood the website. Rosie was almost positive that the only language requirement she'd seen listed was English, but maybe she'd read it wrong and the whole program was in French. "Who have we here?"

"Henry Yi and, uh, Rosie . . ."

"Radeke," Rosie supplied automatically, relieved to hear English.

"Radeke. Right. Rosie Radeke and Henry Yi, reporting for duty."

"Our Chicago arrivals." The woman crossed something off her list. Now that Rosie really looked at her, she was younger than Rosie had thought. Maybe just out of college.

Her dark hair was cut short, showing off simple pearl earrings and a perfectly tied silk scarf knotted at her neck. So many of these French women were wearing scarves! Had Rosie missed a memo somewhere? The only scarf she'd brought had UNIVERSITY OF AKRON and GO ZIPS stitched on it in gold and blue—last year's Christmas present from Cole after he'd been accepted early decision—and it was definitely more functional than fashionable.

"Chicago?" The girl sitting on her suitcase spoke for the first time. She was clutching a tiny paper coffee cup and wearing sunglasses indoors, which was sort of weird, although the fluorescent lighting in the bagages area was pretty aggressive.

"I'm from Bucktown. You know Chicago?" Henry asked.

"Not at all. Deep dish pizza and hot dogs?"

"You've got the important stuff down."

"I'm Yumi." She waved at Rosie and Henry. "From Tokyo."

"That's gotta be a long flight." Henry whistled.

"You have no idea. If my parents loved me enough to fly me direct, it would have been twelve hours and forty-five minutes. But since they don't, it was twenty hours and thirty-one minutes. Thanks, Mom and Dad." Yumi took a sip of her drink and grimaced.

"This was the biggest coffee they would give me," she complained. "Can you believe this *merde*? My Barbies drank bigger coffees."

"It is not the size of the coffee that matters, it is the quality," the woman with the clipboard said.

"Sure. I bet that's what you tell all the baristas." Yumi winked. "My flight landed at five forty-five this morning. Madame Besson and I have had a lot of bonding time."

"Ah yes, of course, my manners. Forgive me." The woman smoothed her scarf, which was already perfectly smooth. "I am Madame Besson. I work in operations at the École."

"Learned a lot about the fascinating world of operations," Yumi said. "Glad we had this special bonding time, Madame B."

"Of course." Madame Besson did not look particularly glad. "As soon as you get your bags, and our students from New York return from *les toilettes*, we may head to the École."

"Speaking of les toilettes . . ." Henry dumped his backpack at Rosie's feet. "I might head that way myself."

"Where in Chicago are you from?" Yumi asked Rosie as Henry wandered off. "Not that I'll know what your neighborhood is when you tell me, but feel free to share."

"I'm not from Chicago. I'm from Ohio. East Liberty, Ohio," Rosie added, as though anyone outside of Maumee County had ever heard of East Liberty.

"East Liberty, huh?" Yumi pushed her sunglasses up on top of her head. "Just how many Liberties does Ohio have?"

"More than enough. Trust me."

"God bless America." Yumi took another swig of her coffee. "My mom's American. Dad's Japanese. I've only ever been to California, though. I've still got a lot more of the country to see."

"Well, maybe you should come to East Liberty. You know what they say about Ohio: So Much to Discover."

"*Really?*" Yumi asked skeptically. "Do *they* really say that?"

"Um. No. Not really. But it's the state slogan."

"Sounds like false advertising."

"What about 'Ohio: It Is a Place,'" Rosie suggested.

"Love it." Yumi grinned, and Rosie grinned back.

"Hey, Yumi." A tall, lanky black guy with closely cropped hair plopped down next to Yumi on her suitcase, his knees folded up like he was sitting on a doll's chair. "You have any more of those green tea Kit Kats?"

Kit Kats again? Maybe they *were* French. Rosie was reconsidering everything she thought she knew about candy.

"No," Yumi said. "You ate them all. And that was supposed to be my stash for the whole semester."

"I'm starving," he moaned, clutching his belly dramatically. Rosie's stomach gurgled loudly in response. "Sounds like I'm not the only one," he teased, but Rosie didn't mind. He teased like she was in on the joke, too.

"Guess I should have gone for that sad-looking plane croissant," she said wryly. "I'm Rosie."

"Marquis." He held out his hand for Rosie to shake. "And airplane pastry is *never* acceptable."

"Agreed." Rosie smiled. "It's nice to meet you. Are you, um, from New York?" Rosie had never met anyone from New York before. She wondered if he'd eaten at any of Chef Laurent's restaurants. Or Marcus Samuelsson's. Or Daniel Boulud's. Or at Jean-Georges. Le Bernardin. Eleven Madison Park. Rosie's mind boggled at the possibilities. In East Liberty, she had the choice between eating at Applebee's or Cracker Barrel. And that was it.

"It's the shirt, huh? Is the shirt too subtle?" Marquis looked down at the silver Brooklyn Nets logo on his T-shirt.

"He's not even *from* Brooklyn; he's from the Upper West Side," Yumi complained. Rosie nodded along like she knew what the difference was between Brooklyn and the Upper West Side.

"One Hundred and Twenty-Sixth Street is not the Upper West Side. It's Harlem."

"According to a think piece I read online, pretty much everything is the Upper West Side now," Yumi announced.

"That doesn't even make any sense—"

"Also Marquis washed dishes at Red Rooster this summer." Red Rooster! That was one of Marcus Samuelsson's restaurants! "*And* he won the *Chopped* Teen Tournament," Yumi continued. "So, you know, he's a boss. Maybe he's almost as good as me. Although I have some doubts about his knife cuts."

"My knife cuts are fine, Yumi!" Marquis ran his hands over his head. "How do you even know that?"

"I googled you while you were in the bathroom."

Rosie prayed Yumi wouldn't google her. Rosie's own online footprint would reveal only the fact that she'd won the Holy Cross Lutheran Church Bake-Off every year since she'd been old enough to enter. And it would probably turn up the article the *East Liberty Gazette* had run after Rosie had been accepted to the École. The headline blared "Recipe for Success" above a terrible picture of an uncomfortable Rosie desperately clutching a whisk. It wasn't exactly *Chopped*. Good gravy. *Chopped*! Rosie was seriously out of her depth.

"Looks like the Midwest is here. Finally. Can we go now?"

Rosie turned around to see who had spoken. This girl had white-blond hair, tumbling in long, loose waves that framed her face. Rosie was never sure exactly what contouring was, but she was pretty sure this girl was contoured. And a quick glance at her feet revealed suede booties with dangerously high heels. Heels! Who wore heels to travel? Or to *cook*? Rosie looked down at her own beat-up gym shoes, and Marquis's immaculate Nikes, and Yumi's lilac high-tops. Rosie's feet, at the very least, fit in. And yet Rosie couldn't help but wish she had a pair of suede booties, even though they were obviously so wrong for the kitchen. This girl just looked so . . . together, in a way that Rosie didn't think people were together in real life. And she found herself wondering with a pang if Henry would think this girl was pretty, not that she had any right to wonder that. She'd only shared row twenty-two with Henry. Nothing more.

"This is Clara Parker-Green," Yumi drawled. "Of the New York Parker-Greens."

"Whatever, Yumi." Clara turned to Madame Besson. "Are we leaving now?"

"I'm Rosie," Rosie said, but if Clara heard her, she didn't acknowledge it. Well. Rosie shouldn't have expected everyone to be as friendly as Henry. And Yumi. And Marquis.

A loud beeping alarm startled Rosie. She jumped and looked around. Was that a fire alarm? Did they have to evacuate?

"It's the belt starting on baggage claim." Clara was definitely looking at Rosie now. "Have you not been to an airport before?" she asked curiously. "Wait a minute—are those plastic pilot wings on your sweatshirt? Like for little kids?"

"Let's go get your stuff." Yumi jumped up and grabbed Rosie's arm before Rosie could die from shame, and pulled her toward the baggage claim carousel with a big number five on it. "Come on, Marquis. You can help us carry it."

"It's not that heavy," Rosie said, but Marquis pushed himself up to standing and ambled along behind them.

"What a friggin' crab," Yumi muttered as they waited in front of the moving conveyor belt. Rosie followed Yumi's narrowed eyes to where Clara was tapping on her iPhone. "She's been here for an hour and she's barely said two words to us."

"Maybe she's tired. One of those people that can't sleep on a plane," Marquis offered.

"Please. Like that's a long flight? I was on a plane for—"

"Twenty hours and thirty-one minutes, yes, we know," he finished for her.

Henry came back from the bathroom and waited with them for their bags. As everyone chatted and laughed and compared the various meals they'd been served on their flights, Rosie's embarrassment faded away, and she realized for the first time that this wasn't just going to be an incredible opportunity to learn from one of her heroes. This was going to be *fun*. Even if, you know, she hadn't been on *Chopped*.

"There's mine!" Rosie felt a weird thrill spotting her bag coming down the ramp, like she'd won a prize. Even though it wasn't a prize, just her lackluster wardrobe. "The green one."

"Who's in the military?" Marquis asked.

"My dad." Rosie stiffened, feeling, somehow, that there was a little less air in the terminal.

"Cool. My uncle's a marine." Marquis grabbed Rosie's bag off the belt and, thankfully, said nothing else about her bag or her dad or the military. A couple minutes later, after three false alarms, Henry grabbed the correct black rolling suitcase off the belt, and they went back to join Clara and Madame Besson.

"Roland is outside with the van," Madame Besson said as she led them outside. Clara didn't introduce herself to Henry, which, in a group of only five people, was so rude Rosie's mom would have spit if she had seen it. Mom. Rosie pulled up her e-mail—she was still connected to the Wi-Fi from the airport—and sure enough, there was an e-mail from Mom waiting for her. All she saw was the subject line—*Proud of you <3*—before hurriedly closing the window. Rosie was worried she'd get swamped by a wave of homesickness that would leave her in a flood of tears, and then Clara would really have reason to sneer at her. But she should still let Mom know she'd landed. So she dashed off a reply—*Landed. Love you*—and sent it before she could think too much about home.

Clara rolled over Marquis's foot with her suitcase and appeared not to notice at all, even as Marquis winced with pain. Maybe everything people said about New Yorkers was true. Although Marquis was perfectly friendly, so maybe it was just a Clara thing. Or maybe Clara was like Cole's high school girlfriend, Mikayla, who had been so beautiful she'd gone on to pose as Miss December in the Cincinnati Ben-Gals calendar, but had been mean as a snake.

They exited through the revolving door, and Rosie waited to feel like she'd really arrived in Paris. But the road outside looked just like the road to O'Hare. And when Rosie climbed into the back row of the van next to Yumi, the van was just a van. And as they drove away from the airport, Rosie waited to see Paris, to *feel* Paris, but all she saw was ugly suburban sprawl and big superstores. It looked way too much like the drive from East Liberty to Cleveland. And it was grayer than she had thought it would be, too.

"Don't worry," Yumi whispered. "Every city is ugly next to the airport. Even the most beautiful city in the world."

Rosie was relieved to hear it.

"Hey, Madame B," Yumi yelled toward the front seat of the van.

"Can you *not*?" Clara asked.

"Madame B." Yumi ignored Clara. "Do you have our roommate assignments?"

"I do not," Madame Besson said, and she turned the radio up—rather pointedly, Rosie thought.

Roommates. Rosie prayed she'd be sharing a room with Yumi—best-case scenario, obviously—but prayed even more fervently that she wouldn't be sharing a room with Clara. Rosie knew she shouldn't judge—she could hear Mom admonishing her for making snap decisions about people—but there was something hard and cold about Clara that scared her. She seemed too glossy and perfect. And like someone who definitely wouldn't tolerate the level of clutter that Rosie was accustomed to.

Accustomed to. Like anything about the École would be anything Rosie was accustomed to.

CHAPTER FIVE

Henry

"N ow *that's* more like it," Marquis said as the van bumped its way along narrow cobblestone roads.

"We have entered Le Marais," Madame Besson announced. "Le Marais is one of the oldest neighborhoods in Paris, home to more buildings from before the revolution than anywhere else. We are nearly at the École."

The van executed a particularly harrowing turn, and Henry saw a blue-and-white street sign framed in green right outside his window, slapped onto the side of the building: RUE DES MINIMES. The van started to slow and paused at the entrance of what looked like a castle. Henry goggled at the enormous wrought iron gate set into an even larger stone arch, big enough that the van could drive through. He got a pretty good look at some seriously fancy stonework as the van pulled into a cobblestone courtyard.

"What *is* this place?" Marquis asked.

"This is the École Denis Laurent, of course," Madame Besson said.

Henry didn't know anything about the history of architecture, and he'd barely passed the unit on the French Revolution, but even he could tell this was some Marie Antoinette–level stuff. The building was shaped sort of like a U, with the cobblestone courtyard in the middle. There were two floors with enormous windows, each with its own balcony. Smaller windows, round with white trim around the window panes, poked out of what looked like a third floor under the roof. This was a *mansion*. An estate.

"Yeah, but . . . what *is* this building? Or, uh, what was it?" Marquis pressed.

"It is the Hôtel des Minimes," Madame Besson said.

"It's a hotel?" Rosie asked. Henry could hear the confusion in her voice.

"No. It's a *hôtel*," Clara corrected, emphasizing even more the fact that Madame Besson hadn't pronounced the *h*. "It's not like a hotel in English. It just means a big townhouse, like a place the nobility used to live in before the revolution."

"Correct," Madame Besson said, pleased.

A townhouse. Henry had seen some nice townhouses in Bucktown—some of his classmates lived in places that had to be worth at least a million dollars—but this wasn't a townhouse. It was a palace. And it was certainly unlike anything Henry had seen before. This was where he was going to *live*?

"The Comte de Crossé built the Hôtel des Minimes between 1651 and 1655 as his in-town residence," Madame Besson explained. "It is the smallest of the *hôtels particuliers* still standing today."

This was the *smallest*?! It looked almost as big as Henry's school back home. Maybe bigger. Quite possibly as big as a whole block in Chicago.

"It had fallen into quite the state of disrepair before Chef Laurent purchased it and converted it into the École. You may leave the van now."

Henry was too shocked to move, and it seemed like everyone else was, too. Except Clara, who was the first to follow Madame Besson out of the van. The rest of them straggled out after her, Rosie bringing up the rear, and Henry watched her staring up at the building, mouth hanging open slightly as her eyes darted from window to window.

"It's crazy, right?" Henry asked, dawdling at her side.

"It's *insane*." She shook her head. "It's bigger than town hall. And the police station and the firehouse put together. The only thing in East Liberty that's this big is the Walmart."

"East Liberty?"

"Ohio," she clarified. "Home."

"You're not from Chicago?" Henry shouldn't have assumed she was from Chicago. Millions of flights from all over the world went through O'Hare every day. She could have been from anywhere. But Henry found himself disproportionately disappointed by the fact that Rosie wouldn't be back in Chicago when this was all over. Even though he knew it was way too early to be thinking about *when this was all over*.

"Nope. Cleveland and Columbus have closer airports, but O'Hare's got more flights."

"Collect your things. This way, please." Madame Besson started walking toward the front door. Henry grabbed his suitcase out of the back of the van, and stopped short of grabbing Rosie's, too. Should he carry it for her? Was that cool or condescending? Henry wished he had any idea what he was doing. But Rosie made the decision for him by taking her bag and following Madame Besson. "You have not much time to eat and change before your first lesson."

They were starting already? Today? Boy, these guys did not waste any time. Rosie looked at him and raised her eyebrows, a subtle signal of disbelief.

The front door was ridiculously enormous, but Henry was surprised to see that inside, the École wasn't quite so overwhelming. The five of them stood clustered in a foyer, and yes, the staircase was big, but it was carpeted with a sensible maroon runner. There was no chandelier hanging from the ceiling and no naked angel babies painted on the walls. It was a lot less intimidating than he'd expected it to be. The cream-colored walls were decorated with black-and-white pictures of food hung in mismatched frames, and there was a ceramic vase with a flower arrangement standing on the antique-looking hall table. Henry dumped his bag on the floor along with everybody else's.

"To your right is the dining hall. Please take a sandwich and return promptly. There will be time to explore later," Madame Besson promised. The dining hall had sturdy wooden tables with plain chairs, and the hardwood floors were scattered with dings and nicks. Portraits decorated the walls, and Henry stepped closer to inspect one. Underneath the photo of a woman in chef's whites, a little golden plaque proclaimed:

MALLORY ORBACH, JAMES BEARD RISING STAR CHEF OF THE YEAR. The next one was DARNELL SIMS, THREE-TIME *CHOPPED* CHAMPION. Then EMILIO PUCCHETTI, CHEFS OF AMERICA PASTRY CHEF OF THE YEAR. And then one he recognized—EVAN PARK, TOP CHEF. Henry had watched the whole season. He reached out to touch the golden plaque, for luck, as if all the things these chefs had accomplished since leaving the École might magically rub off and transfer over to him. Because this, right here, was everything he wanted. And with the École Denis Laurent on his resume, he'd be able to do all of this and more.

Henry turned away from the portraits to see everyone clustered around a table with a wicker basket full of sandwiches and a bunch of bottled waters. He hurried over and took a baguette filled with what looked like ham and cheese, wrapped in wax paper. He bit off the end that wasn't in paper. Delicious. The ham was salty, the cheese was creamy, and the baguette had the most spectacular chew he'd ever encountered in bread.

Rosie, next to him, hesitated in front of the basket of sandwiches, looking them over.

"Pretty sure they're all the same," he said.

"No, it's not that . . . I was just wondering if I should take two," she said sheepishly. "At home, with my brothers, you kind of have to take any opportunity you can to grab food and hold on to it. They're like walking garbage disposals."

"Brothers? How many do you have?"

"Four."

"Four?!" Henry exclaimed. He couldn't imagine having so many siblings. He could barely handle one Alice.

"Now, please," Madame Besson said.

Henry grabbed a second sandwich and stuffed it into the crook of Rosie's elbow. For a minute, she looked like she might put it back, but then kept it, grinning, which left Henry wondering how it was possible that making Rosie smile had become so important to him so quickly.

Henry and Rosie hurried behind the others and grabbed their stuff. They struggled up the stairs, balancing bags and baguettes. The dorms, Madame Besson explained, were on the third floor. Girls' dorms in the east wing and boys' in the west. Boys were never allowed in the east wing and girls were never allowed in the west wing. Curfew and quiet hours were strictly enforced. And she, Madame Besson, lived in the central wing along with some of the other staff, and would be personally enforcing the rules. Henry, of course, was already familiar with these policies. They were pretty much the only reason Mom had gotten on board with him coming to the École.

"I will escort the ladies to their dorms. Gentlemen, please head to the west wing. Henry, you are in room 304W, and Marquis, you are in 305W."

"That kind of sounds to me like you *did* have our roommate assignments the whole time," Yumi accused.

"Come along." Madame Besson ignored Yumi and swept down the hall. Rosie waved at Henry with her half-eaten sandwich as she walked away from him.

Henry and Marquis followed the center wing to the end, then turned and headed into the west wing. Up here, the ceiling was much lower, and the windows were round, like big portholes. Between the windows there were more black-and-white photographs, mostly street scenes of Paris, but a few of a young Chef Laurent in the kitchen.

"Gotta admire a guy who chooses to decorate with his own face," Marquis noted when Henry paused to look more closely at one of the pictures of Chef Laurent. "Maybe I'll put up some glamour shots of me in my room."

Henry laughed, and they resumed their journey into the west wing. Rooms 304W and 305W were right across the hall from each other. When Henry went to open the door, however, it opened from the inside before he could even touch the doorknob.

"My friend! Yes! At last, you are here!" There was a giant filling up the entire doorframe. This guy had the approximate build of a refrigerator. He leaned down to hug Henry, and Henry felt his heels start to lift off the ground. "Please, please do come in." He stepped out of the doorway, and Henry followed, exchanging one last glance with Marquis before he did so. Marquis looked like he was stifling a laugh.

The inside of the room looked a lot like what Henry imagined a college dorm would look like. There were two narrow beds pushed against opposite plain white walls, two desks with chairs, and two sets of dresser drawers, all made of the same blond wood. The window was small but let in more light than he had expected, especially considering how gray it was outside. One of the beds had a blue-and-white woolen throw neatly folded at the end of the maroon comforter the École had provided. Henry rolled his suitcase next to the other bed.

"I'm Henry, man. It's nice to meet you," he said to his beaming roommate. A thick curtain of blond hair hung down to the boy's eyes, and he shook it away every few seconds, reminding Henry, not unpleasantly, of an Old English sheepdog.

"Ah, Henry, yes! So nice to meet you. I am Hampus."

Hampus. That was not a name Henry had ever heard before.

"Where are you from, Hampus?"

"Jukkasjärvi."

Henry stared at his roommate, not entirely sure whether that had been a place or a sneeze.

"It is a small town in northern Sweden. Near Kiruna. You have heard of Kiruna, perhaps?"

Henry had not, in fact, heard of Kiruna.

"It is not surprising. Sweden is a big place with many small places within it. Where have you traveled from this day, Henry?"

"Chicago."

"Chicago!" Hampus's eyes lit up. "You have been to Alinea, yes?"

"I wish." Dinner at Alinea cost, like, three hundred bucks. Dad had promised he'd take Henry when he graduated. Of course, Mom only said *We'll see* whenever Dad brought that up. Mom would probably end up taking him to the Cheesecake Factory.

"Ah. Too bad. Someday, perhaps?"

"Hope so."

"Perhaps when your new friend Hampus comes to see America, yes?" Hampus laughed.

"Perhaps," Henry agreed, laughing along with him. Henry suspected he'd have a hard time feeling bummed living with Hampus. The guy was a six-foot-seven bundle of pure enthusiasm.

"My friend. Henry. You should put on your jacket, yes?" Hampus suggested. "It is almost time for our first lesson."

His jacket. It was lying on his bed, neatly folded, a chef's coat of pure white, the École's insignia embroidered above the left chest pocket. He couldn't believe it. His very own set of chef's whites.

Henry tore off his hoodie and shrugged on his jacket, pulling it on over his T-shirt, his fingers shaking as he did up the buttons.

It fit perfectly.

CHAPTER SIX
Rosie

Rosie was the only student who didn't have a knife kit. It seemed statistically impossible, that out of twenty students, Rosie was the only person who didn't have one. If it had been so essential to bring a knife kit, then it should have been on the packing list, which it most emphatically was *not*. Rosie had cross-referenced and highlighted and checked that thing within an inch of its life. And zero kitchen supplies had been mentioned. It had been *implied*, Rosie thought, that everything they'd need for class would be provided. So she hadn't thought to bring anything. Certainly no knife kit, which she didn't even own.

Standing at her table near the back of the room, Rosie's eyes traveled from knife kit to knife kit. Her own station looked oddly empty, a gleaming expanse of chrome and not much else. The whole setup of the room reminded her of *MasterChef*, or, oddly enough, of her chem class last year, except there was an enormous kitchen with multiple oven ranges where

Ms. Emond's desk had been, and the whiteboard was on rollers off to the side, not mounted to the wall. There were two columns of five tables facing the front of the room, each table long enough for two students to share, and each equipped with two ovens, two gas ranges, and two wooden cutting boards. Her very own oven. Rosie ran her hand along the temperature knob, unable to resist touching it. The oven was so spotless there wasn't so much as a fingerprint on it.

The table was set up for two, but Rosie was alone. Her roommate hadn't been in her room when she'd dropped her stuff off, and by the time Rosie had made it down to the classroom, the only people she knew were already at full tables. Henry stood next to a blond giant at the front of the room—presumably, his roommate—and Marquis was at the table across from them, next to a dark-haired guy Rosie hadn't met yet.

Yumi was a couple rows behind Marquis, but unfortunately the station next to Yumi was occupied by Clara and her gleaming white-blond hair. Rosie couldn't fathom why, exactly, Yumi would have chosen to stand next to Clara.

Rosie looked away from Yumi's station, her eyes roaming around the room. This was, by far, the nicest kitchen she'd ever seen in her entire life. The only other professional kitchen she'd been in was at the Cracker Barrel where Mom worked, and that was a cramped, windowless expanse of chrome, dominated by the industrial oven and its adjacent trays of cooling biscuits, and the huge dishwashing station that churned out an endless supply of clean plates. Unlike at Cracker Barrel, there was just so much *space* in the kitchen here at the École. And it was so bright! The windows all along one side let in light that warmed the cream-colored walls and reflected off the gleaming copper pots and pans that hung from every available surface. Rosie wondered what was in the giant stainless steel fridges, and in each of the jars and containers nestled into the built-in shelving on the walls. One wall had the largest spice rack Rosie had ever seen. Another had more kinds of flour than the whole baking aisle at the Walmart back home—she saw all-purpose flour, cake flour, bread flour, pastry flour, doppio zero flour, and something darker, probably buckwheat. Rosie wished she could run over and open the tubs, and rub the flour between her fingers. She'd never seen or felt doppio zero in real life, but knew it was supposed to be the secret to tender pasta. Next to the flour was something she wanted to explore even more— sugar. Granulated sugar, caster sugar, confectioners' sugar, pearl sugar, cane sugar, demerara, turbinado, muscovado, light and dark brown—Rosie's mind boggled at the possibilities of all the different things she could make with these sugars, how each choice would fundamentally alter the nature of whatever she baked: change the crumb structure, the color, the texture, *everything*.

"*Attention, étudiants.*" A woman in chef's whites, older than Madame Besson—maybe about Rosie's mom's age—walked to the front of the room and clapped her hands twice. The conversational murmur immediately died down. "*Bienvenue à l'École Denis Laurent.* I am Chef Martinet, and when Chef Laurent is away, I run the École Denis Laurent."

Chef Laurent was away? Rosie's heart plummeted to the bottom of her gut. How could he not be here? She had assumed she'd be learning from *him*, not from this stern-looking woman with deep frown lines etched around her mouth. Rosie tried to hide her disappointment, but she felt a wave of loss, of uncertainty, of fear that maybe this wasn't the right place for her. She had decided to apply because of Chef Laurent. What if this whole thing had been a mistake? Was she going to *cry*?! No. Of course not. That would be *ridiculous*. Out of the corner of her eye, Rosie saw Clara looking at her curiously. Stop it, Rosie, she told herself. Rosie looked behind her, away from Clara, blinking, trying to get it together.

She locked eyes with a guy at the back of the room and choked on a gasp. Because it wasn't just a guy, it was Bodie Tal. *Bodie Tal.* He must have registered her recognize him, because he winked. Rosie quickly looked back up at Chef Martinet.

Bodie Tal. Rosie had never had posters of CW stars or pop singers hanging up in her locker, but even she could admit she'd always had a bit of a thing for Bodie Tal. Which was, admittedly, a weird celebrity crush, since Bodie was definitely more of a celebrity in the food world than in the general population. It was no coincidence that the issues of *People* magazine Rosie splurged on just *happened* to feature articles on Bodie in the kitchen with his dad, noted "bad boy of baking," superstar pastry chef Dash Bray. Dash had never married Bodie's mom, Israeli model Sendi Tal, but he was obviously a big part of Bodie's life. Rosie had seen Bodie many times on Dash's Food Network show, *Cake Bomb*, and as a guest judge on *Cupcake Wars*, *Cake Wars*, and *Kids Baking Championship*. Rosie knew enough about him to know that he loved cream cheese frosting, but he didn't like American buttercream, and he wasn't impressed by cakes that looked amazing but didn't have solid flavor profiles or the proper texture. In short, she knew *way* too much about him. He'd definitely become more notorious in the past couple months, though, because of the controversy surrounding the ad campaign he'd done for Calvin Klein, modeling with his dad. A lot of family decency groups had been really upset that a sixteen-year-old had been modeling something so revealing. She'd seen Bodie Tal in his underwear! His *very small* underwear. And now, here he was, standing behind her. *Winking*.

She sneaked another look at him. His eyes, the same gray-blue as his dad's, were even more striking in real life. His hair was buzzed, showing off the high cheekbones, strong jawline, and full lips he'd inherited from his model mother. And he'd pushed the arms of his chef's jacket up to reveal the full sleeves of tattoos Rosie had obviously seen in his underwear ad. Were sixteen-year-olds even *allowed* to get tattooed? Was that legal? Or did laws not matter when you were basically culinary royalty? Wait a minute—wasn't he Chef Laurent's *godson*? Rosie was pretty sure she'd read that somewhere. She must have still been staring, because Bodie Tal mouthed at her, "Pay attention." But he smiled right after, so she knew he was joking. Bodie Tal. Joking. With *her*. Rosie blushed and vowed to focus on Chef Martinet from now on.

"We will now watch a video that will introduce you to life at the École," Chef Martinet announced. So Rosie had definitely missed the welcome speech. Great. Chef Martinet had probably thanked everyone for bringing their knife kits. "Madame Besson, you may play the video now."

Madame Besson, seated at the back of the room, reached

up to dim the lights, just as a South Asian girl in chef's whites bustled in the door by Chef Martinet, her thick black ponytail bouncing as she hustled past.

"Sorry, sorry. Terribly sorry," she muttered as she made her way through the aisle of tables, a deep blush rising in her cheeks. Rosie cringed on her behalf as every single student stared.

"Punctuality is, of course, to be expected at all times." Chef Martinet wasn't even looking at Rosie, and still, Rosie shivered. "Lateness is disrespect. And I will tolerate no disrespect in my kitchen."

Rosie shifted even farther to one side of her bench, trying to indicate, wordlessly, that there was more than enough space for the girl, who threw Rosie a grateful look, then slung her knife kit onto the vacant station.

"Madame Besson, the video. And the windows, please."

"What a fantastic way to make a first impression," the girl mumbled as shades lowered simultaneously over all the windows. Stirring music played as the École's logo illuminated the whiteboard. "Bloody brilliant. Mum threw a wobbly at St. Pancras and I missed my train. And now the ground will probably swallow me whole because this has got to be a waking nightmare."

"Threw a wobbly?" Rosie whispered, keeping her eyes straight ahead on the video, hoping that Chef Martinet wouldn't catch them talking. Still photos of Chef Laurent in the kitchen, surrounded by teen chefs, bounced across the screen, and Rosie wondered idly why he'd been here with *them* but wasn't here now.

"Shrieking, wailing, rending of the garments. Dad had to

physically restrain her at the end there so I could make a run for it. Couldn't bear to let her baby go, that sort of thing. Being the youngest of five is a bloody nightmare."

"I'm one of five!" Had she been too loud? They both froze, their eyes darting around the room. Rosie waited for heads to turn, for an admonishment to come from Chef Martinet, but nothing happened. Everyone was still focused on the screen, where Chef Laurent was tasting something with a wooden spoon. One of five! Rosie couldn't believe it. She so rarely met another one.

"Really? Wicked! Where are you?"

"Right in the middle. Number three."

"Ah." She nodded. "My sister Maryam's always saying that's the worst, but I think being the baby has some distinct disadvantages. I'm Priya, by the way."

"Rosie. Nice to meet you." They shook hands under the table. A low murmur of giggles rumbled through the room—on the video screen, Chef Laurent appeared to be playing soccer in the courtyard with a group of students. Somehow, Rosie was having a hard time imagining Chef Laurent participating in something like that. He took his work in the kitchen way too seriously to mess around with something as trivial as sports.

In fact, Rosie knew Chef Laurent was opening a restaurant in Hong Kong—he'd been blogging about it for weeks. Maybe he'd be back after that, filling the kitchen with his famous laugh, and the sour-faced Chef Martinet would be just a distant memory.

"Hopefully this isn't a seriously creepy question," Priya whispered, "but is there any chance you've got a pink rabbit sitting on your bed?"

"I do." Rosie probably should have been embarrassed that Priya had seen Bun-bun, but she didn't care. The ball of anxiety about who her roommate would be untangled itself and vanished in an instant.

"Dorm Room 304E?"

"304E," Rosie confirmed.

"Wicked! Oh, this is going to be *such* a treat. Back home I share a room with *two* of my sisters. Having only one roommate is utter luxury."

"I'm just excited to shower in a place that doesn't always smell like sweaty gym clothes."

Priya wrinkled her nose.

"My brothers can work up kind of a stank," Rosie clarified.

The lights flickered back on as Priya laughed. Rosie blinked.

"I hope you have enjoyed this video," Madame Martinet said. "It has, I trust, given you a sense of what life will be like here at the École." Rosie had missed the whole thing, and therefore had zero sense of what life would be like at the École. "I promise you, however, it will not be all football with Chef Laurent."

A couple titters of nervous laughter.

"When will we meet Chef Laurent?" A slight guy with glasses, standing at the bench behind Henry's, had his hand up in the air.

"Most likely you will not." Chef Martinet sniffed. "And in the future, you will wait to be called on."

The hand slowly lowered back down.

Most likely you will not?! At this point, Rosie's heart felt like it had leaped free of her chest cavity and gone wandering off to points unknown, possibly to drown its sorrows in a vat of cookie dough. How could she be at the École Denis Laurent and *not meet Chef Laurent*?!

Was it silly that she'd expected him to be here? Maybe Rosie should have known he'd be busy with his restaurants and his TV show and his cookbooks, too busy to spend all day in the classroom with a bunch of teenagers. But she couldn't help feeling the way she had when she'd first realized that Mom and Santa Claus had the exact same handwriting. Rosie tried to dispel her visions of proudly presenting a perfect tarte tatin to Chef Laurent and dragged her attention back to Chef Martinet, still talking at the front of the room.

"You will have your academic classes, you will have time to yourselves, but mostly, you will be here, in my kitchen, and it is here that I will get to know you. I know you a bit from your applications, of course, but I cannot truly know you until I have tasted your food. It is a failure of the application process." Chef Martinet shrugged. "So think of this semester as the next part of your application. There is no guarantee of admittance to the spring semester at the École until you have proved yourself during the fall semester. We will reevaluate your status after our first final exam. Chef Laurent keeps only the best of the best at the École, and it is not uncommon for students to be sent home midway through the year."

A low buzz of discontent swept through the room. Rosie exchanged a worried glance with Priya and was somewhat relieved to see that she wasn't the only one freaking out.

"She'd chuck us out, then?" Priya whispered furiously. "Halfway through the school year? If what we put on the plate doesn't measure up?"

"That's what it sounds like," Rosie whispered back. She

reached into the pocket of her chef's pants, where she'd put the wings Henry had gotten for her. Stuffing them in her pocket after she'd changed into her whites had been an afterthought, a whim, but as she turned them over in her palm, running her fingers along the ridges, she felt comforted.

"I didn't realize we'd be cooking for our lives," Priya whispered. "That wasn't on the bloody application. I'm going to chunder all over this spotless table."

From the green cast on Priya's cheeks, Rosie assumed *chunder* meant vomit. And Rosie didn't blame her. No Chef Laurent. A very distinct possibility they'd be kicked out if they didn't measure up. Priya wasn't the only one at their table who might chunder. Rosie clutched her wings tighter, feeling the sharp edge of the plastic cut into her palm.

Chef Martinet cleared her throat, and finally, the room was quiet.

"So today, before we begin to learn the building blocks of cooking, I will taste your food," she said. "Madame Besson, the timer, please."

She was tasting their food. Today. This was it. The first dish that would determine if they belonged here. That chundering feeling was rising up. Rosie rotated the wings over and over in her palm, faster and faster, and looked up to the front of the room, to Henry, but all she could see was the back of his head. And beyond his head, where the video had been before, there was now a countdown timer projected on the whiteboard, set at twenty minutes. Rosie's heart rate started picking up speed. Good gravy. This was just like *Top Chef*! Or *Chopped*! Or a math quiz!

"Eggs are one of the most versatile ingredients a chef has at his or her disposal." Chef Martinet picked up a small ceramic container displaying six brown eggs and cradled it in her hands. "In twenty minutes, please prepare a classic French omelet."

The timer clicked to 19:59, and the kitchen erupted into chaos.

CHAPTER SEVEN

Henry

Twenty minutes was a long time to make an omelet. Except, of course, if you were in a brand-new kitchen, and you knew where absolutely nothing was. And you'd just found out that everything you cooked from here on out would be a determining factor in whether or not you got to stay at your dream school. No pressure, right?

Eggs. Butter. Salt. Pepper. That was all he needed. Henry looked at the mad crush of people thronging in front of the wall of stainless steel fridges and decided there was nothing to do but try to bob and weave his way in there.

"Henry! My friend!" Hampus grabbed Henry's arm. "I will get the nonstick pans, yes? You will get the eggs?"

"Got it," Henry said gratefully. "Try to see if you can find two wooden forks, too, okay?"

"Okay." Hampus looked surprised but nodded in agreement. With a wooden fork, you could still stir the eggs as they scrambled in the pan, but you wouldn't scratch the nonstick surface like you might with a metal fork, which would ruin everything. To make a real French omelet, the pan had to be perfectly nonstick. No scratches or dings or anything. Any imperfections in the pan showed up in the omelet.

They went their separate ways, and Henry wondered if this was how everyone on *Top Chef* felt. Adrenaline coursed through his veins, yes, but he didn't feel scared. He felt ready. Like he could run a marathon or jump out of a plane. Or cook an omelet, he thought wryly. You know what? Let Chef Martinet judge his food. He could do this. He knew he could. And he would make sure there was no doubt in her mind—or anyone else's—that Henry would be here for the second semester. Because maybe Chef Laurent would be back in the kitchen for the spring. And there was *no way* Henry was going to miss out on his chance to cook with Chef Laurent.

Henry finally made it up to the fridge door, ducked under the armpit of a white girl with pink hair, and managed to liberate a wax-paper-wrapped block of what looked like some very fancy butter and a carton of six eggs. Next, he ran to the back of the room, where he'd noticed a rack of spices. He grabbed a jar of large-flake salt, a wooden pepper grinder, and a small bag of white peppercorns. Henry headed back to his station, where Hampus had already placed a nonstick frying pan on his burner.

"I did not light your burner yet, Henry! But we are ready to rock and roll, yes?"

"Ready to, uh, rock and roll. Yes." Henry found himself talking directly to Hampus's bangs. Hampus had clipped them up, away from his forehead, so they stuck straight up like a tiny little hirsute unicorn horn, which was hard to look away from, but no. Time to focus. Henry cracked three eggs into the mixing bowl Hampus had thoughtfully grabbed and began whisking them together with the wooden fork. There was no need to add milk—a common misconception—not to an omelet, and not to scrambled eggs, either. Henry thanked all of his lucky stars that he was so obsessed with *Serious Eats* that he'd tested out practically every recipe they had on their website, including, of course, the classic French omelet recipe. He'd had a lot of practice with this one, because it was hard, and the first couple times he'd done it, it had come out raw in the middle, and Henry never let a recipe beat him. He had to keep going back and back until he'd gotten it right. And this one he knew how to get right.

The gas flame roared to life as Henry turned the knob on his range. He plopped a thumb's length of butter into the pan and left it there to melt on medium heat. All he needed now were eggs, a couple grinds of pepper, a few pinches of salt—always more salt than people think you should use—and he'd be ready to go.

As he waited for the butter to melt, Henry looked around. A handful of people were grating cheese at their stations. This was kind of an unfair test, actually, now that he thought about it. Sure, maybe Chef Martinet was also testing people on whether or not they knew what a French omelet was, but Henry thought that was kind of bogus for the first day—if you didn't know what a French omelet was, you were automatically screwed. Unlike your classic American diner omelet, French omelets didn't have cheese. And the fold was different. And, well, Henry knew absolutely nothing about the omelets of other countries. Was there, like, a Swedish omelet? Henry glanced over at Hampus's station, but there were no extra ingredients in evidence. Maybe there was no such thing as a Swedish omelet. Or maybe Hampus just knew what a French omelet was.

The butter began foaming. Henry poured in his eggs, stirring with the wooden fork and shaking the pan. The key was to keep stirring and scraping, breaking up any curds as they started to form. Henry pushed any liquid bits to the edges, until, finally, it started to set. He took the pan off the heat, tilted it, and used his fork to fold it in half, rolling and scooting it until the edges were tucked under. But now he needed a plate. Crap. He'd forgotten a plate.

"Hampus, do you have—?"

"Two steps ahead of you, my friend!"

A plain white ceramic plate materialized under Henry's nose. Henry grabbed it gratefully.

"Did you *warm* the plates?" Henry asked in disbelief.

"That was the second step." Hampus winked. "From the two steps of which I was ahead of you."

"Nice touch, man." Henry set the plate down on his station and slid the omelet onto it. Obviously he couldn't taste it, but it *looked* perfect: a fat little yellow caterpillar.

Ringing, not unlike the fire alarm at Henry's school, echoed through the kitchen, unbelievably loudly. The timer on the whiteboard turned red, flashing 00:00 as it pulsated like a beating heart. Henry looked around for a clean dishtowel, didn't see one, and dragged the sleeve of his jacket across his sweaty forehead. So much for keeping his chef's whites perfectly white. He had a feeling the jacket wouldn't smell too fresh by the end of the day, either.

"And that is the time!" Chef Martinet added unnecessarily. "Plates down, knives down, please step away from your stations."

Henry glanced over at Hampus's station. He was relieved to see a perfect-looking French omelet there.

"I will begin in the front," Chef Martinet said. "Do not worry, those of you in the back. I understand your omelets may have cooled by the time I arrive."

Henry should have realized that choosing this station meant he'd be going first. Oh well. At least he'd get it over with, right? It would be worse, surely, to have to wait the whole time for Chef Martinet to judge him. Well, that's what he tried to tell himself, anyway, as Chef Martinet approached his station. He slid the plate a bit closer to the edge, like that would make him—and his omelet—more ready, somehow, as he prayed to whatever kitchen gods there might be that his dish was cooked right.

"Fork, Madame Besson." Chef Martinet held out her hand. Madame Besson hustled up from the back of the room and placed a plain silver fork in her outstretched palm.

Not raw in the middle, Henry prayed. Please, not raw in the middle.

Henry watched Chef Martinet's fork descend, seemingly in slow motion. As she used it to cut the omelet neatly in half, Henry thought he might scream from the tension, then maybe cry in relief that the omelet was, in fact, cooked all the way through. Chef Martinet speared a small bite of omelet, then brought it up to her mouth. Was Henry going to pass out? Because of an omelet? God, he hoped not. That would be even worse than walking in late. Probably.

Chef Martinet chewed, then cocked her head, making eye contact with Henry for the first time.

"It is perfect," she pronounced, and Henry resolved right then that he was going to write the *Serious Eats* staff the nicest thank-you e-mail of all time. And maybe figure out if there was a way he could send them a gift basket or something. *Perfect.* He couldn't believe it. And he couldn't wait to tell Dad, who would probably say he wasn't surprised at all, but Henry was surprised. He'd thought he was a good cook, but he hadn't known whether or not he'd be good enough to measure up here, where *everyone* was good. And he certainly hadn't thought he was good enough to be *perfect.*

"Needs more salt." Henry came back to earth. Chef Martinet had already moved on to Hampus's omelet. Henry shot Hampus a sympathetic look and received a good-natured shrug in response. As critiques went, that wasn't so bad. That was something he'd heard Tom Colicchio say hundreds of times on *Top Chef*, even to people who'd made it all the way to the final four. Even the best of the best were frequent victims of under-seasoning.

After leaving Henry and Hampus's table, Chef Martinet praised the "technical excellence" of Clara's omelet and told Yumi hers had a "sloppy fold," which wasn't all that bad. Things didn't really get awkward until she tasted the omelet made by the girl with the pink hair. As Chef Martinet explained that French omelets were different from American omelets, that hers was folded incorrectly and it certainly shouldn't have cheese, the girl started to turn the same color as her hair.

And she wasn't the only one to have cooked the wrong type of omelet. Moving on to the rows in the middle of the room, Chef Martinet found plenty to criticize whether the students had made the wrong omelets or the right kind. Out of everyone in their class, only Henry, Clara, and Marquis met with her approval.

And then Chef Martinet was at Rosie's row. All he could see through the smattering of students was the edge of her toffee-colored braid. He shuffled around until he could catch sight of her face, which was unnaturally pale. She looked like she was about to throw up. Henry hoped her omelet was okay. He couldn't see it from his angle, no matter how he shifted or ducked.

"Henry," Hampus whispered urgently. "Are you having to pee?"

"I'm fine, man," Henry whispered back, reddening as he came to a standstill. "Don't worry about it."

Rosie. He prayed that she wouldn't be embarrassed, like the girl with the pink hair.

"The shape is wrong," Chef Martinet said, pointing her fork at the student who shared Rosie's table, the girl who had come in late. "This is not a French omelet. And *mon dieu*! More cheese!" Chef Martinet sniffed disapprovingly. "The cook of the eggs, at least, is fine. Not overdone."

Now it was Rosie's turn. Henry felt almost more nervous than when Chef Martinet had tasted *his* omelet.

"Again, the shape is wrong." Chef Martinet sighed, and Henry's heart sank right along with her sigh. "Again, there should be no cheese." Henry squirmed, trying to catch Rosie's eye, but she was looking down at the floor, head bent, trying to hide the flush that crept up her cheeks. "The eggs are rubbery. Terribly overcooked. A poor effort."

A poor effort. That couldn't have been easy to hear. It looked like the girl next to Rosie might have grabbed her hand and squeezed. Henry hoped she had. Henry wished he was back there so he could let her know that it was okay, that it was just the first day, and this test was bogus, anyway. And omelets were better with cheese, and best when they came off the flat top at a diner, and maybe this was one case where the French didn't really know what they were talking about. Just like their obsession with meat spreads. What was that all about, anyway? Pâté was okay, but honestly, nothing to get all that excited about.

Chef Martinet moved on from Rosie's station, and Henry tried to keep shooting Rosie telepathic messages of support as he watched the instructor taste the omelet of a black guy with wire-rimmed glasses Henry hadn't met yet, who stood next to a white guy with a buzz cut Henry hadn't met either. There was something familiar about the white guy. Henry frowned, squinting at him, like that might help him place him, somehow. Was he from Chicago?

Then Hampus inhaled sharply.

"It is Bodie Tal," Hampus whispered.

Bodie Tal. The name was familiar. Just like his face.

"Is he, uh, famous or something?" Henry asked.

In the back of the room, Chef Martinet moved on to Bodie Tal's omelet, cut a neat forkful, and chewed contemplatively.

"Oh yes. He is most famous. In Sweden, we have *Kaka Bomba*. I think it is *The Cake Bombs* in America, yes? Do you have this?"

"*Cake Bomb*," Henry corrected automatically. "With Dash Bray."

And then it clicked. Bodie Tal was Dash Bray's son. *Cake Bomb* wasn't Henry's favorite Food Network show—he really wasn't that interested in pastry—but he'd caught parts of it often enough that he remembered Bodie now.

"A real celebrity." Hampus seemed practically starstruck. Henry didn't totally understand *why*. It wasn't like Bodie Tal was *really* famous. His *dad* was famous. Bodie Tal was just famous-adjacent. Like Blue Ivy. But Dash Bray was no Beyoncé.

"Not enough salt," Chef Martinet pronounced as she left Bodie's station.

"Perhaps I am not in such bad company, then, hey, Henry?" Hampus jostled Henry's shoulder. But as Henry watched Rosie quickly wipe something off her face that he hoped wasn't a tear, he could barely return Hampus's smile.

CHAPTER EIGHT

Rosie

"Well, I think we can all agree that was a complete and utter disaster." Priya plonked her tray down next to Rosie's, the beef stew threatening to spill over the side of her ceramic bowl as it wobbled.

"She said I had a *sloppy fold*. A SLOPPY FOLD!" Yumi viciously tore off the end of her dinner roll. "A sloppy fold. That sounds borderline obscene." She stuffed the roll in her mouth and chewed angrily.

"Priya, Yumi; Yumi, Priya," Rosie said, introducing the two of them. They nodded at each other in solidarity. Rosie took a spoonful of her stew. It was good: warm, earthy, comforting. Rich, but not too rich. The beef practically fell apart in her spoon. It reminded her of Nana's pot roast, minus the Lipton Recipe Secrets Onion Soup Mix.

"At least you knew what a French omelet *was*," Priya pointed out. "I swear to you I'd never seen that bloody thing before in my life. I thought all omelets came in half-moons."

"Me too." Rosie nodded in agreement. She'd thought all omelets looked like the ones at Cracker Barrel. Wrong. So wrong. And what was worse, she hadn't even made a *good* diner omelet. She didn't understand how it had happened. Rosie knew how to make an omelet. She'd made them before, plenty of times. Sometimes, for big weekend breakfasts before her brothers' soccer games, she'd set up her own omelet station in the kitchen back home, filling prep bowls with different toppings, although invariably everyone just wanted cheese. But every single one of those cheese omelets was light-years better than the one she'd produced today, when it really mattered. *A poor effort.* Rosie's cheeks burned with the shame of it all over again. She took another bite of stew and tried to forget, although she wasn't sure she'd ever get those words out of her head.

"Is it even good? A French omelet?" Priya asked. "Looked rather dodgy, if you ask me. A rolled-up bit of egg and nothing else? No thank you."

"They're not bad, if you get the texture right." Yumi reached across the table, lifted Rosie's roll right off her tray, and bit into it. "They can be really fluffy."

"I'd still rather have a regular old cheese omelet," Rosie said, trying not to stare too longingly at her rapidly disappearing roll. "It just seems wrong, an omelet with no cheese. What's the point? Why not just scramble the eggs, then?"

"Agreed," Priya said. "D'you think Martinet'll wait till the end of the semester to chuck us out, then, or just put us out of our misery now?"

"No way." Yumi shook her head vigorously. "I'm not letting

that *oni* chuck me anywhere. She'd have to get me onto that plane by brute force, and I'd fight her every step of the way. With my teeth if necessary."

"What's an oni?" Rosie asked.

"It's like a demon. Google it."

Rosie pulled out her phone, and her whole lock screen was full of notifications. She did the math in her head . . . lunchtime in Ohio. Nothing from Cole, who'd been sucked into the vortex of freshman year. Nothing from Reed, who was undoubtedly still sucked into the vortex of *Assassin's Creed*, like he'd been all summer. She tapped onto the series of texts from Ricky.

Ricky

Hey Rosie where are the mixing bowls?

Ricky

Is there like a special kind of spoon you're supposed to use?

Ricky

This spoon feels kind of small

Ricky

Yeah this is def the wrong spoon

Ricky

Is mixing with your hands, like, artisanal?

Ricky

That's a technique, right?

Ricky

Do you know where Mom keeps the extra paper towels?

Ricky

We didn't have blueberries so I put in grape jelly. Basically the same?

Ricky

Hmm I don't think this oven cleaner is working

Ricky

Also how do you disable the smoke alarm?

What on earth was Ricky making?! By the time she opened the next text, she was full of trepidation.

Mom

This is Owen on Mom's phone. I asked Ricky to make me blueberry muffins, like you do. He did not do a good job.

Then there was a picture of Owen holding a charred lump of something that Rosie sincerely hoped neither of her brothers had attempted to eat. She burst out laughing at the sight of his face, smeared with soot and grape jelly.

"Did you find it?" Yumi asked.

"Um. Almost." Quickly, Rosie fired off a text to Owen:

Rosie

> DO NOT EAT THAT!!! DO NOT ASK RICKY TO BAKE FOR YOU! Will send you muffin recipe later—you can do it yourself! ☺

Then she attached a gif of an iguana wearing sunglasses, because why not. And then a text to Ricky:

Rosie

> Mixing with hands is v. artisanal but only if hands are CLEAN. Grape jelly is not the same as blueberries. Extra paper towels are under the sink. Use wooden spoons to mix—they're in drawer to left of stove underneath cabinets with mixing bowls. But in future, please refrain from cooking anything that's not a Totino's pizza roll for the health and safety of all involved.

Finally, Rosie Google-image-searched the oni. She flipped her phone around to show Priya the picture of the big, horned, red demon.

"Oh, Chef Martinet is most assuredly an oni," Priya said.

"And I refuse to be defeated by a demon. So just wait until tomorrow, because I'm going to cook something so spectacular, Chef Martinet will be *begging* me to stay. At the end of this year, they'll probably rename the school the École de Cuisine Yumi Osaki-Weissman."

Rosie wished she had Yumi's confidence. She felt so *confused* by her omelet disaster, it was hard to ignore the possibility of being asked to leave. If Rosie couldn't make an omelet, did she even deserve to be here?

Rosie looked back down at her phone, opening her e-mail. There was a new one from Mom, with the subject line: *How's it going?*

What would she even say?

Well, I'm a terrible cook who can't even slap together an omelet, but at least I have people to sit with at dinner?

No way. She couldn't let her mother know how badly she'd done. Mom had been so sure Rosie would excel at the École. But she couldn't ignore her forever. She'd e-mail her back. Later. Tonight. When she could think of a way to put a positive spin on the whole omelet situation.

"Excuse me. What do you think you're doing?"

Rosie looked up from her phone at the sound of Yumi's voice and stuffed it back into her pocket. Henry and Marquis stood across from her, trays in hands. Her eyes met Henry's, and Rosie thought that if she saw anything sympathetic lurking around in there, even the smallest hint of pity, she'd start crying into her stew. Or fling the bowl against the wall. She could almost hear the satisfying crack of china, see the dribbles of brown stew travel down the cream-colored paint, feel the hush in the room as conversation stopped.

What would Mom think, if she knew Rosie was contemplating chucking crockery across the room? She wouldn't believe it. Good Rosie. Quiet Rosie. Responsible Rosie. Rosie didn't *throw things.* Rosie shouldn't even be thinking about throwing things. She stuck her hand back in her pocket and curled it around the plastic wings, then looked up at Henry.

Henry smiled at her, and his eyes crinkled. They seemed to say, *Wasn't today crazy?* and not, *You are a huge loser who can't even cook a friggin' omelet*, and so that was okay, and so Rosie didn't throw anything. She took her hand back out of her pocket and took another bite of stew.

"Uh, sitting?" Marquis said as he put his tray down next to Yumi's.

"Um, no. Nope, nope, nope." Yumi swung her legs across the seat, blocking Marquis from sitting. "Sorry, golden boys. This table is reserved for omelet losers only."

"Come on. There are no omelet losers here. That test wasn't even fair." Henry walked around the table and put his tray down next to Rosie's. She felt her cheeks getting warm as he pulled out his chair and sat.

"The only thing worse than being an omelet loser is being an omelet sore loser. Move your legs."

Grumbling, Yumi did as Marquis asked.

"It was just the first day." Henry took a bite of his stew. "Hey, this is pretty good," he said, surprised.

"Duh," Yumi said. "They can't have crappy cafeteria food at a *cooking school*. That would just make them look bad."

Rosie had been surprised it was good, too. She'd been expecting something like the hot food at East Liberty High, which was barely edible, and best eaten only under the direst of circumstances.

"Makes sense. So the stew is good. And the omelets weren't that bad. Nobody's was," Henry said, and Rosie stiffened as his leg brushed hers. "Sorry," he said.

"No worries," she said, breezily. She hoped it was breezy. She'd been aiming for breezy. But she couldn't deny the current of electricity that had run up her thigh at the slightest brush of his leg. Had he felt, it, too? Rosie cast a shy look over at Henry. He was chasing a piece of carrot around his bowl, attempting to lever it onto his spoon. Probably not, then.

"Rather easy for you to say, Mr. Perfect," Priya said.

"Mr. Perfect. Now there's a nickname I'd be okay with," Yumi said wistfully. "Guess what Clara started calling me after the omelet incident. When she wasn't busy rubbing her 'technical excellence' in my face," she added darkly, propping her elbows up on the table as she leaned in. *"Sloppy Fold."*

Marquis guffawed, the sound of his laughter echoing through the dining hall. A couple people at other tables turned to look at them.

"Sorry, sorry," he apologized, wiping tears of laughter from his eyes. Yumi shot him a look that would have incinerated a weaker being. "Chill, Sloppy Fold. Don't look so serious."

"That was an awful thing for her to call you," Rosie said. Yumi nodded her agreement, then transferred her death-stare away from Marquis and over to a table up by the salad bar, where Clara was holding court, sitting in between the girl with the pink hair and Bodie Tal. Of course she was. Rosie couldn't have imagined Bodie Tal sitting next to any other girl here. Except, maybe, the girl with the pink hair, who was just as beautiful as Clara, but cool in an alternative way, with her black winged eyeliner and that cotton candy hair, like the punk Barbie to Bodie's hipster Ken. Maybe the École wouldn't be all that different from East Liberty High. Sure, it wasn't the football players and the cheerleaders sitting together here, but it was the same sort of system. The cool people, Rosie mused, must always be able to find each other, wherever they go. Maybe they had some sort of tracking device implanted so they could locate each other. Like homing pigeons.

Rosie found herself almost mesmerized as Clara tossed her white-blond hair over one shoulder, laughing at whatever Bodie had said like it was the funniest thing that had ever happened. Well, sure. Rosie would be having the time of her life, too, if she'd cooked an excellent omelet instead of her own "poor effort."

"Oh, I'm most definitely cursed." Yumi dunked the last bit of Rosie's roll into her stew. "Nothing else would account for me being stuck sharing a room with that blond nightmare."

"You don't get along, then?" Priya asked. Everyone looked at her. "What? Maybe the whole . . . um . . . *sloppy fold* situation . . . was a bit of an outlier?" Priya had whispered the words *sloppy fold*, like they'd be less offensive at a lower volume.

"Definitely not an outlier," Yumi said. "She's the worst. The literal worst."

"Then *why* did you decide to share a table with her?" Rosie asked.

"It's not as if I had a choice, did I?" Yumi looked around at all of them. "Miss Bossy Boots plunked her knife kit down, glanced at the spot next to her, and then she gave me this *look*, like, *Are you intimidated, loser?* and obviously I couldn't back down, could I?" Rosie felt she definitely could have backed down. But then again, Rosie was clearly loser material. Improperly cooked omelet material. Failure material. "You guys weren't downstairs yet"—she gestured vaguely at Rosie and Marquis—"and the spot next to Perfect Boy was already occupied by his giant friend, so that left me sharing a table with Roomie Dearest."

"Hampus," Henry said. He'd almost finished his stew, Rosie noticed. "That's my giant friend. Tall friend. Roommate. He's a really nice guy."

Rosie wondered where he was sitting. He was so tall, he should have been easy to spot. She looked around the room at her fellow students, feeling strange that she'd only met about half of them. There were just twenty in total—she should know everyone. Were they ever going to do, like, an ice-breaker, or something? Rosie thought about the getting-to-know-you games she'd run this summer, when she was a counselor at Bible camp. She tried to imagine standing up in front of the room, saying, *My name is Rosie, and I like rhubarb*, and failed. But still. She'd like to know who everyone was.

"Who's your roommate, Marquis?" Yumi asked, reaching over and grabbing the roll off his tray, too.

"Hands off!"

He tried to grab it back, but before he could, Yumi licked it.

"Licking? Seriously, Yumi! You don't mess around!"

"I do not." She took a big bite. "Who's your roommate?"

"Fernando. He's, uh . . . over there." Marquis pointed up to the table by the salad bar, the Bodie Tal table. Rosie guessed he meant the tan guy with dark curly hair, sitting across from the pink-haired girl. "He's Spanish. From Barcelona. Seems cool."

"Wait, Rosie," Henry said. "Who's your roommate?"

"Priya." Rosie realized she hadn't introduced Priya to the boys. She was a terrible roommate. Priya waved cheerily at them. "Priya, meet Henry and Marquis."

"Pleasure," Priya said. "I'm the knob who was late on the very first day."

"You weren't *that* late," Henry said, and Rosie wondered if this was something he always did, the way he seemed to try to make everyone feel better, to let them know that things weren't so bad.

"Late enough. And my omelet was bollocks, so that's my doom sorted. D'you think Chef Martinet will purchase my ticket back home for me? Or will I have to get it myself?"

"You know what? Screw those omelets."

"Henry!" Yumi teased. "My God! The language!"

"Seriously. It was the *first day*. Those omelets don't matter."

"Sloppy Fold over here might beg to differ," Marquis said.

"I will literally murder you." Yumi pointed her butter knife at him.

"With that knife? Good luck," Marquis said.

"I know where you live," Yumi threatened him. "When you least expect it, I will end you."

"No girls in the boys' hall. Strictly enforced. Weren't you listening to Madame Besson?" Marquis asked.

"Madame Besson can't protect you from my terrible vengeance."

"You know what matters?" Henry said, his volume rising as he talked over Yumi and Marquis. "We're here. In *Paris*."

"Paris," Rosie whispered, because, quite honestly, she still couldn't totally believe it. *In an old house in Paris . . .* Her first memory of Paris, leaning against Dad's chest as he read *Madeline*. Paris, a place where little girls were fearless and pooh-poohed tigers at the zoo, no matter how big their teeth were. Rosie's favorite page, the one where they broke their bread. Rosie pointing at the table, asking *What are they eating, Dad?* And you couldn't tell from the picture, not really, but he'd make it up, inventing wildly fantastical dinners eaten by twelve little girls in two straight lines.

"Here. In Paris," Henry said. "At the École Denis Laurent. At a place thousands of people wanted to be, and *we* made it."

"Hear, hear," Priya cheered.

"We are here to cook. And to eat. And for *adventure*. And that's what matters. Not some dumb omelet," Henry concluded.

"Is this the end of your inspirational speech?" Yumi asked.

"Shh, you're ruining it," Priya said.

"Um, yeah. That's the end," Henry said, seeming to shrink into himself a bit. "Sorry. I didn't meant to get quite so . . . weird . . . about everything."

"You're right, Henry. Who cares about the omelets?" Honestly, Rosie cared very much about the omelets. But she could try to pretend she didn't. "What matters is being here. Learning. And exploring."

"God, I can't wait to explore," Priya said wistfully. "I've only ever been here with my mum before, and she barely let me off the leash. Certainly not enough to do anything interesting." She stifled a yawn. "Maybe exploring tomorrow, though. I'm knackered."

"*You're* knackered?" Yumi asked skeptically. "I was on a plane for—"

"Twenty hours and thirty-one minutes," Rosie, Henry, and Marquis said right along with Yumi, then they all burst into laughter as Priya looked at them, befuddled.

Maybe Henry was right. Maybe the omelet didn't matter. Maybe what mattered was *this*.

CHAPTER NINE

Henry

Henry's feet were suffocating. That was his first thought. He scrabbled up to sitting, kicked the covers aside, and pulled off his socks. His eyes adjusting to the darkness, he looked across the room to see Hampus sleeping contentedly, a black silk sleep mask pulled over his eyes. Paris. The École. Right. Henry must have passed out the minute he lay down. He hadn't even remembered to take his socks off—or his jeans, for that matter. Apparently, he'd fallen asleep fully dressed.

Sighing, Henry reached over to the nightstand to check his phone. Four a.m.? Seriously? His alarm was set to go off at seven o'clock and he knew he could have used three more hours of sleep, but he was wide-awake now. Stupid jet lag. Stupid brain. Quietly, Henry got out of bed and slipped into the hallway, shutting the door behind him. Maybe a drink of water would help.

The lights in the hall were on but dim. He padded into the bathroom, splashing water on his face from the tap. Henry scrutinized his face in the mirror. He looked awful. Like something that might pop out of your TV in a horror movie.

Back out in the hall, Henry hesitated in front of his door. He didn't want to wake Hampus up, but the last thing he wanted to do was lie in bed and stare at the walls. So he just kept wandering, walking past Marquis's room, and others belonging to guys he didn't know, until, at the end of the hall, there was a door without a number on it.

He tried it, because why not, and much to his surprise, it swung open. Henry stepped through, climbed up a flight of plain stairs in a whitewashed hallway, and, pushing open the door at the top, found himself on the roof.

It was cool up here but not cold, and Henry loved the rush of the air on his skin. Breathing deeply, he looked out past the edge of the rooftop and saw hundreds of other rooftops spread out before him, illuminated here and there by the glow of streetlights.

"I still don't understand *why* you ate it."

He wasn't alone. Farther along the roof, near another door, a figure in plaid pajama pants and an enormous navy sweatshirt paced back and forth. It was Rosie, her hair piled in a messy bun on top of her head, a phone pressed against her ear.

"Well, of course Owen didn't eat it. You know what? Here's a good rule of thumb: going forward, if Owen doesn't eat something, you don't eat it, either."

Crap. He didn't want to scare her, and he didn't want her to think he was eavesdropping. Henry froze in the doorway, unsure of where to go, or what to do.

Rosie burst out laughing. "No, I wouldn't consider *pooping purple* 'an adventure.'" She turned and saw him. Henry tried to look as un-creepy as possible but was having difficulty deciding what the most casual way to stand in a doorframe was. "Ricky, I gotta go. Sure. Yeah. Put Mom on one more time. But then I gotta go."

She was waving at him now and walking toward him, smiling, so maybe he *had* figured out a really good, super-casual doorway lean.

"Good night, Mom." She was close enough that Henry could see her mouth "Sorry" as she pointed to the phone. Henry shrugged and flapped his hands at her in a way that he hoped looked like he was telling her to take her time. "I'm going to sleep now. Yes, literally right now. I promise." She held up crossed fingers. Henry stifled a laugh. "Love you, too." Rosie hung up and slipped the phone into the pouch of her sweatshirt. "Sorry about that."

"No, I'm sorry," Henry said. "I didn't mean to interrupt."

"You didn't. Promise," she said. "And it's okay; you can close the door. The one I came through didn't lock."

Henry let the door swing shut behind him with a creak and stepped onto the roof, closer to her.

"How long have you been up here?" he asked.

"Three a.m.?" She shrugged. "I think? Gosh, was I really on the phone for that long? I don't know. All of a sudden I was just . . . awake."

"Yeah. Me too." Even in the dark, Henry could see her so clearly. She tugged on the ends of her sleeves, pulling them down farther over her hands. "Did you know we could come up here?"

"No. I just found a staircase at the end of the girls' hall. Actually . . . can we be up here?" She peered at him. "You know, the whole no-boys-and-girls-on-the-same-hall thing."

"I'm not on your hall," Henry said.

"True. And I'm not on your hall," she said.

"So . . . I think we're good."

"It's a very literal interpretation of the rules."

"One that I'd be happy to explain to Madame Besson, if she comes charging up here in her nightie."

"Nightie?" Rosie chuckled.

"What? Is that a weird word? Nightgown?"

"I don't know. Maybe? It just sounded funny. Come on." Rosie started walking to the middle of the roof. "We can sit over here."

Henry followed her over to some kind of mechanical something—a fan, maybe—and sat next to her, his back leaning against the metal whatever-it-was. They sat quietly for a moment, looking up at the night sky. Henry knew the sun wouldn't rise for hours yet, but he imagined he could almost see the first faint traces of dawn approaching. Next to him, Rosie shifted, drawing her knees up and tenting them beneath her sweatshirt.

"I can make an omelet, Henry," she said quietly.

"I'm sure you can."

"No. Really. I know how to cook an omelet." He was startled by her sudden vehemence. "A *good* omelet. I make them *all the time*. And I have never—*never*—done anything like what I did today."

"I believe you."

She turned to him, her brown eyes dark, and looked at him like she was searching for something.

"Thanks," she said eventually, and Henry wondered if

she found what she was looking for. "Today was beyond embarrassing." She slumped even farther down, almost her entire body engulfed by the sweatshirt.

"Worse than asking a flight attendant for plastic wings?"

"Much, much worse," she said, but she was smiling now. "I'd rather ask a million flight attendants for a million wings."

"What would you even do with a million wings?"

"Fly anywhere I wanted."

And there was a wistful quality to the way she said it that made the joke Henry had poised on his lips stay there. If Henry had a million wings, he wouldn't want to fly anywhere. He wanted to be here. With her.

"What's your favorite omelet?" Henry asked.

"No more omelets," she groaned.

"Come on. Face the dragon. Favorite omelet."

"Ugh. Fine." She sighed. "Cheese. I'm boring. But a really, really sharp cheddar. And so much cheese that it oozes out and winds around the tines of your fork and is difficult to eat."

"That's the best," he agreed, able to picture the pull of a forkful of melted cheddar so clearly in his mind. Dinner suddenly seemed like a long time ago.

"Do you have a favorite omelet? And, just in case you weren't sure, this is the weirdest getting-to-know-you game I've ever played," Rosie added.

"Do you think I could get everyone to go around the room tomorrow and name their favorite omelet?"

"If anyone could, it would be you."

Henry didn't know exactly what she meant by that, but it pleased him, nonetheless.

"Favorite omelet. Come on."

"Hmm. Okay. This place in my neighborhood, the Bongo Room, does a potato and chorizo omelet I really like."

"Potatoes *in* the omelet?"

"Yeah. And on the side. Extra crispy. They're *really* good."

"Double potatoes? You're a potato maniac," she teased.

"You have no idea. I'm a potato fanatic. Potatoes make everything better."

"I think you said *potato* when you meant to say *chocolate*."

"Potatoes are better than chocolate," Henry scoffed.

"Now I *know* you're a maniac."

"And yet, here you are, alone on the roof with me, in the middle of the night."

"Hey, I'm not worried about me," Rosie said. "I'm worried about any innocent potatoes that might wander by."

"I wouldn't eat a perambulatory potato."

"A *perambulatory potato*?" Rosie practically spat through her laughter. "What is that, your band name?"

"Yeah." He grinned. "Wanna play the tambourine?"

"I'd be honored."

She was smiling now, really smiling, and Henry hoped that stupid omelet test was all but forgotten. A yawn broke through her smile, and Henry wondered what time it was now.

"We probably shouldn't fall asleep right now, huh?" Henry asked reluctantly.

"Definitely not." Rosie shook her head. "Can you imagine what would happen if Madame Besson found us up here?"

"My mom would murder me," Henry said. Which was probably the lamest thing he could have said. But it was true.

"My mom would be so surprised she'd have some kind of cardiac episode. And then *I'd* be responsible for murder."

Henry laughed. But he didn't stand up yet. And neither did she. He realized how close they were sitting, almost huddled together against the wind, their backs pressed against the metal thing, her leg not quite touching his, but nearly. Henry watched her blink once, then twice, her long lashes briefly covering her widening eyes. He wondered what would happen if he leaned in, closed his eyes, if her lips would be there to meet his. And then Henry found himself leaning in, closer to her, his leg pressing against hers as he moved.

Rosie froze several inches away from him, and her eyes popped wide open.

"Henry," she whispered. "Did you hear that?"

"Hear what?"

"That creaking sound. It sounded like the door."

Henry hadn't heard anything. But he hadn't exactly been paying attention. Rosie peeked her head around the metal structure, then immediately popped back to face him.

"It's Madame Besson," she said, white-faced. "Smoking."

"Is she wearing a nightie?" he asked, deadpan.

"Not the time for jokes!" she whispered, but she was laughing, silently. "What are we gonna do? She can't see us up here."

"It's okay," Henry said, not sure if the pounding of his heart was from almost kissing Rosie or from being afraid Madame Besson might catch them. "We'll just hide up here and be quiet until she leaves."

"Quiet," Rosie agreed. She mimed locking her lips and throwing away the key, and then she pulled her knees back under her sweatshirt, scooting in closer to the metal thing and closer to Henry.

Henry thought he could hear Madame Besson exhaling farther down on the roof, but it was probably only in his mind. They sat together, silent, almost motionless, waiting to hear the creak of the door. They'd been about to kiss before Madame Besson had arrived. Hadn't they? Or had *he* been leaning in for a kiss Rosie was about to dodge, before she was saved in the nick of time by the creaking door? Henry wished he could tell, but short of asking Rosie—mortifying—he didn't know how. Eventually, Madame Besson left, and after waiting to make sure it was safe, Rosie and Henry silently disappeared down two separate staircases, nodding good-bye to each other, still afraid to make any noise. Back in his room, Henry was unsure if Madame Besson had saved him from making a total idiot of himself, or completely ruined the moment.

★★★★

Later that morning, Henry's alarm jolted him awake. He opened his eyes and was greeted by the sight of Hampus doing squats in his boxers.

Henry shuffled down the hall to the boys' bathroom, still mostly asleep, showered, still mostly asleep, and put away two chocolate croissants downstairs at breakfast without ever really waking up.

"These are the circumstances in which one drinks coffee," Yumi said as she sat across from him at breakfast, clutching her mug like she was afraid someone was going to take it away from her. Henry didn't drink coffee. He couldn't stand the taste. Yumi suggested that now might be a good time to start, and as Henry blinked at her, he wondered if she had a point.

Henry was starting to wonder if seeing Rosie on the rooftop might have been a dream. She looked way too well rested. No dark circles under her eyes, no frizz escaping from her neat braid, nothing. There was even a faint crease on one of her cheeks from, Henry assumed, her pillowcase. Maybe all of it—including the moment Henry almost kissed her—had been a jet-lag-induced dream.

Even when they got down to the kitchen and class started, Henry couldn't wake up. Hampus coughed delicately, and Henry jumped. He must have closed his eyes for a minute. Just a minute. But Chef Martinet was still focused on the large steel pot heating up on the range at the front of the classroom, and not on him. Maybe he wouldn't be falling asleep if they were doing something a little bit more interesting. Today, they were learning how to boil water. *Boil. Water.* Henry wondered if their next lesson would be watching paint dry.

Apparently, this was a classic culinary school thing. First, they'd learn how to boil water. Then, they'd move on to knife cuts. And then somewhere down the road, they'd actually start cooking. Henry would have enjoyed making that omelet more if he'd known he would be relegated to boiling water for the foreseeable future.

Chef Martinet instructed them to boil two quarts of water in a saucier. Sighing, Henry started looking around for a pot. Well, not a pot. A saucier. Which was kind of like if a pot and a frying pan had a baby—the base was as wide as a frying pan, but the edges were straight, like a pot, and they were only a couple inches tall. He wondered what they were going to be boiling water for. The saucier was way too shallow for pasta. Poached eggs, maybe? Maybe they were on some kind of egg spree. That kind of made sense. Eggs were about as fundamental as you could get.

Without the countdown timer ticking away on the whiteboard, people were moving through the kitchen much more civilly. Most of the pots and pans seemed to be hanging from the ceiling near the walls toward the back of the room, their copper surfaces gleaming in the sunlight like they were part of a magazine spread.

By the time Henry got there, there was only one person left: Bodie Tal. He handed the saucier in his hands to Henry.

"Oh, uh, thanks," Henry said awkwardly.

"No worries." Bodie grabbed his own saucier. "Can you believe this?" He leaned in conspiratorially. "Boiling water? Seriously? Is this some kind of joke?"

"I don't think Chef Martinet jokes."

The two of them glanced toward the front of the room where Chef Martinet stood by her saucier. She looked like she'd just bitten into a lemon. Bodie laughed.

"I'm Bodie, man."

"Henry."

They clasped arms in some sort of bro-y handshake that Henry was pretty sure he'd executed incorrectly.

"Henry, with the perfect omelet. Right?" Bodie said.

"That was yesterday. This is a brand-new day. Yeah, sure, I can make an omelet. But can I *boil water*?!"

Bodie laughed again. Henry was shocked by how, well, normal he seemed. He'd expected the guy to be completely full of himself. To name-drop his dad at any and all opportunities.

"Hi, guys," Rosie said as she approached them. She rose up on her toes, reached once, wobbled, reached again, and just barely made contact with the bottom of the saucier. "Oops," she said as she tipped sideways, bumping Henry with her shoulder, now almost as close to him as she was on the roof. What would have happened last night, if Madame Besson hadn't needed a cigarette? Would they have kissed? Would everything be different now? He wanted desperately to know if she would have kissed him, if she was thinking about last night, too, but he felt so awkward about the whole thing, he could barely even look at her.

"Here you go." Bodie grabbed the saucier, lifting it easily off the hook, and handed it to Rosie.

"Thanks," she said, and a faint tremor of what Henry could identify only as fear passed through him. Rosie *blushed*. The same end-of-season-raspberry blush he'd seen before now blossomed in both cheeks and traveled down her neck, disappearing beneath her chef's jacket. No. Henry could *not* think about what was beneath Rosie's chef's jacket. Definitely not right now. Not in class.

"No worries," Bodie said breezily. "I'm on saucier distribution duty today." He grinned at Henry. "I'm Bodie."

"Rosie," she said, adding "It's nice to meet you," before turning to leave with her saucier.

As Henry walked back to his station at the front of the room, he glanced back at Bodie. Was it him, or did Bodie's gaze linger on Rosie as she bent over the range? Henry walked right into Hampus's broad back because he'd been looking behind him, and he cursed himself for not watching where he was going. You *had* to pay attention in a kitchen. If you didn't, people got hurt.

Rosie was wrong—Henry wasn't a potato maniac. He was a literal maniac. Determined to stop obsessing over something that wasn't there, Henry went to fill his saucier and began to boil water.

CHAPTER TEN

Rosie

"Don't look behind you. Stop! I said don't look!"

Priya's hands encircled Rosie's wrists as she drew Rosie close to her, her nails digging into the soft flesh of the underside of Rosie's arms.

"Ow! Priya, I'm not looking. I was never looking."

Priya relaxed her grip, but barely.

"Were you. Just talking. To *Bodie Tal*?" Priya hissed.

"Um. Yes," Rosie said. Why did that simple yes make the kitchen start to feel a bit warm?

"What did he *say*? What did *you* say? Did he look the same as he does on telly?"

"Priya." Rosie tutted. "Come on. You've been in the same room with him for days. You know what he looks like."

"But not up close! Not talking close! Oh God, Bodie Tal!" Priya was practically swooning. Rosie half expected her to start fanning herself with a dish towel. "The episode of *Paul*

Hollywood: City Bakes where Bodie shows Paul around LA changed my *life*. Bodie makes a donut–ice cream sandwich! Shirtless! And then he eats it! *Shirtless!* And it's all drippy!"

"That's not sanitary."

"It was a beautiful moment and I shan't have you say a word against it. So? What did he *say*?"

"Um . . ." Rosie was having a hard time remembering what, exactly, he'd said. What she did remember was the gray-blue of his eyes. And how strong his arms had looked when he'd reached up to grab the saucier for her. She'd found herself wishing that his chef's jacket would ride up a bit so she could see, in real life, a glimpse of the abs she knew were under there. Sadly, the jacket had been plenty long enough. "Something about pots?"

"Something about pots," Priya repeated, disappointment evident on her face. "Pots."

"Yeah. Pots."

"Don't look behind you!" Priya's nails were digging into Rosie's wrists again. "Don't look!"

"Priya, I'm not!"

"He's. *Coming*."

And by the time Priya hissed the last syllable of *coming*, there he was, Bodie Tal. At their table. Fully clothed and not eating any kind of ice cream sandwich.

"Just coming to check on the saucier," Bodie said, his hands stuck casually into his pockets, the sleeves of his chef's jacket pulled up. Rosie struggled not to stare at his tattoos. She saw a whisk, and a skull and crossbones, and what she thought might have been a pair of peaches. From behind her, Rosie heard a faint wheezing sound that she hoped wasn't Priya hyperventilating. "Wanted to make sure I'd gotten you a good one."

"So it's like a full-service saucier delivery," Rosie said.

"Exactly," Bodie said, and he laughed. Rosie had made *Bodie Tal* laugh. Priya wheezed even louder.

"Bodie! Man!" The guy who shared Bodie's table was waving at him. "Your water is doing something weird."

"How does *water* do something weird?" Rosie asked.

"I'm very talented."

Priya pinched Rosie. Rosie swatted her hand away. Priya pinched her again. Bodie looked back and forth between the two of them, amused. Rosie slapped Priya's hand again, harder than she'd meant to.

"Ow, Rosie!" Priya hissed.

"Sorry!" Rosie whispered.

"Bodie!" Bodie's table partner was still waving. "Come fix it! I'm not dealing with this!"

"Excuse me, ladies." Bodie shrugged and walked back over to his station.

Priya leaned over and Rosie caught her wrist mid-pinch. The two of them stood that way, frozen, smiles plastered on their faces, until Bodie was safely back at his station and not looking at them anymore.

"Stop attacking me!" Rosie said. "I mean it. No pinches, no pokes, no grabbing!"

"I'm not attacking you! I'm *prodding* you because you're not producing a proper response."

"A proper response to what?"

"Um, hello? He was flirting with you!" Priya left her mouth hanging wide open as she turned to stare at Bodie Tal, who was busy fussing with his saucier on the stove. Rosie was tempted to tell her to close her mouth or a fly would get in there, like Mom would have.

"No, he wasn't," Rosie scoffed. Priya was being ridiculous. Guys didn't *flirt* with Rosie. They asked her for highlighters, or to remind them what the homework was. But they didn't flirt with her. And Bodie Tal, of all people, certainly wouldn't flirt with her. His last girlfriend had been an Aerie model, for goodness' sake.

"Maybe you're unable to recognize proper flirting. It could be a condition. Like having a vitamin deficiency."

"I can—" But Rosie found her protest dying on her lips before she even finished the sentence. *Could* she recognize flirting? Maybe she should tell Priya about what happened on the roof last night. Because she had really thought Henry had been about to kiss her, but then nothing happened, even after Madame Besson was safely downstairs. And then he'd been falling asleep at breakfast, and so *weird* over by the sauciers, like he couldn't even look at her.

"Rosie?"

"Huh?"

"What is it?" Priya asked curiously.

"Nothing." Better to say nothing. Because who knew what Henry meant? Or almost meant? Or what he was thinking now? The fact that he couldn't even look at her meant one of two things: either it had all been in her head, or Henry instantly regretted trying to kiss her. And Rosie didn't really want to talk about either of those depressing possibilities.

"Certainly doesn't seem like nothing."

"It was. Come on. Boil your water." Rosie gently turned Priya to the stove.

"Water is boring," Priya moaned. "I want to talk about Bodie."

"You can drool over Bodie later." Rosie ignited Priya's burner. "Maybe if you're lucky, they'll serve ice cream for lunch, and Bodie will eat it with his shirt off."

"Don't get my hopes up!"

They boiled their water without any more visits from Bodie Tal, and even though there wasn't any ice cream at lunch, Rosie was still happy to be in the cafeteria and done with boiling water for the day. Priya peeled off to grab a drink first, and Rosie stepped into the lunch line behind Clara. Even after spending all morning in the kitchen, not a hair in Clara's fancy fishtail braid was out of place. Dismayed, Rosie looked down at her own sloppy braid, frizzy strands escaping every which way. How did Clara do it? Was it hairspray? Some kind of secret braid alchemy Rosie wasn't privy to? Maybe she'd learned it at the same time she learned to boil water "with precision." Rosie still wasn't sure how Clara could be better at boiling water than everyone else, but Rosie was starting to feel like there was a lot she didn't understand in Chef Martinet's kitchen.

"We're going out tonight, right?" the girl with the pink hair asked, looking back over her shoulder to talk to Clara.

"Obviously."

"Curfew's a real downer, though."

"Ugh, I know, Elodie. Don't get me started." Clara stopped to scoop some farro onto her plate. "Nothing in Paris happens before midnight."

Privately, Rosie felt plenty happened before midnight. Like the first two hours of a good night's sleep. But Clara and the girl with the pink hair—Elodie—didn't ask her opinion. Rosie spooned some of the arugula-farro salad onto her own plate and headed to her table.

She slid into the seat she now thought of as hers, next to the empty seat she now thought of as Henry's. Yumi and Marquis were already there, and then Priya joined them, and Hampus, and Rosie found herself waiting for Henry, pushing her salad around the plate without really eating any of it. Which was silly. Good gravy! She could *eat* without him. Just to prove she could, she took a big bite.

"We should go out," Henry said, so fast she almost thought she hadn't heard it. He stood behind her with his tray, ostensibly about to sit in the empty chair next to her, so she felt rather than saw him. And her whole body froze. Henry wanted to go out. With her. Henry was *asking her out*?!

Rosie wished she didn't have so much salad in her mouth. She tried to swallow it all, in one huge lump, and then coughed a little as she forced it down. She hadn't imagined last night. Henry *must* have been about to kiss her. Because here he was, asking her out. She had to answer. What was she going to *say*?!

Yes, obviously. Right? Yes. She was going to say yes. And the idea of saying yes made her feel kind of nauseous, but the idea of saying anything *but* yes made her whole being shrivel up like an overcooked mushroom. She imagined the two of them going somewhere, together. Alone. They'd hold hands. Kiss, maybe. For real this time, with no interruptions from Madame Besson. Rosie had to say yes. But her throat felt like it had closed up, and she was having trouble saying anything.

Rosie stuck her hand into her pocket and curled her fingers around the little plastic pilot's wings she kept bringing with her everywhere, squeezing them once for good luck. Yes, she thought. Rosie, say yes.

"Duh, loser," Yumi said. Somehow the fact that there was a piece of arugula stuck next to one of her incisors did nothing to diminish her tone of authority. "It's Saturday night. Of course we're going out."

Priya tapped discreetly on her own incisor, and when Yumi smiled, the arugula was gone. And so was Rosie's feeling of excitement. Of course Henry wasn't *asking her out*. He just wanted to *go out*. Like, out of the building. A perfectly reasonable thing to want to do. Rosie bent her head over her salad and tried to hide her flaming cheeks behind her hair as Henry sat next to her.

She ate quietly while ideas about what to do tonight pingponged around her. Rosie still couldn't quite believe that they were allowed to leave the École and explore on their own— especially at night. Yes, they had a ten o'clock curfew, but as long as they were back in the dorm by ten, they could go anywhere they wanted. Rosie had a ten o'clock curfew back home, too, but she couldn't remember the last time she'd been out after dinner. Certainly not on her own. It was her older brothers who had always been going to some party, trying to sneak back in without waking anyone up.

A wave of homesickness washed over Rosie as she thought of being back in her bed in Ohio, listening to Ricky and Cole whisper as they crept past her door. Under the table, Rosie pulled out her phone and clicked open Mom's most recent e-mail.

Hi, sweetie! I'm sure your omelet was great—I know you make the best ham and cheese in East Liberty! (Shhh, don't tell the guys at work! ☺) Doing anything fun this weekend with your new friends? Don't forget to wear comfortable shoes for walking around! And take pictures. Lots of pictures! Oh—here's a picture of Owen with his meerkat habitat diorama. He wanted to show you. Love you bunches! Miss you!

Rosie scrolled down to see a beaming Owen standing in the kitchen, clutching a wobbly-looking model of what was apparently a meerkat habitat while Reed skulked in the background, attempting to avoid the camera. Well, at least Rosie had successfully sold Mom on the fiction that her omelet was okay. The lie made her feel kind of squirmy, but it was better than telling Mom her first couple days at the École had been a bit of a disaster. As she held it, Rosie's phone vibrated with a notification:

Ricky

BREAKFAST OF CHAMPIONS!!!!!!!!!!

In the picture that popped up next, he was eating Cinnamon Toast Crunch out of an orange bucket from Home Depot. Rosie laughed.

Rosie

Why are you up so early??

Ricky

FIFA qualifiers streaming them live on my phone

Rosie

and why are you eating out of a bucket?

Ricky

I couldn't find any bowls so I improvised

Ricky

Very avant-garde and chef-y, right?

Ricky

Like that guy you like who serves corn ice cream in a corn cob?

Ricky

Corn ice cream sounds weird, Ro

Ricky

Also where are the bowls?

Rosie paused to take a bite of her salad before composing her response.

Rosie

Dominique Ansel is a pastry GENIUS and if he makes corn ice cream, I'm sure it's delicious. Also think about how sweet corn can be? It totally makes sense. Anyway, you should tell Dominique about your cereal-bucket innovation. I'm sure he'd be impressed. And bowls are in the same place they've been for YEARS, in the cabinet to the left of the sink.

And upon further reflection, she added . . .

Rosie

> Please tell me you washed that bucket

Rosie saw the three dots pop up that meant Ricky was typing, but then they disappeared without any new text. Which didn't make Rosie feel confident that her brother hadn't accidentally ingested something lethal. But there wasn't much she could do about that from France. So Rosie slipped her phone back into her pocket and finished her lunch.

★★★★

Later that night, when they were getting ready to go out, Rosie had nearly forgotten her Henry-not-actually-asking-her-out embarrassment. Nearly.

"Why am I even reading this?" Yumi muttered from her position on the floor, lying on her stomach, stripy-socked feet poking up into the air. She flipped another page in the magazine. "Seriously. Why? I don't even know who any of these people are."

"You will come to know them, and you will come to love them," Priya said, her voice slightly garbled as she carefully smudged eyeliner across her lower lash line, a task that apparently had to be accomplished with one's mouth hanging wide open. Rosie sat across from her, cross-legged on Priya's bed, holding up a small circular mirror so Priya could do her makeup in their room and not in the communal bathroom down the hall. The bathroom *seemed* like it should be big enough for ten girls, with its multiple stalls and four showers, but it had been a bit of a madhouse that morning as everyone tried to get ready before class. And right now, Rosie was willing to bet that all of the available sink space was covered in makeup bags and dangerously hot curling irons and girls jostling for space.

"Why is this magazine so aggressive?" Yumi flipped another page. "I mean, *HELLO!* What's that exclamation point about? It doesn't need to *shout* at me."

"We have *OK!* in America," Rosie said. "I think that's worse. It's aggressively declaring its mediocrity."

"*HELLO!* is simply greeting you enthusiastically." Priya switched to her other eye. Rosie moved the mirror slightly, tracking her. "Oh, Yumi, I'm so glad you'll now be fully updated on the whereabouts of the royals."

"These royals need to calm it down," Yumi said. "They're *everywhere*. Charity functions. Schools. The Serengeti. Is there any inch of your country that isn't crawling with royals?"

"Pretty sure the Serengeti isn't in England," Rosie said.

"Shoreditch, at the very least, is a decidedly royals-free zone," Priya assured them.

"There are way too many of them. Are you *sure* all these people are really royal?" Yumi squinted at the magazine. "None of them look familiar."

"There are always more royals than you think," Priya said meditatively, like running into princes was just a thing that happened, sort of like you might run into your mailman at Walmart and feel weird about it, unsure if you were supposed to say hi or not.

"Hat game's on point, though," Yumi said. "Can I tear out this picture for my inspo board?"

"*That* hat? That hat's inspiring you?" Rosie asked skeptically.

The hat looked like a sea creature rendered inanimate. Yumi shrugged.

"Who is that? Eugenie?" Priya glanced away from the mirror, down at the image of a startled-looking woman in a hat that seemed about to take flight from her head. "Yeah, go for it. How did I do?" she asked Rosie.

"Perfect," Rosie said. The shimmery copper eye shadow made Priya's eyes look enormous, and her eyelashes were so thick and dark, they looked like a different species from Rosie's eyelashes. Rosie's eyelashes turned blond at the tips, giving the impression that they disappeared millimeters before they actually did. Rosie had seen a picture of a naked mole rat in one of Owen's animal books and had thought they'd had pretty similar features, when it came to eyelashes.

"I don't know *why* you're making an effort," Yumi said. "Not that your makeup's not bangin', because it is, but I don't think there's anyone here worth putting makeup on for."

"Are you having a laugh?" Priya asked, aghast. "Have you even *looked* at Bodie Tal? The boy is seriously fit."

"If you like that D-list celebrity baby kind of thing." Yumi sniffed.

"Rosie. Back me up?" Priya pleaded.

"He's cute," Rosie admitted, recalling her jacket-riding-up fantasy.

"Are you blushing?" Yumi demanded. "Is that a blush? *Are you kidding me?!*"

"No female is immune to the charms of Bodie Tal," Priya said triumphantly.

"I'm immune. I'm extremely immune. He's overrated. And

definitely not as cute as he thinks he is. You know the ego on that guy needs its own chair in the cafeteria."

"He helped me get a pot," Rosie said in a near-whisper.

"I'm sorry, what was that?" Yumi cupped her hand to her ear.

"He helped me get a pot!" Rosie said, and now she was the one who was shouting. "He helped me get a pot," she said, at a more normal volume, although this was now the third time she'd said it, and it was no less weird or random than the first time she'd said it. But Priya was nodding at her sagely, like the pot was, in fact, of great import.

"He got you a pot?" Yumi slow-clapped sarcastically. "Well, let's get the young man a Nobel Peace Prize. A pot. You've got to be friggin' kidding me."

"No one's saying he needs a prize," Priya said. "Just that he's insanely gorgeous. And speaking of insanely gorgeous . . ." Priya turned to Rosie, waggling her eyebrows. "Can I do your makeup? Please? But only if you want, of course," she added hurriedly. "You're lovely as is. But I'd be happy to. My sisters and I always do each other's makeup."

"Makeup is a tool of the patriarchy," Yumi said from the floor. She'd flopped over onto her back, but her feet were still up in the air, kicking tiny little flutter kicks, like she was swimming.

"Bollocks," Priya scoffed. "It's *fun*. Rosie? What do you think?"

"Sure," Rosie said. "Why not?" Because, honestly, *why not*? Maybe going-out Rosie always wore makeup. Nobody here knew any differently. How odd, Rosie thought, and how freeing, to be in a place where nobody knew anything about her.

There was freedom in that, a freedom that made Rosie feel like she was really breathing for the first time in a long time, pulling in deep lungfuls of air, when before she'd only been able to get shallow gasps.

Rosie closed her eyes as Priya instructed and felt the whisper of a brush over her eyelids. Tickly, but nice. Unlike the eyeliner, which turned out to be literal torture. She blinked uncontrollably as Priya made repeated attempts to stab her in the eyeball. Or that's what it felt like, anyway. She continued to blink as the mascara went on, and if she ended up resembling anything other than a waterlogged panda, she'd be downright shocked.

"Perfect." Priya smudged her thumb under Rosie's left eye. "Would you like to see?"

"You look the same," Yumi said, deadpan. "You looked fine before and you look fine now. This is all a conspiracy by Big Makeup to steal money from women's paychecks. It's worse than the wage gap."

"Honestly." Priya tutted as she held the mirror up for Rosie. She reached up an experimental finger to poke one of her eyelashes, unable to believe they were really that long, or that dark. That they were hers. She wondered what Henry would think. If he'd even notice. If he'd think she looked different at all. If maybe she always looked like this, he'd actually ask her out. Rosie blinked at her reflection again. He'd probably think she looked the same. She was, after all, still Rosie. Even if a Rosie who wore makeup and went out on a Saturday night was almost unrecognizable.

"Can we get out of here?" Yumi stood up, chucking the magazine onto Priya's bed. "You guys ready, finally?"

"We're ready." Priya patted Rosie's knee twice, like Mom would have. Rosie closed one eye, looking at the silver shimmer on her eyelid.

"Great. We're ready to go." Yumi already had her leather jacket on. "Does anyone even know where we're going?"

Rosie didn't know. But she couldn't wait to get there.

CHAPTER ELEVEN

Henry

S o here we are," Marquis said as they waited in the courtyard outside the École. Henry rocked back and forth, rolling his gym shoes over the cobblestones. It was darker than he'd thought it would be at seven p.m. And colder. Not Chicago cold, but cold enough that he probably should have worn something warmer than a hoodie. He'd considered running back in to grab something warmer at least a dozen times, but hadn't, worried he'd miss Rosie. Which made no sense, because Marquis could have just asked them to wait, but Henry felt, fervently, that he had to be here when she got here. That it would be unlucky or something if he wasn't. "Think they'll be here soon?"

"Dunno. Probably." Henry cast an anxious glance up at the windows on the girls' side of the third floor. He saw nothing but the golden glow of lights in the windows, which were oddly shimmery. Was it raining? No. Please no. Henry felt something small hit the top of his head. Then another something. Yup, definitely a drizzle. Perfect.

"You sure you wanna go out, man?" Marquis was squinting up at the sky. "We could just hang out in the common room or something. Bet there's some weird French TV we could watch."

"No way." Henry pulled his hood up, which did absolutely nothing. Now he just felt wet cotton instead of wet hair. "We're going out."

Not that there was anything wrong with the common room. It was pretty cool, actually. The common room was on the first floor, across the hall from the cafeteria, and just as big—it looked like it had also been a ballroom back in the day. But now it was full of comfy chairs and huge couches and, yes, a TV. Definitely an awesome place to hang out, and certainly a lot drier than wherever it was they'd end up going. But he wanted to actually go *out* with Rosie, away from the building, into Paris, where it felt like anything might be possible. Like Henry might even be able to muster up the courage to *really* ask her out. And to kiss her, finally, with no Madame Besson in sight. He couldn't stop replaying that moment on the roof over and over again, wondering what would have happened if they hadn't been interrupted.

He had to kiss her. He had to at least *try*. Or he was going to lose his mind.

"It's raining," Marquis said, stating the obvious.

"If we wait for a dry night, we'll never go anywhere," Henry argued. "It rains a lot in Paris."

"Fine. You win," Marquis capitulated. "I guess it'll be good to get out of here for a while. I wasn't emotionally prepared for school on Saturday."

Henry agreed. True, it was a half day, and true, it was cooking, not actual school, but still. There was something weird about not having the full weekend. And they hadn't even started their academic classes yet. That would come Monday. Henry was trying to imagine having his cooking classes and math and English in the same day, and struggling.

The door opened, but it wasn't Rosie who came out. It was Bodie Tal, wearing a distressed leather jacket.

"Henry, right?" Bodie asked, pulling a hand out of his pocket.

"Yeah. Hey." Again with the bro handshake. Henry still felt like he was doing it wrong.

"Bodie, this is Marquis," Henry said.

"Marquis! Hey, man!" Somehow the bro handshake looked a lot more natural when Bodie and Marquis did it. Was there something wrong with Henry's hand? Was he missing some kind of bro chromosome? "*Chopped* teen grand champion. Dad said that pain perdu you did with the Ho Hos in the final round was killer."

"Thanks, man. I appreciate it." Marquis grinned.

"Dude." Henry found himself at a loss for words. "You won *Chopped*?!"

"He didn't just win it. He destroyed it. Dad was a guest judge—said it wasn't even close."

"It wasn't," Marquis said, and Bodie laughed.

"Hey, I think I'm meeting up with Fernando and Clara and Elodie at some club," Bodie said. "You guys wanna come with?"

"At *seven p.m.*?" Henry asked. Henry had never been to a

club before. But he had a pretty good idea that seven p.m. wasn't the right time to go to one.

"Yeah, I don't know." Bodie rolled his eyes. "Fernando was pretty set on it."

"He's a determined guy," Marquis said. "That dude squeezed himself into the tightest pair of pants I've ever seen in my life. It was, like, a twenty-minute struggle to get them on. I was worried that he was going to ask me for help."

Henry thought of Hampus's now-familiar early morning squats-in-boxers routine. Things could definitely be worse.

"Well, think about the club," Bodie said. "It's over on the Rue des Haudriettes if you wanna come later."

And with one last "See ya," Bodie Tal headed out into the night.

"*Chopped*? Seriously? *Chopped*?" Henry asked.

"Yes. Seriously. *Chopped*. So where are we going?"

"I don't want to go to a club." Even thinking about going to a club with Rosie made Henry feel all sweaty and weird. Dancing was not his strong suit.

"Yeah, nothing about that look screams *I'm ready to hit the clubs*." Henry knew Marquis was teasing, but he couldn't resist tugging at the hem of his shirt self-consciously. He'd spent way too long picking out this specific long-sleeved tee, hoodie, and jeans, which were in no appreciable way different than any of his other long-sleeved tees, hoodies, and jeans. "Am I missing something? Do *you* know where we're going?"

"Um . . . no," Henry admitted.

Probably a thing he should have figured out by now. But that was one of the biggest problems with this entire enterprise— he'd *never* had a plan.

When he'd stood behind Rosie and blurted *We should go out*, Henry didn't even really know *what* he was saying. He *wanted* to ask her out. But he didn't think standing behind her and blurting out weird declarative statements was the way to go about it. Not that he really knew what the right way to go about it was. He had an absurd vision of himself dropping a note off at Rosie's station that read, *Will you go out with me? Check Yes or No* with little boxes. Or asking Priya to ask Rosie if she liked him. All of his dating ideas came straight out of third grade.

Which is why he'd been relieved when Yumi had commandeered the conversation, assuming he'd been talking to the entire table.

"Okay, well, what do you want to do? Get some food?"

"Food is good." Henry looked back up at the windows. Food *was* good. They could all get something to eat together. And then, maybe, on the walk back, Henry could get Rosie to hang back a bit, and it would be even *better* than sitting on a roof, the two of them alone, on the streets of Paris. . . .

"You're being weird, man." Marquis assessed Henry critically. "Like . . . twitchy, somehow."

"Not being weird."

"You are, but that's okay. I can take over."

"Take over?"

"Relax." Marquis clapped Henry on the shoulder. "I don't know what's going on right now, but relax. I got this."

The door to the École swung open with such force that it banged against the stone doorframe. Backlit by the glow from within, there they were: Yumi, Priya, and Rosie. *Rosie.* Henry had never seen her with her hair down before. It tumbled, almost to her waist, curling softly, like a Disney princess's. And there was something different about her eyes. They seemed bigger, somehow, and darker, with the same shine the rain had given the cobblestones in the courtyard.

"Okay, boys." Yumi hopped down the stone steps, neatly sidestepping a rapidly forming puddle in a dip on the bottommost stair. Rosie hung back with Priya, helping as Priya struggled to open a very capable-looking black umbrella. "Where are you taking me?"

"I'm about to change your life," Marquis said.

"Is that *Hamilton*?" Yumi asked, consternation evident on her face. "Are *you* Elizabeth Schuyler?"

"Uh . . . maybe?"

The umbrella whooshed open with an audible *pop*, and Rosie and Priya hurried down the stairs beneath it.

"Then by all means, lead the way," Yumi said. "Where are we going, again?"

"You'll see when we get there."

"But I want to know *now*."

Yumi and Marquis were already making their way out of the courtyard, bickering as they went. Henry stepped back to walk with Rosie and Priya.

"I think there's room under here," Rosie offered, tipping the angle of the umbrella up to let him in.

"There's room for everyone under this umbrella. The thing's bloody enormous," Priya said as Henry ducked under the umbrella to stand with Rosie. "I'm worried Mum thinks I'll melt if I get wet. Like the Wicked Witch of the West."

Henry knew they were allowed to leave the École, but it still felt illicit to exit the courtyard, cross through the wrought iron gates, and turn down the Rue des Minimes. Large as it was, the École disappeared from view entirely as they rounded the corner and turned onto another street, the vast building swallowed up by the twists and turns of the medieval city.

Marquis led them down a street so narrow it wasn't a street at all—more of an alley, really. Henry spotted a small restaurant with a couple lingering over an empty plate and two small cups of coffee in the large window. Two glass lamps with real flames inside flickered on either side of a blue door, and painted on a sign that swung out into the alley above the doorway, he saw a French word he definitely knew. *Crêpes.*

"Crêpes," Yumi said lustily. "It may be a cliché, but it's a cliché for a reason."

Crêpes were perfect. Casual, but delicious, *obviously* the right choice for their first real night out in Paris. Henry owed Marquis. Big-time.

"Crêpes," Rosie said, smiling up at the sign. "The only crêpes I've ever had came from a Bob Evans. Or the ones I tried to make myself, but it's hard without the right pan."

"It's impossible," Henry agreed. When he'd tried, they'd come out sort of thick and gummy. "We have this awesome crêpe stand at the farmers market back home, though. I go every Sunday, in the summer."

"These'll be even better," Marquis said. "Trust me."

Henry held open the door, and after only a few minutes of struggle with the umbrella—he eventually subdued it—they filed inside.

Within, the restaurant was even narrower than the alley outside. There were only four tables, total. But the smell—the *smell*—Henry wanted to bottle it. He looked over to see that Rosie had closed her eyes, and was inhaling deeply.

A woman in a gray T-shirt and a white canvas apron leaned out from the open kitchen, her elbows resting on the pass-through. It seemed like the kitchen here was even smaller than the one in his family's restaurant back home, which Henry had thought would have been impossible. She said something in French, which sounded friendly, not that he could understand any of it. Henry thought he might have caught *bonjour*, but he couldn't even be confident in that. She said something else and gestured toward a table, then waited expectantly.

"*D'accord.*" Marquis nodded at her, smiling. "She says we should just push the tables together."

"You understood that?" Henry asked as they started moving chairs and pushing tables.

"I understood enough." Marquis lined up the last chair. Henry wondered if he could maneuver his way into sitting next to Rosie without looking too obvious. "I've been taking French since sixth grade."

"I'm jealous," Rosie said, as she slid into the chair next to where Henry was standing. *She* sat next to *him*! Henry couldn't help the grin that broke out across his face. "We've only got Spanish at my school."

"I've been taking French for ages, and I'm still rubbish," Priya said, shaking her head. "That sounded like a load of bla-de-bla to me."

"We'll learn," Rosie said, smiling at her. "French class starts on Monday, remember?"

"Ugh, don't remind me." Yumi groaned. "I don't want to

take classes. I just want to *cook*. I wish the École was a free pass out of school for the year."

Henry agreed. His grades had *never* been good. He couldn't imagine it would be any different here.

A bell tinkled at the door, and it opened to reveal Hampus, much to Henry's astonishment.

"Hampus!" Henry waved at him, like he couldn't see them. There were only seven people in the whole restaurant. "How did you *find* us?"

Hampus made his way to their table, struggling to navigate his considerable bulk and two bulging canvas tote bags through the tiny restaurant. "It was not challenging," he said, settling himself into the vacant chair at the head of the table. "This is the best crêperie in Le Marais. And quite close. And I thought to myself, on a night like this, what would be better than a crêpe?"

"Brilliant deduction, Holmes," Priya said, a smile tugging at the corners of her lips.

"What have you been up to?" Henry asked.

"Foraging!"

"Foraging?" Yumi asked, eyes narrowed, confused. "Like a squirrel?"

"Squirrel? What is squirrel?" Hampus asked, intrigued.

Henry thought of how to describe a squirrel. A more appealing rat? A rodent with a furry tail? Then Rosie drew her hands up into paws, nibbling at an imaginary acorn as she chattered, looking for all the world like a large, blondish squirrel.

"Yes! I know this animal! It is *ekorre*!" Hampus cheered.

Rosie dropped her hands into her lap, flushed, like she'd

just realized she'd busted out a killer squirrel impression in the middle of a restaurant. Which she had.

"You must be *lethal* at charades," Henry marveled.

"My brother," she muttered. "My littlest brother. He, um, he likes animals."

"So you've been running around Paris like a giant ekorre?" Yumi asked, looking at Hampus.

"Yes. Like the ekorre, I have found many treasures."

Hampus nearly upended the table as he reached beneath it to grab his canvas bags. As she leaned forward to look inside, Rosie's leg brushed Henry's, and this time, she didn't apologize, or move it away.

He hadn't eaten a bite yet, but it was official: this was the best crêperie in Paris.

And Henry was going to kiss her. Tonight.

CHAPTER TWELVE

Rosie

Rosie could not believe she had just gone full-on squirrel. In a *restaurant*. In front of two literal strangers, and five other people who weren't strangers but were still *new*.

Thankfully, no one was staring at Rosie like she was a giant freak. Rosie could have kissed Yumi, who had skillfully turned the conversation away from her and back toward Hampus, who was excitedly grabbing bunches of greens out of his tote bag and shaking them enthusiastically, spraying little clods of dirt on the table. Rosie leaned in like she was paying attention, but she wasn't. She was trying to remember the last time she'd gone out like this, with friends. She *used* to go to Applebee's with her friends and eat greasy cheeseburger egg rolls until she thought she might barf, but she hadn't gone in forever. She hadn't really gone anywhere in forever.

"So they're weeds," Priya said, as Rosie drifted back into the conversation.

"Yes! There is much to be found foraging, even in these urban environments!" Hampus gestured to his weeds. "Of course, back home, there is much more to be found—mosses, lichens, all sorts of things—but even here, among the cobblestones, there is something."

"I like this one," Henry said. Rosie almost jumped as she realized he was eating weeds straight out of Hampus's tote bag. "It's kind of peppery."

"Dude, you are going to get a *disease*." Yumi shook her head. "Who knows what happened to that weed before you ate it? A dog could have peed on it!"

"Honestly, Yumi, we're about to eat," Priya said. "Can you not talk about weeing?"

"Many great chefs are foragers," Hampus countered. "And I have seen many videos of urban foragers as well. You know Maangchi?"

"*You* know Maangchi?" Henry asked, grabbing a different weed, disregarding Yumi's warning. "Ooo," he said as he chewed. "Bitter."

"Maangchi?" Rosie asked.

"She's a Korean food blogger," Henry said after he swallowed. "I'm surprised you've heard of her in Sweden."

"Jukkasjärvi is very small, Henry," Hampus said. "There are very few restaurants, and even fewer where one is able to eat foods from different places around the world. I learn from the internet." Rosie certainly empathized with that. "I would very much like to try kimchi, but I cannot get the ingredients. It is impossible."

"Come to Chicago," Henry said. "My dad'll feed you so much kimchi you'll be sweating it out of your pores."

"I've never had kimchi, either," Rosie said. "But I'd love to try it."

Henry looked like he was about to say something, but before he could, the waitress appeared with menus and left a stack on their table. Rosie picked up the single laminated sheet of paper with two columns, one labeled *Gallettes* with a numbered list of different items, the other *Crêpes Sucres*. Hmm. The only gallettes Rosie knew were free-form tarts with fruit fillings. But that couldn't have been right. She scanned the numbered list below *Gallettes*—*Oeuf. Jambon. Gruyère.* Gruyère! That was a cheese! Definitely not a fruit tart, then.

"A gallette," Hampus mused. "It is buckwheat flour, is it not?"

"Yeah." Marquis nodded as his eyes scanned the menu. "Gallettes are crêpes made with buckwheat flour and savory toppings."

"Ooo, even I know some of these," Priya said. "Oeuf. Jambon. Egg. Ham. I really must have paid attention during that breakfast unit. Gets a bit dodgy once we head toward lunch foods, unfortunately. Sucre. Hmm. What's a sucre, then?"

"Sugar," Rosie answered. That was a word that certainly popped up often enough on the baking blogs she read. So those must have been the sweet crêpes. Here and there Rosie could pick out words that made sense—*fruits, chocolat, bananes*—and she wanted some of everything.

"I don't know what any of this means, but I'm pretty sure I want one of everything," Henry said quietly as everyone at the table asked Marquis translation questions, the conversation flowing around them. Rosie looked up at him quickly. "What?" he asked.

"Are you telepathic?"

"No. But I *am* planning to order an absolutely insane, truly disgusting amount of food," Henry said. There was something about the way Henry smiled at her that made Rosie not embarrassed about briefly turning into a squirrel anymore, that made her feel like nothing she did could possibly be embarrassing. And there was something about the way he said what he wanted that made ordering an absolutely insane, truly disgusting amount of food seem like the right thing—no, the only thing—to do. "And what I really need is for you to save me from myself."

"So . . . you *don't* want me to let you order an insane amount of food?"

"Rosie! Please!" Henry looked shocked. "Let's get one thing straight right now—I will always, always order an insane amount of food. And no one can stop me, so don't even try."

"So you need me to . . . ?"

"To help me eat it."

"That I can do," she said, and Henry held up his hand for a high five. She smacked his palm and found herself wishing the high five wasn't the briefest, least romantic form of physical contact the world had ever known.

Eventually, the waitress came by and took their orders, which involved lots of pointing and some dismal attempts at French. Whenever Rosie tried to say *sucre*, it stuck in the back of her throat, and she couldn't quite figure out how many syllables it was supposed to have. But she could point, and that was clear enough.

For as long as it had taken them to order, the food arrived in almost an instant. The waitress arrived bearing plates of crêpes stacked two deep on her arms, dropped them off at the table, and returned with more.

The gallettes were darker, a nut-brown from the buckwheat flour, and folded from a circle into a square, with the savory toppings peeping through invitingly. Rosie saw what looked like goat cheese on Yumi's plate. And maybe ratatouille on Marquis's. And over on the plate between her and Henry—ugh, a fat yellow egg stared back at her. Rosie still hadn't forgiven eggs for the whole omelet debacle.

"It's called oeuf miroir," Henry said, poking the yolk with his fork almost reverentially, as Marquis and Yumi debated whether or not they should wait for everyone to get their food before they started eating. Yumi, her cheeks full of goat cheese, was firmly on the side of *not*. "It means *egg mirror*. Or *mirror egg*. I think. It looks kind of like a mirror, yeah? And then there's ham and Gruyère underneath. Here, you can have the first bite."

Rosie loved Gruyère. And that egg *did* look perfect. Maybe she could put aside her egg grudge. Just this one time. And so she took her fork and knife and cut a small square off the side of the plate.

Good gravy. The flavors exploded in her mouth. Buckwheat flour was a revelation—nuttier than she'd expected, not like a nut, really, but she couldn't think of any other way to say it. It had a subtle flavor all its own, crisp edges from where it had been seared on the hot pan, and a perfectly soft, almost spongy texture within, where the Gruyère melted into the salty ham, and before Rosie knew it, she'd eaten three bites.

"Get some yolk!" Henry encouraged, pushing the plate closer toward her. "This yolk is *everything*. It adds this, like . . . creamy . . . fattiness . . . none of these words are right. . . ."

"Maybe we'll learn the right words in French class on Monday," Rosie suggested, taking the smallest bite of egg yolk. It was delicious. Stupid eggs.

"I have a feeling we'll be stuck with *Hi, my name is Henry* for the foreseeable future," he said glumly. Rosie was surprised. She couldn't wait to start French class. Henry, obviously, felt otherwise.

"Priya, is that banana and Nutella?" Yumi shrieked from across the table. "I didn't know you were so *basic*," she teased.

"Sod off," Priya said good-naturedly. "It's the greatest combination known to man."

Three more crêpes materialized in front of Henry and Rosie, one of which had three slices of banana and a drizzle of Nutella on top.

"I got banana-Nutella, too," he said, grinning. "Guess that makes me basic."

Next to the gallettes with their savory fillings, and even the banana-Nutella crêpe with its seductive chocolaty drizzle across the top, and especially next to whatever monstrosity Henry had ordered topped with three scoops of vanilla ice cream, the crêpe au sucre Rosie had selected certainly looked plain. It was a slim triangle dusted with sugar, but Rosie swore the sugar was sparkling in the dim light of the restaurant. She cut a tiny triangle off the tip and took a bite. Now this, this was everything. It *was* simple, but in the way that reminded Rosie that sometimes the simplest things were the best. The crêpe was golden and buttery and the caramelized sugar crunchy before it dissolved instantly, melting on Rosie's tongue. It couldn't be anything more than butter, sugar, flour, and milk. And yet . . . those simple ingredients were transformed into something transcendent. And that, Rosie thought, was exactly the power of cooking.

The banana-Nutella was addictive. And the crêpe with the ice cream was obviously delicious, if slightly insane. But Rosie found herself most enjoying the simple crêpe au sucre.

The mountains of crêpes disappeared at an alarmingly rapid pace. Eventually, only Henry was still eating, working doggedly through his mountain of ice cream.

"I'm stuffed," Yumi groaned from across the table, clutching her belly. "Henry, how are you still going?"

"Sheer determination and force of will," he said, and Rosie laughed. She had always thought she had the biggest sweet tooth in the world, but Henry was putting her to shame.

"Warning, everyone: it's nine forty-five," Priya announced.

"Finished just in time," Henry said, and sure enough, he had chased the last melting bits of ice cream around the plate and put down his spoon.

"You sure you don't want to lick the plate?" Rosie teased.

"Maybe next time." Henry smiled. "When we know each other a little bit better."

Rosie blushed as his eyes met hers, pleased, but suddenly shy about holding eye contact. Especially after some of Henry's hair fell in front of his eyes, and Rosie was possessed by an almost irrepressible urge to smooth it away from his face and run her fingers through his hair. To keep herself from assaulting the side of his head, Rosie pressed her finger to the plate, picking up a few lingering sugar crystals, and stuck her finger in her mouth. Apparently, *she* was the one who wanted to lick her plate.

The waitress seemed content to let them sit there all evening, but Rosie was glad that no one was willing to risk missing curfew. Yumi got the bill with what Rosie was quickly recognizing as her signature flair, and Marquis helped them decode the check. They'd be back at the École with plenty of time to spare.

Despite all the crêpes in her belly, as they burst out of the restaurant and into the street, Rosie felt lighter than she had in months. Longer than that, maybe. Clutching Priya's arm and laughing about nothing, really, Rosie followed the group back to the École.

"Hey, Rosie," Henry called from behind her.

Rosie squeezed Priya's arm and let her run on ahead, stopping and turning to see Henry loitering in front of a shop window with a neon-green cross.

"What do you think this place is?" he asked.

"Um . . . a pharmacy?" Rosie answered.

"How did you—"

She pointed up at the gold letters spelling out PHARMACIE over the door.

"Right." He laughed as he reached up to scratch the back of his neck. Except he didn't really laugh, he said, "Heh-heh-heh," in a strange, strangled voice. "Obviously. Heh-heh-heh."

"Henry, are you—?"

"Let's walk," he said abruptly.

"Um . . . okay?"

He was being weird. *Really* weird. Rosie watched his eyes dart from side to side as he walked down the sidewalk, hands jammed into his pockets. Then he stopped, just as abruptly as he'd started, and looked at her.

Wait. Was it happening? Like, actually happening this time, with no Madame Besson barging in with a cigarette? Rosie licked her lips nervously. What should she do? Should she lean in?

"Rosie?" he said, like he was asking a question.

"Henry," she answered, hoping this was finally their moment.

"It's nine fifty-seven!" Priya called from somewhere ahead of them in the darkness.

"Nine fifty-seven," Rosie repeated, panic gripping her. "Henry! Come on!"

She started running, sprinting as fast as she could toward Priya's voice, determined not to be late. After only a couple strides her chest burned and her legs ached—running was pure evil—but she had to get back to the École. Rosie heard Henry running alongside her. Gosh, she hoped it was dark enough that he couldn't see how red and sweaty she was. Henry reached the gates a few paces before Rosie did, holding it open behind him as she slipped through. She stopped for a moment to catch her breath, feeling the uncomfortable prickle of sweat at her temples.

"Hold that gate!"

Rosie held the gate, as she turned to see who was yelling behind her. It was Bodie Tal, sprinting ahead of three others—Elodie and Clara, their arms around each other's waists, and a guy with dark hair shuffling behind them. Maybe Fernando, Marquis's roommate.

"Hey," Bodie said, nodding at Rosie, like he knew her, which he did, technically. Sort of. She was still having trouble processing Bodie Tal as a person she actually *knew*, not as someone on a TV show or in a *People* magazine article. Rosie realized she was staring, so she nodded back at him, then lifted her hair over one shoulder, the weight of it suddenly clammy against her neck. "Did we make it?" he asked.

"It's nine fifty-seven," Rosie said, surprised by how cool her voice sounded, how detached, like she was just telling the time to a random passerby. Not *Bodie Tal.*

She had to stop thinking of him as *Bodie Tal* and start thinking of him as Bodie, a guy in her class. Otherwise she'd do something embarrassing like ask him to sign her arm.

"That's a miracle." He ran a hand over the back of his head, bristling the short hair there, like it was unfamiliar to him. "Those two were walking so slowly I thought we'd never make it. You can't wear *heels* on *cobblestones*," he said derisively.

"They're not that slow." Rosie watched Clara and Elodie progress through the courtyard. "Just a little unsteady. Kind of like baby giraffes."

He laughed, and his eyes crinkled when he smiled, and he looked less like *Bodie Tal,* and more like, well, just some guy. Some exceptionally cute guy, but still. Someone who was human. Like her.

Something shoved Rosie—hard—and she stumbled forward. She was vaguely conscious of Bodie scrabbling the air, reaching for her, but she was in front of him, too far away, and she landed with a thud on her knees and her palms, a horrible jarring sensation traveling up her wrists. Oh no, her *wrists.* Her wrists had to be okay. She needed them to whisk, and to flip, and to stir, and to do, well, everything. Gingerly, she pushed herself up so she was kneeling, barely mindful of the wet cobblestones soaking her jeans—her *good* jeans, the nice ones that she'd found at the Salvation Army over in Alliance.

She rolled her wrists one way, then the other, but there was no sharp pain, no disturbing crackles or pops—just soreness that would, hopefully, be gone by morning.

"Clara!" Bodie said sharply. "What's wrong with you?"

"Sorry," Clara said, and there was a bit of a slur to her *sorry*. Rosie looked up at her quickly. Was she *drunk*?

"It was an accident," Elodie said quickly, and Rosie thought there was a bit of a slur to her voice, too. Maybe. She wasn't sure. Rosie looked up at them from her place on the pavement, and they seemed impossibly tall, their legs long and thin, as they towered over her.

"Rosie! Are you okay?" Henry asked. He was already at the door of the École, but he'd turned around, concern furrowing on his brow, and was coming back. For her. "Let me help you up."

"No worries," Bodie said, and as he spoke, he extended a hand down, and Rosie could see all of his tattoos snaking their way up his arm, disappearing under the sleeve of his T-shirt. How was he not freezing? "I've got it."

And so Rosie took Bodie's hand, and she let herself be pulled up.

CHAPTER THIRTEEN

Henry

Henry didn't even know what had happened last night. He'd asked Rosie to hang back with him, like he'd planned, but then he'd chickened out. Repeatedly. And when he'd *finally* been about to do something, Rosie had literally run away. Not *because* he'd been about to kiss her, but still—not great. So Henry had chased her back to the École, psyching himself up to kiss her as soon as they made it safely through the gates. He had thought Rosie was right behind him, and then he looked back, and she was on the ground. And then Bodie was helping her up, and Henry wished he'd been there instead. He could have helped her up, then pulled her close to him and kissed her, and that would have been the *perfect moment*. But he hadn't been there. Bodie had. And it *sucked*.

Even though Henry had been back in his room at the perfectly responsible—too responsible, honestly—stroke of ten o'clock, he'd stayed up way too late. Because all he could think about was how spectacularly he'd failed at trying to kiss

Rosie. And when he'd tried to distract himself by checking his e-mail, there had been one from Mom, asking if he felt prepared for his classes to start on Monday, double-checking that she had the correct list of subjects, and reminding him that she expected a full report on all of his grades. Had she asked anything about what he'd cooked? Or eaten? Had she even mentioned the omelet, which Henry *knew* Dad must have told her about?

Of course she hadn't. Because she didn't care about any of it. Didn't care about anything that really mattered.

So when Hampus had asked him if he wanted to watch some Swedish show on his laptop—with subtitles, obviously—of course Henry had said yes. The last thing he wanted to do was think about Mom and school starting on Monday, or even worse, blowing things with Rosie. They'd binge-watched almost an entire season of *Bron/Broen*, and Henry must have crawled into bed at some point, because he'd slept until eleven a.m. Well, he'd been woken briefly by Hampus's early-morning-squats routine, but he'd rolled right back over and gone to sleep, and Hampus was gone by the time Henry woke up for real. Foraging, presumably. Or maybe running? The passionate dedication to the squats seemed to imply some sort of fitness regime. Personally, Henry couldn't think of anything he wanted to do less than run. He just wanted to eat.

Downstairs, Henry poked his head into the dining room. All the tables were empty, including, unfortunately, the serving tables at the head of the room. Too late for breakfast and too early for lunch. What he wanted, what he *really* wanted, he realized suddenly, was a Coke. He hadn't had one since arriving in France, and right now, nothing sounded better than an ice-cold soda. He needed to shake off his Swedish TV hangover.

Outside the École, the sun struggled to peek through the clouds, swaddling Le Marais in a light that looked much more like early-morning than almost-noon. Henry wandered away from school, no direction in mind, hoping to find somewhere, anywhere, with Coke. The wind picked up, sending an old bit of newspaper scuttling across the road, and Henry got a whiff of something incredible. *Bread.* Someone was baking bread. Hopefully, it was a bakery. And hopefully, it was open.

As Henry turned onto the next street, the smell got stronger. He literally followed his nose, like he was a cartoon dog salivating as he zoomed toward a bone. That scent was *unreal.* It had to be coming from a bakery. Only commercial ovens could produce a smell that strong. Right?

Right. Because there it was, a shop sitting proudly on the corner lot, almost like a tiny, two-story version of the Flatiron Building he remembered from his family's trip to New York City last Christmas. There were blue-and-white-striped round awnings over the windows and the door, and BOULANGERIE painted in flowing gold script on the glass. As Henry got closer, he could see the displays: a veritable mountain of baguettes and some kind of fat, round loaf; tarts with shiny fruits glistening on cake stands; decadent éclairs displayed like cigars in a box. Two women left the shop, talking, baguettes under their arms, pale pink pastry boxes in their hands. Henry nodded at them, waited for the steps to clear, and pushed his way into the boulangerie, the golden bell tinkling behind him as the door shut.

"Bonjour!" The man behind the counter greeted Henry enthusiastically, smiling through a neatly trimmed beard and wiping his hands on his apron, small eddies of flour floating into the air as he did so. Rosie would love it here, Henry thought. He'd have to show her.

He'd only meant to get a croissant, something to tide him over before lunch. But pretty soon he'd pointed at a croissant and what he was pretty sure was a chocolate croissant. And something else that looked kind of like a croissant but was shaped like a half-moon. And a little roll with a crimped sort of bottom and a round shiny top, with another little round piece of bread on top, almost like a hat. And an éclair, because he was in France, so he should probably get an éclair. And a baguette, for the same reason.

And then Henry saw it. The tart. It was small, so small it could fit in the palm of his hand, and filled with some kind of fruit—apple, probably, or maybe pear or some kind of stone fruit—but the fruit was sliced so thin that Henry couldn't tell what it was. Each slice was arranged like the petal of a flower, so that the tart looked exactly like a rose. A buttery, sugary, edible pastry rose. He'd bring it back to the dorm for Rosie. He'd wait for her in the common room, and then he'd see what she thought about the lamination in the croissants and the crumb structure of the bread and the way everything tasted, and maybe she'd forget about how weird he'd been last night. As always, food would save the day. Henry pointed excitedly at the tart.

The man said something else to Henry and laughed, and Henry just laughed along with him. Probably a joke about how much food he'd ordered. Maybe in a few months this would all be routine, and he could just walk into a boulangerie and get one thing, but right now, everything was new, and everything was irresistible.

There was clearly some kind of system that Henry didn't understand, where the croissants and the roll went into a small bag, but the éclair and the tart each went into their own small boxes tied with twine, and the baguette went into its own long, skinny bag, and so Henry left the boulangerie juggling four parcels. For a minute there, he'd thought the guy behind the counter would have to come help him with the door.

The sun had struggled out from behind the clouds, changing the soft lemon-yellow light into a bright force that caused him to blink. Then he blinked again, because there she was—Rosie. She was standing across the street, drinking a small glass bottle of Coke, her braid resting on one shoulder. He blinked again, and she was still there. A smile broke across her face, reminding Henry, in a horrible, cheesy way, of the way the sun had broken through the clouds that morning. And she walked toward him.

"Did you order an insane amount of food again?" she asked.

"This is a very normal amount of food." Henry attempted to gesture at all of his boxes and bags, but his hands were so full, all he could do was shrug.

"Sure. A nice light snack for one," Rosie teased.

"I'm sorry about last night," he blurted out.

She looked at him quizzically.

"When you fell," he clarified. "Are you okay?"

"Totally okay." She smiled. "Didn't even rip my jeans."

"I'm sorry I wasn't there. I thought you were behind me but . . ."

"No worries," she said breezily. "Bodie was right there."

Bodie was right there. And he knew it was just a throwaway comment, not the kind of thing that he should ascribe some kind of deep symbolic meaning to, but it bothered him nonetheless.

"Come on," she said. "Let me help you carry all this." Before he knew it, she'd grabbed one of the small twine-tied boxes and the baguette. She bent her head toward the baguette and inhaled deeply, *mmm*ing as she did so, before she stopped abruptly, and looked up at him with wide eyes. "Oh gosh. I just smelled your bread. I just *smelled* your *bread*!" She seemed almost panicked. "I'm so sorry. That was so weird. Do you want me to get you another one? I can get you another one."

"You can just eat the half you smelled." Henry laughed. "I need help eating all of this anyway. I'm glad I ran into you."

"Me too," she said, and Henry's heart leaped at the soft smile she shared with him. Forget Bodie. Now, Henry was *right here*.

"Any chance you're willing to trade a sip of that Coke for some delicious pastry?" he asked.

"Here." She thrust the bottle toward him, and he took it, gladly. "It tastes a little different, somehow? But still good. I felt so embarrassed, heading out to look for pop this morning. *So* not Parisian. Pretty much the epitome of a tacky American tourist. But I missed it." She shrugged, helplessly. "Almost everywhere was closed. I wandered around for, like, twenty minutes before I found a place that was open and selling pop."

"I'd actually headed out this morning looking for Coke, too," Henry confessed. He took one more sip—a small one— then handed it back to her as they started walking. "Guess I'm not ready to trade in my American vices for black coffee and cigarettes."

"It can be our secret," Rosie said. "Like a Sunday Morning

Secret Soda Society. Should we find somewhere to sit so we can eat?"

"Definitely," Henry said emphatically as they started wandering down the street. "A Sunday Morning Secret Soda Society. I like it. I need someone to enable my tacky American habits."

"Well, then, I'm definitely your girl." *Your girl.* Henry tucked that away for later, something to turn over and over again in his mind. "You can't get much more American than East Liberty, Ohio. We have an award-winning Memorial Day Parade."

"They give out *awards* for *parades*?"

"They'll give out awards for anything," she said, neatly hopping over a puddle that had pooled into a depression in the cobblestones. "My littlest brother, Owen, won an award for being Quietest Worker last year, which just inexplicably depresses me, for some reason. The idea of him working away so quietly. Although I guess it's supposed to be a good thing."

"Littlest. Of your four brothers, right?"

"Right," she said. "Cole's the oldest, then Ricky, then it's me, then Reed, then Owen, the baby. Not a baby anymore, but he's still *the baby*, you know? What about you? Do you have any siblings? Wait—you do. A sister, right? You mentioned her on the plane." Henry was surprised she remembered. "The one who doesn't like 'weird' foods."

Henry explained about Alice and her cello and her terrible taste in food, and the fact that she was somehow, for a ten-year-old girl, pretty terrifying, even though she still had a nightlight. They turned a corner and walked underneath a large stone archway built into a redbrick building, and it deposited them into a square unlike any Henry had seen before.

"What is this place?" Rosie asked, and Henry could only

shake his head. "This seems famous. Is it famous, do you think?"

"Everything in Paris seems famous," Henry said, and it was true, but watching Rosie look around her, there was something about this place that just seemed even more special than usual.

Or maybe it was her.

CHAPTER FOURTEEN

Rosie

In some ways, Rosie thought, it looked a little bit like the square in East Liberty in the middle of downtown, with the gazebo where polka bands sometimes played in the summer, and older couples brought beach chairs and coolers and danced as the fireflies came out. But then Rosie almost laughed out loud, because although, yes, this place was in the shape of a square, it was *nothing* like anything in East Liberty.

This square was wide, with a big statue of a guy on a horse in the middle. There were four triangular grassy areas in each corner, each with its own large fountain, impressive even without water running. There were large trees in the middle, surrounding the statue of the guy on the horse, their leaves still green and fulsome. And then there was everything *around* the square, too! It looked like another castle, like the École, only made of red bricks, and much, much larger. It enclosed the entire park on all four sides. What *was* it? Did people *live* there? Rosie could feel herself gawping up at the windows poking out of the blue slate roofs. Were there people behind them? Eating breakfast? Drinking coffee? Folding laundry? Just living their ordinary lives, in this extraordinary place? She couldn't imagine.

Henry had started down one of the paths, toward a fountain. She hurried to catch up. He stepped over a low fence—it was only ankle high—and onto one of the grassy areas. Rosie hesitated for a moment but didn't see any signs telling them to stay off the grass.

"It's not wet," Henry said, and Rosie joined him, sitting cross-legged. He opened the small brown bag and held it toward her, and she could smell the butter. Notably, though, there was no grease soaking the bottom of the bag, like when Mom brought home donuts. She peered in.

"I think it's a croissant. And a chocolate croissant. And some kind of roll. And some other thing I didn't know what it was."

"Chausson aux pommes," Rosie said, pulling it from the bag. She was pretty sure anyway—it had the distinctive half-moon shape, and the slashes on top let her see a peek of what looked like apple filling.

"What's that?"

Rosie stilled as Henry shifted closer to her. He was just looking at the pastry, and she knew that, but still. He was close, and he smelled warm, and sleepy. And male.

"It's kind of like an apple croissant," she said, ignoring the rapid rise of her heartbeat. "Or an apple strudel. An apple turnover, I guess."

"Try it."

"You should have the first bite. You got it."

"I insist," Henry said, and he wouldn't take it from her. So she bit in, and the pastry flaked instantly, then yielded into sweet, soft cinnamon apples. It was so good that she had to imagine this would be the best thing she'd try today. But then Henry was grinning, chocolate smeared on his face, and he passed her the pain au chocolat, and she thought that had to be the best thing. But then the classic croissant was so perfect, each layer of lamination distinct, and then the brioche was dangerously rich, yet so light at the same time, and the éclair's filling was perfectly smooth, and the baguette made Rosie rethink what, exactly, the stuff she'd been eating for the last sixteen years was, because it couldn't possibly be bread, not like this . . . and before she knew it, they were surrounded by nothing but crumbs and flakes of croissant, and Rosie groaned, flopping onto her back, as her stomach rose up like a beach ball before her.

"I'm ready to call it," Henry said. "Paris is the best place on earth."

Rosie laughed, but she didn't disagree. She'd eaten so many pastries in her life—a lot of which she'd baked herself, enough of which she hadn't—but she'd never had anything like this before. All of it so simple, yet so complex, each bite a discovery. She had so much to learn. But she didn't feel intimidated by that. She just felt profoundly grateful to be here, to be *able* to learn, in a place where people had clearly perfected the thing she cared most about in the world. Screw eggs. She was here to *bake.*

"I think I could eat an infinite amount of croissants," Henry said. "Of all different kinds. Put anything in a croissant, and I'll eat it."

"It's brioche for me," Rosie murmured. "I don't know why, because, intellectually, I *know* it's rich—it's so buttery and it's got egg yolks and all these things bread doesn't normally have—but it feels so light and fluffy, it just disappears."

"Do you think we should head back to the École so we don't miss lunch?"

Rosie groaned in response.

"I was just teasing. Kind of."

Rosie turned her head to consider him, wondering if he could possibly still be hungry after all that food, if she'd finally found someone who could eat even more baked goods than she could. The grass tickled her cheek and she tried not to think about what kinds of Parisian bugs might or might not be crawling all over her. Henry was lying on his side, elbow in the grass, head propped up in his hand, and it struck her again how *near* he was. It didn't help that she could see the bulge of his very distracting bicep through his long-sleeved shirt, and now all Rosie could think about was what Henry's arms would feel like wrapped around her.

"I almost forgot! There's one more." Henry popped up to a seated position in a manner that was far too sprightly for someone who had just consumed that much butter.

"More? Are you trying to kill me?" Rosie laughed, maybe a little too loudly, like that would keep Henry from guessing she'd been ogling his arms.

"I saved the best for last."

By the time Rosie struggled to sit up, Henry sat in front of her with a pink pastry box. He lifted the lid, and Rosie peered inside to see a tiny apple rose tart, the "petals" impossibly thin, caramelized and shining with a dusting of sugar.

"It's a rose—get it?" Henry said, and Rosie felt her breath catch in her throat.

"It's beautiful." Carefully, Rosie lifted the tart out of the box. "Look at how thin the petals are—they must have used a mandoline. And the bake on the bottom is so even. It's hard to be so accurate with something so small."

"Are you going to analyze it or eat it?" he joked.

It looked delicious, but she almost didn't want to eat it. Henry had gotten her a rose, something far more beautiful than any flower could ever be. She wished she could keep it in her room forever, but that was part of the magic of food. It didn't last. It couldn't. Each bite was only a moment that transformed into a memory. So she bit into the tart, and then handed the other half over to Henry.

"Saved the best bite for last," she said after swallowing.

"Guess you weren't too full after all."

"I am *definitely* too full."

"Not too full to explore," he said. "Come on. Let's go."

Rosie groaned in protest, but when Henry stretched out his hands to her, she took them and let him help her up. His grip was strong, and his hands weren't greasy at all, despite their buttery feast. Rosie wasn't sure if she imagined it, or if he held on a bit longer than was necessary once she got to her feet.

"What are we exploring?" Rosie asked.

"Anything you want," he answered, hopping over the low fence. "What are you curious about?"

"Who's that guy on the horse?" She pointed to the statue. "What are these buildings? Are they homes? A hotel?"

"I was thinking we'd explore *Paris*, not just, you know, this park. But why not? Let's start small."

They made their way over to the bronze statue, stopping to dump their empty bags and boxes in a trash can, and stood, gazing up at the man on the horse. LOUIS XIII, the plaque said. Must have been a king of France. About what Rosie expected. She was more curious about what was inside the buildings ringing the square. They followed one of the white gravelly paths until it led them right up to a surprisingly modern automated sliding glass door.

"Is this a museum?" Henry asked, peering in. "I think that's a security guard. Is it open to the public?"

Rosie noticed a small, weather-beaten gray stone plaque with gold lettering.

"*Maison de Victor Hugo*," Rosie read out loud, pretty confident she'd said *maison* wrong. "So . . . Victor Hugo must have lived here. The author?"

"Probably. *Les Miz*, right?"

"Yeah. And *The Hunchback of Notre Dame*, too." Rosie hadn't read anything by Victor Hugo—she felt silly talking about him. "Is Notre Dame around here?"

"I don't think it's far?" Henry cocked his head, like he thought that might help him judge the distance. "I do *not* know enough about Paris. I should have done more research before I came here. But I was too busy trying to make sure I could *brunoise* an onion flawlessly."

"I should have done more of that," Rosie said ruefully. "We'll probably start knife cuts next week, and spoiler alert: my knife cuts are probably worse than my eggs."

"Just wait until we start having to bake. Then you'll kick all of our asses." He said it so casually, not like he was trying to pump her up, or stroke her ego, just like it was a fact. "I can't even bake a boxed cake mix. They always come out with craters."

"That's not your fault. Boxed cake mix is crap," Rosie said vehemently, and Henry laughed. "What! It is!"

"Your birthday must be a minefield."

"I make my own cake," Rosie said.

"That surprises me not at all. So?" He jerked his head toward the door. "Should we go in? Check it out? See what we can learn about the life and times of Victor Hugo?"

"Not today," Rosie said. With the sun on her face, warming her, she couldn't quite bear the idea of heading indoors. "It's so nice outside. Maybe we should just walk around?"

"That sounds awesome," he said. "Should we find the Seine? I feel like it's weird we haven't seen it."

"Totally," Rosie agreed. "That's the one bit of Paris geography I know: there is a river in the middle of the city, and it's called the Seine."

"Also sums up everything I know. Let's go find it."

They crossed under an archway next to the Victor Hugo house, leaving the square, and Rosie promised herself that she'd look it up on Google Maps later so she could figure out what it was. Back out in the streets, Paris had definitely woken up a little bit. They passed an older couple walking in nearly identical coats, and then a dad holding hands with a little girl, her hair in one long braid down her back. Every couple steps, he'd pick her up and swing her down the sidewalk as she roared with laughter. Rosie looked away, trying to shut out the burning in her eyes and the painful prick in the back of her throat.

"You okay?"

Henry was watching her, concerned, like she was about to cry. Which she *wasn't*.

"Of course," Rosie said brightly, too brightly, and the concern in his eyes went nowhere. "Look!" She pointed, directing his attention away from her, anywhere but at her. "There it is!"

And, luckily, there it was, or otherwise, Rosie would have looked legit crazy-pants. They had made it to the banks of the Seine—whether it was the left bank or the right bank neither of them knew, but they *did* know that was a designation. Rosie ran the last couple feet up to the edge of the river, resting her arms on the low stone wall. There were things that looked like big green boxes along the wall near her, most decorated with graffiti; no idea what those were. She looked down and saw yet another road, lined with trees, and next to that was the Seine. Wide and brownish-green, but appealing nonetheless, for some reason she couldn't quite articulate.

"It flooded, when my dad was here," Henry said.

"Your dad was here?"

"For culinary school. Before he met my mom and they had me. It rained so much, the Seine overflowed and flooded that road down there. Well, maybe not literally that stretch of road, but you know what I mean."

"Your dad's a chef?" Rosie asked. Here she was. Talking about dads. And she was *fine.* She fought against a memory that threatened to claw its way to the surface: her own father swinging her along the sidewalk as they walked to the ice cream truck, her braid bouncing, the summer heat warm on her back. No. *Fine.* She was fine. She pushed it away and turned toward Henry, taking in the determined set of his jaw.

"Yeah. He's incredible," Henry said emphatically, like he

had to prove it. "You might not know it if you came to the restaurant—not that the restaurant's not good, because it is—but he can just do *more*."

"And that's what you want. More," Rosie said, and then couldn't believe she'd said something like that.

But he didn't say she didn't know him, or how dare she, or anything like that. He just turned his eyes away from the Seine, looked at her, and said, "Yeah. Exactly. I want *more*."

And Rosie didn't say it out loud, but for the first time, she could admit to herself that she did, too. That was the reason she'd applied. The reason she wanted to leave East Liberty. To see more. To do more. To cook things that didn't just win bake-offs in church basements, but dishes that could be served in the finest restaurants in the world. To have a life that was more than she had dared to want for herself.

Rosie wanted *more*. And something about the way Henry looked at her made Rosie feel like she was *already* more, more than she'd let herself believe. And almost before she'd decided she was going to do it, she rose up slightly and pressed her lips against his.

He tasted like apples and caramelized sugar. Surprised, he hesitated for a moment, and then his hands were around her waist, pulling Rosie into his chest. She threaded her arms around his neck, deepening the kiss. Henry groaned softly as his tongue met hers, and Rosie felt like she was somehow both shivering and warm all over. Her heart pounded like it did when she had to run, but unlike running, Rosie never wanted this to stop.

For the first time in her life, Rosie had found something she liked better than baking.

CHAPTER FIFTEEN

Henry

School in France was *awesome*.

Okay, fine, it was still school, and it still sucked, but Henry couldn't have cared less. Because he may have been stuck in four hours of academic classes every morning, but he was stuck in those classes with Rosie. Rosie, who had *kissed him*. Henry could still barely believe it had really happened, that they had made out for what felt like hours before heading back to the École to eat dinner with their friends with matching goofy grins on their faces. In pre-calc, Henry started coloring in some of the squares in his graph paper to keep himself from doodling *Rosie, Rosie, Rosie* like a fifth grader.

All of the academic classrooms were on the second floor in a previously unexplored area of the École. He'd sat next to Rosie in the room where Monsieur Reynaud taught France and Europe: 1700–2000, in Mr. Bertram's English class, in Ms. Cooper's Environmental Science class, Madame Huppert's French class, and here in pre-calc. But Henry couldn't have said with confidence what they'd done in any of those classes. He was too busy thinking about Rosie. And when he could kiss her again. And where he should take her when he asked her out. And how soon would be too soon to ask her to be his girlfriend. Or if that was a lame thing to ask? Was it just supposed to be, like, understood? Henry still had no idea what he was doing. But he didn't care, because Rosie had kissed him.

This morning, Henry hadn't even minded being woken up by Hampus, who had, presumably, already finished his squats routine, because he was standing, showered and dressed, mere inches from Henry's face, when he shouted, "HENRY! IT IS THE FIRST DAY OF SCHOOL!" Henry responded with a sound kind of like "Nnnnghhh," but then he remembered that *Rosie had kissed him*, and he'd grinned through his shower and with a mouth full of toothpaste and all the way down to breakfast, where he ran into Rosie in front of the pain au chocolat, and the way she smiled at him almost killed him. In a good way. In the *best* way.

"And that's it!" Ms. Whitman said. Class was over? Already? Henry admired the snakelike pattern he'd doodled down the side of his paper. "Homework's in the bin on your way out the door—grab it, and I'll see you tomorrow."

Henry sprang to his feet with energy he hadn't felt since before he'd been subjected to four solid hours of learning. He couldn't wait to get to lunch. To talk to Rosie. Maybe he'd even hold her hand while they waited in line for food. Right now, Henry felt like *anything* was possible.

"Henry, can I talk to you for a minute?"

Ms. Whitman stopped his rocket-fueled progression out of pre-calc. Henry dragged his feet up to her desk, waiting for her to tell him off for doodling all class. But when he finally met her eyes, she was smiling at him like he'd raised his hand for every question.

"I got the nicest e-mail from your mom this weekend," she said.

And just like that, Henry plummeted back down to earth. Whatever Ms. Whitman was about to say, he knew it wasn't going to be good.

"I think it's so great that you want to focus on extra academic work while you're here. You know, there's a lot of business involved in running a restaurant. It's not all dicing cilantro!"

"You don't dice cilantro," Henry stammered, although that was the least of it. He didn't buy any of the BS Mom might have fed Ms. Whitman about the business of running a restaurant. This was part of some horrible plan to make his college applications look more enticing. Mom was probably hoping he'd write an admissions essay entitled "How a Math Packet in Paris Revolutionized My Relationship with Numbers" or something equally asinine.

"I've devised a curriculum that I think is going to be really exciting," Ms. Whitman continued, apparently unconcerned about the proper way to prepare cilantro. "It's a combination of accelerated math work, an introduction to econ, and some real-world business development that I think you'll really enjoy."

"Econ? Business development?" Henry parroted, not sure who was more delusional: Mom or Ms. Whitman. "I'm sorry, I don't—"

"This is so great!" Ms. Whitman cut him off. "You know," she added conspiratorially, "so many of the students here treat math as an afterthought. It's really such a treat to have someone who is taking his academic course load as seriously as he takes his work in the kitchen."

Henry emitted a strangled noise of distress. Ms. Whitman took it as an exclamation of enthusiasm.

"I'm thinking maybe three check-ins a week to begin? Before class starts in the morning probably makes the most sense."

"Before class?!" With Ms. Whitman talking a mile a minute Henry could barely get a word in edgewise. What was happening?!

"Let's say Monday, Wednesday, Friday. Here's your first packet." Ms. Whitman rummaged around on her desk and handed Henry a depressingly thick pile of paper. "See you in class tomorrow! And bright and early on Wednesday! Let's say seven, okay?"

"Seven?!"

"Seven it is!"

Before he could say anything else, Ms. Whitman shooed him off to lunch and shut the door behind him. Had Henry just committed himself to an *extra* math class? He had to stop this. But it wasn't Ms. Whitman he needed to stop—it was Mom.

"Whoa. Henry. Are you okay?" Rosie was waiting for him in the hall, looking up at him like he might pass out. Which, at the moment, felt like a distinct possibility.

"Yeah, yeah, I'm fine." What time was it in Chicago? Henry didn't care. He was calling Mom *now*. "Just, um, just go to lunch. I'll meet you there."

"You sure?"

"Sure. Yeah. Sure. I'm sure." Henry nodded at her vigorously, trying to paste a simulacrum of a smile on his face, trying to get her to leave before he *lost it*. And she must have bought it at least a little bit, because Rosie disappeared down the hall, only looking back once.

Henry pulled his phone out of his pocket and dialed.

"Henry?" Mom answered groggily. "Is everything okay?"

"No, everything is not okay!" Maybe he was being a bit dramatic. But he was *pissed*. "What did you tell Ms. Whitman?"

"Oh, that."

"C'mon, Mom," Henry wheedled. "*More* work? I barely have any free time here already."

"Alice showed me your Instagram. If you have time to take pictures of bread, you have time to focus on academics."

Alice. Henry was going to kill her.

"I'm not doing it," Henry said.

"Of course you are," Mom said matter-of-factly. "If you don't do it, you can't stay at the École."

The bottom dropped out from Henry's stomach. She wouldn't do that. She *couldn't*.

"You can't be serious," Henry said. "Does Dad agree with that?"

Henry waited as he heard shuffling noises.

"Henry?" Dad answered, sounding even groggier than Mom had. "What time is it?"

"Did you know about this?" Henry demanded. "This . . . math?" He said *math* like the vile curse it was.

"Oh . . . uh, er . . . yes." Henry's heart sank. If Dad had been complicit in this, Henry had no chance. "It's just a little bit of extra work."

It wasn't, though. The stack of papers Ms. Whitman had

handed him was enormous. And he had to get through all of it before *Wednesday*?!

More rustling noises, and then Mom was back on the phone.

"Are we clear, Henry?"

"I just don't understand why you're doing this to me."

"Don't be so dramatic. I'm trying to *help* you, Henry, not punish you." She sighed. "I'm hoping with some extra work this year, you can get into AP Calculus next fall. Might be a good way to make up for that SAT score."

"In what universe would I get into AP Calculus?" Henry demanded. She'd lost it. She'd completely lost it. AP was not a designation of math to which Henry aspired. "This is a waste of my time. I already know all the math I'd need to run a restaurant. Pretty sure sine and cosine don't factor into it."

"There's more to school than just learning to run a restaurant!" Henry could tell she was starting to lose her cool a bit. "Think about next year. Colleges need to see an advanced, aggressive course load."

"I don't even want to go to college, Mom. I want to go to culinary school."

"Well, forgive me if I think you should have an education that involves reading a book. Discussing philosophy. Proving a theorem. Using your *brain*."

"You use your brain to cook. How do you think chefs develop new recipes?"

"I don't want you limiting yourself. With a college education, you'll open yourself up to so much more possibility—"

"There's only one possibility!" Henry exploded. "For me. There's only one possibility for me. And that's cooking, Mom. It's all I want to do. It's all I *can* do. It's *me*. And I don't understand why you have such a problem with that. Culinary school was good enough for Dad, right? It's good enough for me."

"You know, Henry, when I met your father—"

"Waiting under the CTA heat lamps for the El to arrive at Merchandise Mart, yeah, I know."

Henry had heard this story many times before. His father had offered his mother a sip of the hot chocolate he'd taken home from the restaurant he'd been working at in the loop at the time, and the two of them had stayed under the heat lamps for hours, talking so much that they hadn't noticed the trains passing by. Henry had a hard time reconciling that carefree young CPA who took a chance on his dad's dreams with the mom he knew who never drank sweetened beverages and seemed to view the restaurant as nothing more than a series of spreadsheets.

"I had no idea how much of our lives running the restaurant would consume," she continued like Henry hadn't interrupted her. "No idea. Weekends, evenings, holidays. Your father spent your entire infancy in the kitchen—fourteen, sixteen hours a day, while I was alone with you, trying to balance the books, trying to make the restaurant turn a profit."

"And you *did* it, Mom. But this is different. I've been in the restaurant my whole life. I know what it's like."

"No, you don't, Henry. Not really." Henry tried not to bristle at her dismissive tone. "Helping out at the register on the weekends is not the same as being responsible for the entire business."

Henry heard her inhale and then exhale, like she was trying to calm down. *He* was the one who needed to calm down. Fine. He hadn't run his own restaurant. But that didn't mean he had no idea what he was in for. And, quite frankly, he thought the idea of spending sixteen hours in a kitchen sounded pretty great.

"She just wants you to have options, Henry."

"Dad?"

Apparently Mom had handed off the phone. Henry could hear rustling noises, and his father pacing around, probably walking into the hallway.

"She's not saying *no*. She's not saying *never*. This isn't like when I told my parents I wanted to be a chef and they kicked me out of the house."

"I know." In the face of what his dad had gone through with his grandparents, who had arrived from Korea with expectations for their son that in no way included working in a kitchen, Henry felt embarrassed complaining about a math packet.

"But my parents came around. Eventually. And your mother will, too. This isn't really about school. It's about her wanting you to be able to do whatever you want to do, and right now, she sees pulling up your grades—and putting in some more time with your math work—as the best way to make that happen."

"But I suck at math."

"I don't think you suck at math. I think it just doesn't interest you enough to try."

Sometimes, Dad was too perceptive for his own good.

"You're smart, Henry. I know you can do it if you focus. Did you or did you not singlehandedly make a beef Wellington when you were only twelve?"

"I did." Henry didn't want to smile. But it was happening.

"See? This extra work will be nothing for you. Math is easy. Medium rare is hard."

Henry laughed, remembering the astonished and delighted look on Dad's face when he'd cut into the Wellington so long ago, the flaky puff pastry yielding to reveal the perfect pink of medium rare. It was one of his favorite food memories.

"You've got this, Henry," Dad said gently. "I know you can keep your grades up if you try. Show Mom you can get all As this semester, and go show Chef you're the best one in the kitchen."

Sighing, Henry thanked his dad, hung up, and put the phone back in his pocket. He was grateful to Dad for understanding, but the unfairness of it all still gnawed at him. Extra math was the last thing he wanted to do.

Henry was half tempted to head back up to his room to sulk. But the idea of stewing in his room, alone, just made him feel worse. At least if he went to lunch he could drown his sorrows in the École's excellent hot chocolate. So he headed down the stairs to the cafeteria.

"Quiche!" Rosie announced excitedly as he walked through the door. She was waiting with two plates, each with two slices of quiche. "Did you know that it's called quiche Lorraine because the original quiche recipe came from the Lorraine region of France, near Germany?" she asked as she handed him a plate. "The recipe first appeared as early as 1373, although some people say it didn't have bacon then, and some people say it didn't have cheese then. Food history is always kind of foggy."

"Thanks." He grabbed the plate from her, wincing a little as her eyes widened at his short response. Maybe he was still more annoyed at Mom than he'd thought.

"Henry," she said, her voice low. "Are you sure you're okay?"

"Yeah. Yeah, I'm okay," he said tersely. "I'm fine."

Great. She looked hurt. But Henry didn't want to talk about it. And the more he thought about not wanting to talk about it, the more annoyed he felt. It was like that snake eating its tail, like Rosie had mentioned back when they'd first met.

Rosie and Henry sat down together at their usual table, everyone busy eating lunch. He could feel Rosie looking at him. Self-consciously, Henry stabbed a forkful of quiche as Marquis talked about Advanced French.

"There's a crazy range of ability in that class. It makes *no sense*. They've thrown everyone who has any sort of background in French together." Marquis rolled his eyes. "Seydou is fluent, and then this one can't even remember how to form the *pluparfait*."

"I panicked!" Priya protested. "I can pluparfait under normal circumstances!"

"Who is Seydou?" Hampus asked. Henry took another stabby forkful of quiche.

"He's from Senegal. Which is why he's fluent. Over there." Marquis waved at the table next to them, and the guy with wire-rimmed glasses who shared Bodie Tal's table in class waved back, grinning at them. "The teacher said he could just pick a book he liked and read it during class and write a report on it."

"I wish I could just sit in the back of the class reading," Yumi said wistfully. "Madame Huppert made us talk. Out loud. In front of *everyone*."

"You *love* talking," Marquis said. "Or at least I assume you do. Because you never stop."

"I love talking in a *casual* way, on subjects I have chosen myself, in one of the two languages I happen to be fluent in, which is more than most people here can say. Except for that Seydou guy. And Hampus. And Fernando, probably. And maybe lots of other people here. Oh, forget it. I'm not special."

"Henry," Rosie said quietly, again. "What's going on? Do you want to talk? We could go somewhere—"

"I'm *fine*," he barked, loudly enough that everyone stopped talking, even Yumi. Henry felt hot as they all turned to stare at him, and then he felt awful as he registered the confusion and hurt in Rosie's eyes. "Sorry," he muttered immediately. "I'm sorry, I just . . . I don't want to talk about it, okay?"

"Totally okay," she said, but she couldn't quite meet his gaze as she took another bite of her quiche.

Sighing, Henry turned back to his lunch, and let the conversation flow around him.

CHAPTER SIXTEEN
Rosie

Rosie was right—knife cuts came next. And she had also been right that her knife cuts were terrible. The students at the École had cut up thousands of onions and carrots this week, all in an effort to improve their knife skills. They'd started off on Monday learning the different names for ways to cut vegetables: *julienne* meant vegetables cut in long skinny sticks, *batonnet* meant thicker sticks, and *batons* were the thickest. And then there was Rosie's personal nightmare, the dices, all the different-size cubes, the difference between them marked only by a millimeter on Chef's ruler.

It probably didn't help that she was having such a hard time paying attention in class, finding herself constantly distracted by staring at the back of Henry's head. What had *happened*? One day they were making out, and the next, it was like he wanted nothing to do with her. Did she do something wrong? Or maybe—and this was the fear that kept haunting Rosie as she tried to dice—even though he'd *seemed* enthusiastic, maybe Henry hadn't wanted to kiss her at all. After all, *she* had kissed *him*. Maybe he had just gone along with it to be nice. Or maybe he had cooled off because he didn't want her to get the wrong idea, didn't want her to expect him to be her boyfriend or something.

Rosie desperately wanted to talk to Priya and Yumi about it. She'd almost told them a dozen times. But she was too embarrassed to admit to them that she'd thrown herself at Henry, and she didn't want to make things weird for everybody else. At least Henry had warmed up a bit since that awful lunch where he'd snapped at her, but he still wasn't himself. He was moody, and distracted, and it seemed like kissing Rosie was the very last thing he wanted to do.

After a long Thursday afternoon of dicing, dicing, and more dicing, Rosie wanted to ask Priya to explain guys to her. But instead, she asked her about vegetables.

"How are you doing it?" Rosie asked Priya as they waited in line to dump their vegetables into a huge plastic tub at the front of the room. At least the vegetables they'd cut up weren't going right into the trash. Maybe they were going into their meals here at the École. Maybe one day next week Rosie would recognize one of her own improperly squared carrots as it found its way onto her fork.

"Doing what?" Priya asked.

"How do you cut everything so precisely? How do you know what two millimeters looks like?" The only people in line behind them were Bodie and Seydou. At the beginning of the week, Rosie probably would have been too embarrassed to talk about her lack of skills in a place other people might hear. But it certainly wasn't a secret anymore. She'd failed her way through a whole week of knife cuts, and thanks to Chef Martinet's loud and frequent criticisms, everyone knew it.

"I don't *know* what two millimeters look like. It's not as though I'm measuring with my mind's eye, thinking, *Ooo, yes, that's two millimeters bang on. Well done, Priya.*" Priya reached the front of the line and dumped the contents of her board into the bin, using the back of her knife to scrape away a couple clinging bits of onion. "I just know what it looks like because I know what it looks like. And you'd know, too, if you'd spent your entire life dicing a billion bloody onions for curries. I'd *love* to not know what a fine dice looks like if that would give me some of those stolen hours back."

"My knife cuts are also not very good," someone volunteered from behind Rosie, his voice low, almost lyrical. Rosie turned to see Seydou talking. "It is all right, because that is why we are here—to learn."

"And here I thought we were only here for the free white coats," Priya teased. Seydou laughed, then stepped to Rosie's side and knocked his veggies into the bin. Liar—his cuts may not have been as precise as Priya's, but they were certainly heaps better than Rosie's.

"I have a theory about you, Rosie," Bodie said.

Surprised that Bodie was talking to her, Rosie dumped her veggies into the bin with more force than was necessary, causing an errant carrot to fly up and tumble onto the floor.

"Do you want to hear my theory?" Bodie asked as he bent over to retrieve the carrot and flicked it into the bin.

"Um. Sure? Okay. Yes. Sure."

That was too many affirmatives. Get a grip, Rosie, she scolded herself. Gosh, why couldn't she just *relax* around him?

Every time Rosie looked at Bodie Tal, she half expected a Food Network chyron to pop up in the lower right-hand corner of her vision.

"I think I've figured you out." Bodie leaned in to dump his veggies, and Rosie could tell he was wearing some kind of aftershave. It smelled . . . spicy, almost, but better than the word *spicy* implied. She took a step back, quickly, away from his heat, away from his scent, away from *him*.

"You've figured me out," Rosie repeated. She very much doubted that. They hadn't had nearly enough interactions for her to be *figured out*.

Priya and Seydou must have left at some point because Bodie and Rosie were alone in the kitchen. All of a sudden, his aftershave seemed to be everywhere. It was even stronger than the onions. Rosie reached into her pocket for her plastic pilot's wings, turning them over and over again, round and round, hoping the repetitive motion would calm her down.

"So my theory"—a lazy grin stretched across his face—"is that you're just like me."

Rosie stared at him. Famous? Tattooed? Buff? She was none of those things.

"I think you're a pastry chef," he said.

"What? How did you know?"

"Because I'm one, too. I mean, I want to be. I'm bored by all this crap. Who cares that I can't cut a billion carrots into equally tiny squares? I don't. I just want to bake. And I think you do, too."

"How could you tell?" she asked.

"Well, for one, your knife cuts are terrible. Which means you probably haven't been chopping many vegetables. Or butchering things." Rosie wasn't even mad when he said her knife cuts were terrible. He was right. "And you measure your salt when you cook with it. Like, you get out the teaspoons. Almost everyone here just tosses salt in until it feels right, which is what a chef would do. A baker would measure it, because baking's more precise." She was surprised he had noticed. "And you take an *insanely* long amount of time to choose what pastries you want at breakfast, but you end up taking one of everything because, I'm assuming, you can't help yourself." Now Rosie was blushing. "And I do the same thing. Except I take one of everything right away because I know it's inevitable."

She didn't know what to say to that. To any of it. He had noticed all these things about her; he had *seen* her, so clearly. She wasn't sure how she felt about being seen like that.

"I think we're the only ones," he said, almost conspiratorially. "The only bakers. Which makes sense, since this isn't a pastry program. But there isn't anything of a similar caliber for pastry. Believe me, I checked. Denis told me we'll get to pastry eventually, though. There's even a specific pastry teacher. We just have to get through all this foundational stuff first."

Denis. It took Rosie a beat too long to realize he meant Chef Laurent, his *godfather*.

"Huh," Rosie said, which was wholly inadequate, given everything he'd just said, but she had no idea how to respond.

"So that was my theory. We're in this together. Alone."

She looked at him, and he looked back at her, and she was completely unsure of how she felt about *this* Bodie Tal, the one who also loved baking and noticed things about her—not the one who was on TV and in *People* magazine.

"Should we get some dinner, then?" he asked. "Maybe there'll be a new kind of roll and you can analyze its crumb structure for a solid three minutes again."

She *had* done that.

Bodie Tal had been looking at her. A lot.

And now, Rosie didn't know how to look at him.

"I'm gonna go, um, change," she blurted, and practically ran out of the kitchen.

He wanted to get dinner. Did that mean he wanted to sit with them? Rosie tried to picture him, squeezed in next to Hampus and across from Priya, and couldn't. He didn't belong with them. He belonged over at the cool table, where no one ever wore their pajamas to breakfast.

Why had he even been looking at her, anyway? Rosie climbed the stairs up to her dorm two at a time, hurtling through the École at unprecedented speeds—speeds she'd definitely never reached in gym class. Bodie couldn't possibly . . . *like* her, could he? Rosie could practically hear Priya insisting that he did. But the whole idea of it was totally insane. Rosie was so . . . ordinary. But still, the idea of Bodie Tal watching her pick out pastries made her feel all clammy. Should she shower? She felt like she needed a shower. But she didn't want to miss dinner, so instead, back in her dorm, she just shucked off her whites and pulled on jeans and a T-shirt. Normal. Rosie needed something normal. She pulled out her phone and saw a new e-mail from Mom, subject line: *CHAMPS!*

It was accompanied by a picture of a muddy Ricky in his soccer uniform, holding Owen upside down as he shrieked with laughter, a surly-looking Reed standing next to them. Rosie loved seeing pictures of her brothers, but she wished she could get one of Mom, too. She had so few pictures of Mom. Mom had spent Rosie's whole childhood behind the camera.

"Ellen, get in this one!" Rosie could still hear her dad say. The last Fourth of July he'd been there, the last Fourth of July they'd done the big barbecue with all their friends and neighbors in the backyard. Mom had taken a picture of Dad at the grill, Rosie standing at his side, already eating her second burger. Mom had protested, but Dad had gotten Mrs. Hansen from down the street to take their picture, and Rosie still had it. Dad showing off his THRILL OF THE GRILL apron, Mom smiling self-consciously in her American flag T-shirt, and Rosie, covered in ketchup, a half-eaten burger in her hands. It was her last picture—one of her only pictures—of just the three of them together.

She'd left it behind, in its frame, in her bedroom at home. She wasn't even sure anymore why she hadn't brought it— maybe she'd been afraid of talking about Dad, afraid of having to answer a polite question about him from someone new, but now, she wished she had it here.

Rosie read mom's e-mail:

> *Another win for East Liberty High last night! Your brother executed a particularly spectacular belly slide that somehow resulted in the winning goal. Ricky went out with the team, and then I took Owen and Reed over to the Dairy Queen in Alliance. It wasn't the same without you telling us about butterfat percentages in different types of ice cream!*

There was another picture beneath that, Owen grinning with Oreo Blizard all over his face, and Reed next to him, attempting to hide in the hood of his sweatshirt. Rosie would have loved a Blizzard. Actually, what she would have loved was Mom. And Ricky and Owen and Cole home from college and even Reed rolling his eyes in the corner. She missed them. All of them. And she missed *normal*. She missed being part of a world where her self-worth wasn't defined by how quickly she could cut a carrot into tiny squares. She missed the safety of her bedroom at home and her pictures of Dad and knowing that Mom was right down the hall, always there for her, whatever she needed.

By the time Rosie made it down to the cafeteria, Bodie was already sitting at his usual table, next to Clara and across from Elodie. Maybe he had just meant *get dinner* like *walk-to-the-cafeteria-since-we're-both-going-to-the-same-place*. Rosie had had a completely bizarre reaction to a totally innocuous phrase. But as she went through the line and grabbed a pan bagnat—basically a fancy French tuna fish sandwich—her neck still felt clammy.

Rosie slid into her chair—the open chair next to Henry—and tried to avoid making eye contact with Priya. But Rosie could practically feel the weight of Priya staring at her from across the table.

"Bodie. Tal," Priya hissed, barely audible, as Yumi and Marquis had a very loud conversation about the relative merits of Sriracha. Rosie shook her head. "Rosie," Priya hissed again. Rosie looked up, trying to give Priya a stern look. Priya didn't look particularly cowed by it.

"Hey." Henry's voice was full of excitement. Rosie turned to look at him and saw something shining in his eyes. Her heart lifted. Finally, he looked like Henry again. "Here."

He pushed a folded-up white linen napkin toward her, with something hidden inside. Curious, she lifted up the edge of the napkin.

Inside, there were three carrot roses, and they were impeccable. Each petal was perfect, becoming smaller and smaller as they neared the heart of the rose. They looked too good to have been made by hand. Picking one up, turning it over in her palm, she couldn't find a single flaw. Rosie remembered the story of Thumbelina, so small she lived in a flower. This was a flower fit for a fairy princess. How could this have come from a carrot?! She half expected the petals to be soft, like a real rose.

Rosie couldn't even cut a carrot into a stick, and Henry could do *this*. She felt unexpected tears pricking at her eyes. What was she even doing here? She was so far behind—maybe her admission had been a mistake. Maybe there was some other Rosie Radeke out there in the world who was *great* at knife cuts and couldn't fathom how her application had been turned down. Right now, all Rosie wanted to do was go home—back to where she belonged. She couldn't do that. But what she could do was get out of there before everyone saw her cry.

She knew Henry hadn't meant to upset her. And looking at his stricken face as she left the table, she wanted to tell him that. But Rosie didn't trust herself to speak.

So she left without saying anything.

CHAPTER SEVENTEEN

Henry

From the outside, Henry was pretty sure that it looked like he had everything under control. And he *did* have everything under control—mostly. He'd been in Ms. Whitman's room Monday, Wednesday, and Friday morning, packet complete. In fact, he'd done his homework for *all* of his classes far more thoroughly than he'd ever done his homework back home. Henry was raising his hand in science, volunteering to read in English, speaking in French, and making timelines in history. He was, in short, busting his ass to make sure that Mom had absolutely nothing to complain about. No way was Ms. Whitman the only teacher she'd e-mailed. They were probably all reporting back to her. And he was going to give them only good stuff to report on.

There was, however, one small problem: Henry was exhausted. And it wasn't just his academic classes he was struggling to stay awake in. Even now, standing in the kitchen in front of Chef Martinet, Henry couldn't stop yawning.

And, of course, there was one big problem: Rosie. He knew he'd been kind of a grumpy jerk—thanks, Mom—and then when he'd tried to apologize with the carrot roses, that had failed spectacularly. He couldn't believe he'd made her *cry*. Although what had he been thinking, showing off his fancy, useless knife cuts when he *knew* Rosie was struggling in class? Oh, that's right—he *hadn't* been thinking.

"Happy Friday," Chef Martinet said, pulling Henry out of his carrot-roses funk. The words sounded so incongruous coming out of her pinched lips that Henry wondered if maybe she'd translated some other phrase into English incorrectly. "Now that we have set up a solid foundation for cooking, we will begin to flex our creative muscles." Wait, what was going on? Henry tried to wake himself up a little more. "Today, we will begin our Dish of the Day. Every Friday you will have a chance to create your own dish—anything you like—using the ingredients we have focused on that week. This is your chance to impress me. Every week, there will be one winning Dish of the Day."

All around Henry, his classmates buzzed excitedly. Hampus thumped him on the back, but even that wasn't enough to clear the fuzz out of his brain.

"What do we get if we win?" Yumi asked, her hand up in the air.

"What do you *get*?" Chef Martinet repeated icily. "You get the satisfaction of a dish well done, Osaki-Weissman." Even the normally indomitable Yumi looked chastened by Chef Martinet. "It is worth mentioning, perhaps, that no student who has won Dish of the Day has ever been asked to leave the École. Madame Besson, if you would."

As Madame Besson rolled the whiteboard to the front of the room, *everyone* was talking. She flipped it over to reveal DISH OF THE DAY written on the top of the whiteboard, with a numbered list of slots for, Henry assumed, the top Dishes of the Day for the rest of the semester. Adrenaline should have been kicking in right about now. Why wasn't it kicking in?! Henry wanted, badly, to see his name in that number one slot—wanted to guarantee his spot in the spring semester—but right now, all he could think about was how good it would feel to lie down.

"All week long," Chef Martinet continued, "you have been practicing your knife cuts on vegetables. Today, please create a vegetarian entrée that showcases a vegetable of your choice. You have the rest of class to create your dish."

Everyone started moving around him, running here and there across the kitchen, grabbing things, loading up with produce. But Henry couldn't move. Couldn't even think. What did he want to make? Vegetables? His mind was totally blank.

Well, he could start by dicing vegetables. That was a pretty safe foundation. Henry grabbed onions and carrots and celery and started chopping, hoping that something would come to him as he worked. And then the knife slipped.

"Crap," Henry muttered as bright red blood squirted out of his thumb. Quickly, he lifted up his hand, trying not to get blood anywhere near the cutting board.

"Here." Rosie was next to him, juggling canisters of what looked like different kinds of flours. She set them down on his station and started pulling him over to the sink. "Wash it first."

As Henry washed his hand with soap and water, she pulled a Band-Aid and a plastic glove out of the pockets of her apron.

"I've got Neosporin, too, but you shouldn't put that on until after you're done cooking," she said. "Just the Band-Aid and the glove for now."

"Why do you have all this stuff?"

"Habit. I come from a very accident-prone family," she said wryly as she dried his thumb with a paper towel. "Did you know it was possible to slice your face open on a zipper?"

"I did not."

"That's why you don't wrestle someone who's wearing a partially-zipped-up hoodie." Carefully, she wrapped the Band-Aid around his thumb. "Also, one time Ricky ate a whole bunch of quarters because Cole dared him to, but Band-Aids didn't help that."

They laughed, and for a moment, Henry felt like things were finally back to normal. Rosie's hands stayed wrapped around his, the slight pressure of her fingers on his thumb finally waking him up.

"I'm sorry," she said suddenly. "The other day—when I cried—it wasn't—"

"*I'm* sorry." Henry was so eager to apologize, he interrupted her. "I don't know what I was thinking—"

"You were thinking it was *nice*. And it was." She squeezed his hand. She still hadn't let go. "I didn't get upset because of the carrots, or because of you. I promise. It was a bad day, and I was homesick, I guess, and thinking about other stuff . . ."

"What other stuff?" Henry asked. "Do you want to—"

"Radeke and Yi!" Chef Martinet trumpeted from the front of the room. "The kitchen is a place for *working*. It is not a place for *holding hands*."

Almost instantly, Rosie turned the color of an overripe

tomato. Henry found himself clearing his throat excessively as Rosie dropped his hand, gathered up her stuff, and raced back to her station like she was trying to set a new land-speed record. Henry picked up a carrot and tried to pretend he was busy working.

Was Rosie embarrassed to be seen holding his hand? It certainly seemed like it, from the way she'd turned bright red and sprinted away from him. And what had Rosie been about to say? Stupid Chef Martinet. Why did she have to pick that exact moment to notice them?

"Henry," Hampus said gently. "You are okay?"

Henry realized he was standing in front of his station, holding a carrot in a death grip, and doing absolutely nothing.

"Yeah. Yeah, I'm fine. I'm just . . . making . . . this . . . carrot."

And that's what he'd do. Carrots. Something spectacular with carrots. Screw his bleeding thumb and Chef Martinet and all of it. Carrots three ways, he thought as he started peeling them. Roasted carrots on a bed of smoked carrot puree, with pickled carrot greens as a garnish. Three ways would be impressive, right?

As Henry roasted and smoked and pickled, he was more awake than he'd been all day. He wished his mom could see him here—maybe she'd finally recognize how much better he was at cooking than pretending he cared about how many times the French had attempted revolutions.

"Time is up!" Chef Martinet announced.

After a quick check to make sure all the carrots were in place, Henry wiped his hands on his apron and looked around the room, his eyes wandering, as they always did, to Rosie. She was bright red and sweaty, her hair matted against her face, strands escaping from her braid every which way. It looked like she'd run a marathon instead of created a vegetarian dish. But she was *smiling*. This was it. Henry could feel it. After a week of Chef Martinet telling Rosie everything she did was wrong, it looked like Rosie had finally gotten it right. And Henry couldn't wait for her to finally have that moment of validation from Chef Martinet. And maybe later tonight they could *really* talk—with no interruptions.

"This dish is very safe, no?"

Henry's attention snapped back to his own plate. He stared at Chef Martinet in disbelief. *Safe?!* Seriously? There was nothing *safe* about attempting three different preparations.

"Every element is technically perfect, but it is not . . . exciting." *Not exciting?!* Henry struggled to keep his emotions from playing across his face. "These carrots could have been made by any competent chef. I have learned nothing about *you* from this dish, Yi."

Henry felt like Chef Martinet had just dumped a bucket of cold water over his head. What did she even mean?! How was a dish supposed to be more *him*?! What was he supposed to do, carve his initials into the carrots?

"The nest is made of butter-poached foraged mushrooms," Hampus was saying. Henry had been so busy fuming he'd missed Chef Martinet's first bite of Hampus's dish: creamy scrambled eggs spilling out of eggshells inside a nest that was, apparently, made of butter-poached foraged mushrooms. It looked so much like a real bird's nest Henry could hardly believe it was mushrooms. "In Sweden, we like our scrambled eggs very, very creamy," Hampus continued. "I have added a simple salad of foraged dandelion greens to offset the richness of the dish."

"This is inspired," Chef Martinet said. "You have made the mushroom the star."

Hampus was beaming so brightly they probably could have turned off all the lights in the kitchen. Henry held out his knuckles for a discreet fist bump under the table as soon as Chef Martinet left. Now, if only things could go this well for Rosie.

He had never seen someone look so hopeful before. Rosie's face made him remember how it felt to be a little kid playing that claw game at the arcade, trying desperately to grab a stuffed animal, sure that this would be the time he'd win. Finally, Chef Martinet made her way to Rosie's station, dipped her spoon into Rosie's dish, and took a bite.

"The vegetables are cooked unevenly because they were prepared unevenly. Again." As Chef Martinet put her spoon down, Rosie's face fell, and Henry's stomach plummeted. "This dish seems very . . . simple."

"It's a play on chicken-and-biscuits," Rosie said in a small voice that barely even sounded like her. "Except it's a vegetarian stew topped with herbed biscuits."

Chef Martinet didn't even respond, just swept off to the next station. And she tasted her way around the room until she announced that Hampus had won Dish of the Day. And of course that was totally deserved and Henry was glad Hampus had earned a spot in the spring semester, but as Henry looked at Rosie's disappointed face, he couldn't feel happy about anything.

★★★★

Hours later, after dinner, Henry was still bummed about his dish not being *him* enough, whatever that meant. Rosie didn't look any happier, either. She sat across from him in a big, over-stuffed chair in the common room. Frowning, she scribbled on a worksheet propped up on her notebook. It was Friday night, and Henry was pretty sure he and Rosie were the only people doing their homework on the weekend. But if Henry didn't get a head start on all of his work today, he'd be swamped. Better to suffer now and get through it.

The numbers in front of Henry went fuzzy. He blinked, trying to clear his head, and looked around the common room. There were a couple people on their laptops, and Cecilia and Anna, from his pre-calc class, were sitting with Seydou and playing some kind of card game. Everyone else was probably out doing something awesome. Hampus had gone foraging, and Priya and Yumi and Marquis had been talking at dinner about trying to find a movie theater playing something in English. Either of those things were infinitely preferable to homework. But Rosie had chosen to stay behind with him, and spending Friday night with her was better than foraging. Even if it involved math.

"You know what bothers me the most?" Rosie said suddenly. "She didn't even *taste the biscuits*. She pushed them aside to get to the vegetables."

"That's messed up," Henry agreed.

"I know! They were a *huge* component of the dish. And they were good—I tasted them after she left. Priya did, too."

"I'm sure they were awesome."

"She's gonna send me home, Henry." Fear. Henry could see it in her eyes. Raw, animal fear, like he saw in the eyes of the rabbits that hopped around Wicker Park if he got too close to them. "This time, I thought, I *really* thought that I'd done an even dice. But apparently not. I don't even know enough to know when I've messed up! She's kicking me out. For sure."

"She's not gonna kick you out," Henry argued. "She's not gonna kick anyone out. She hasn't kicked anyone out yet, right?"

"That's because she's biding her time." Rosie pushed her notebook aside, dropping it on the floor. "Doesn't make sense to kick us out now. She'll wait until we already have our plane tickets home for the holidays, right? Chef Martinet is waiting to trim the fat at the end of the semester when it makes more logistical sense."

"You are not 'the fat.'" Henry air-quoted. "And anyway, fat is delicious."

Rosie wrinkled her nose at him.

"Come on! Think about it . . . a perfectly seared piece of pork belly? That dripping, golden, buttery, crispy, melty fat?" Henry's mouth was practically watering. "Mmm. Who wouldn't want to be the fat?"

"You're a Nutter Butter," she said, but the fear was gone from her eyes when she rolled them at him. "We're breaking down a chicken next week, you know."

"Now *there's* some good fat. Render it down. Cook some potatoes up in that fat. Get 'em all golden and crispy."

"Stop, Henry, you're making me hungry!" Rosie laughed. "Now let me guess—you can break down a chicken in twelve seconds flat." She pointed a pair of finger guns at him, like he was the fastest butcher in the west.

"I'm not that fast."

"But you *have* broken down a chicken before."

"Yeah." Henry stopped himself, just in time, from adding, *"of course."*

"I'm in so much trouble." She dropped her head into her hands, hiding her face.

"It's really not that bad." Henry swung his legs around and moved down to the end of the couch, closer to her. "It's easier than it looks."

"Henry, I can't even cut a *carrot*. What am I going to do with a chicken? Every time I've cooked with chicken before, I just bought it in the shape it needed to be. Breast? Buy the breast. Thigh? Buy the thigh. Whole roast chicken? Buy a whole chicken. Done."

"Maybe you just have a mental block about vegetables. Like an anti-vegetarian. Maybe poultry is your thing."

"Poultry is *not* my thing," Rosie said decisively. "Well, butchering it is not my thing. Eating it? Especially when it's fried and served with mashed potatoes? Then it is very much my thing."

"Ooo, yeah, mashed potatoes. Now that's a *great* potato. Perfectly smooth, whipped to perfection, a big pat of melting butter on top—"

"No more potatoes!" Rosie picked up the small throw pillow on the chair behind her and hit him with it. "I'm serious! Now I'm *starving!*"

She hit him again, and this time, Henry caught the pillow, and they both tugged at it, the pillow suspended between them. Something else was suspended between them, too, a moment when their shared laughter changed to something else. And then Rosie dropped the pillow and it hung limply in his hands. But whatever had just happened, Henry wanted to keep it going.

"You know what?" Henry said. "Let's go find a chicken."

"Find a chicken," Rosie repeated. "What are you talking about?"

"Let's go find a chicken and break it down."

"Okay, yeah, sure, great. Let me go get my chicken-catching hat on." Rosie mimed pulling on some kind of cap. "Seriously. What are you talking about?"

"I mean we're going to break down a chicken right now." Henry stood. "And then you'll see it's not that bad."

"Where are you going to get a chicken?" she asked, but she was pushing herself up, and she'd shoved her notebook into her backpack.

"Downstairs. They've got to be in the walk-in by now."

"Downstairs, like, where we have class?" He was already walking out of the room, spurred by a burst of confidence in the chicken. Rosie followed. "Are we allowed to go in there after class? Is it even *open*?"

"I guess we'll find out."

They turned and headed down the stairs to the big kitchen, the path already a familiar one.

"You can't take a chicken out of the walk-in, Henry. What if they only have enough for each of us?"

"I'll count them. If there's more than twenty, we're good to go."

"I don't want to get in trouble." She paused, right at the threshold.

"They didn't say we *couldn't* get a chicken," he argued.

"Well, I guess that's Chef Martinet's fault, then," she said, and Henry answered her grin with his own. "She should really be more specific about where students can and can't get chickens."

Inside, the kitchen was dark. Henry hit the switch next to the door, and the lights flickered on. The space was so familiar and yet, at night, there was a quality that rendered it foreign. Like Henry felt he should whisper. Or maybe not talk at all. So he crept, silently, to the walk-in, pulling open the heavy steel door and letting the cold air blast them.

"I guess we *can* take a chicken," Rosie said. There was a *wall* of chickens stacked up higher than his head.

"I'll get the chicken. Can you grab a chef's knife—a sharp one—and a cleaver?" Poultry shears would be better. Easier. But Chef Martinet seemed like the kind of person who was going to make them do it with a cleaver.

"Sure," she said. "Believe me, I know where the knives are." And there was something bitter in her voice when she said it.

She was waiting for him at his station when he left the walk-in with the chicken, knife and cleaver on the cutting board, and there was no more bitterness in her voice when she said, "This is probably going to be gross, isn't it?"

"Not gross at all." He plopped the chicken down on the cutting board. It looked like a good one—there was a creamy quality to the fat beneath the skin that made Henry think this chicken had been fed a good diet, or maybe grazed free-range on some farm in the French countryside. "Grab the drumstick and pull it to the side. Don't rip it off—just pull enough that the skin is stretched out."

"I always forget how unpleasant this texture is," Rosie said as she pulled. "Until the next time I'm handling raw chicken, and then I'm reminded all over again."

"Now cut through the skin—just the skin, none of the meat."

Sighing, Rosie picked up the chef's knife and cut. She really *was* bad with a knife. It looked awkward in her hand, like it didn't belong there. Henry always felt like his knife was an extension of himself, like it automatically went where he wanted it to go and did what he wanted it to do. But Rosie's knife looked like it was fighting her.

"Pop the joint."

"What?"

"Pop the joint out of its socket. Just grab the leg and twist. It'll come out easier than you think."

"Ricky dislocated his shoulder once." Rosie shuddered. "On the field, during a game. I'll never forget the popping sound that made."

"This is *not* going to sound like that. Trust me."

"How about you do this first leg?" she asked. "I'll do the second one. Promise."

"Here," he said, and he reached from behind her, his arm alongside hers, the warmth of her pressed against his chest, the faint vanilla smell of her skin. It probably would have been romantic if they hadn't been holding a chicken carcass. "Pull."

They twisted, and the leg popped out of its socket. Rosie turned to Henry, surprised. Her face was so close to his, only a breath away. All Henry had wanted to do since they had kissed was kiss her again, and finally, it felt right. He watched

Rosie's eyes flutter closed and he leaned in, brushing his lips softly against hers.

Something vibrated against his leg. Rosie yelped and shot away from him, leaping back.

"It's my phone!" Henry said shrilly as he pulled the offending device out of his pocket.

"Oh. Um. Ha-ha." Rosie laughed an awkward, strangled laugh. "You should probably get that."

"No, I don't need to—"

"It's fine. Tell your Mom I said hi." She gestured at the screen, where, sure enough, MOM was flashing on top of a baby picture of Henry. *Why* had Henry let his mom program in a *baby picture* of him to display when she called?! If he hadn't been so busy trying not to die of embarrassment, he would have almost been impressed by the new lows of mortification he had sunk to. "It's okay—you can answer it," Rosie whispered.

There was no reason not to. The moment had been pretty thoroughly ruined.

"What?" Henry barked into the phone. "I mean, hello," he amended, noticing Rosie's shocked face.

"What's this B-minus on your English paper?"

"Nice to talk to you, too, Mom," Henry muttered. He pointed to the door and walked out of the kitchen, into the stairwell. Probably better if Rosie didn't overhear this conversation.

"I thought you were going to *try*."

"I *am* trying, Mom." Henry gritted his teeth, trying not to raise his voice. "Mr. Bertram is a really hard grader. I don't think anyone got an A."

"I don't care if everyone gets an A; I care if *you* get an A. I need to see that you're making an effort, Henry," Mom warned him. "Or you're coming home."

"It was one paper, Mom!" Seriously? One B-minus, and she was already threatening to pull him out of the École? Henry was trying. He was trying harder than he'd ever tried before. But what if Henry's best wasn't good enough, and Mom made him leave anyway? Henry couldn't even think about that without flinching, like the idea of leaving the École was a hot griddle that would burn him if he let his hand linger too long near the surface.

"Where do you think grades come from? Papers!"

"I get it, okay?" Henry wanted to get Dad on the phone, wanted Dad to help him explain that this wasn't a big deal. Or maybe he just wanted Dad to reassure him that Henry wasn't in danger of losing everything he'd ever wanted because Mr. Bertram thought his paper suffered from strained transitions, but Henry was so pissed at Mom for ruining the moment—or maybe at himself for not putting his phone on silent—that he just wanted this conversation to end. Immediately. "Look, Mom, I have to go."

"You have to *go*," she repeated. "Go where? Go try to see if you can earn some extra credit by revising your paper? Because that sounds like an excellent idea."

"Yeah. I'll go do that."

He hung up on her. Henry tried to remember what Dad had said about Mom just wanting him to have options, but he was so frustrated that Mom couldn't see the effort he was making, he was having a hard time looking at anything from her point of view.

"Everything okay?" Rosie asked when he made his way back into the kitchen. She was leaning against the counter, her arms wrapped around herself like she was cold.

"Yeah. Yeah, it's fine," he said. "I just have to go do some work on the English paper."

"The one we just got back?" she asked, confused.

"Yeah. It's a whole thing—don't worry about it." The last thing he wanted to do was get into how nuts Mom was being and how scared he was about the possibility of leaving. "We can do a chicken later, okay?"

"Sure."

Rosie smiled at him, and if there was something unsure in her smile, Henry tried not to notice it. So they packed the chicken up in a Ziploc bag, cleaned the cutting board and the knives, and by the time they left, it looked like they had never been there.

When they got back upstairs, Seydou, Anna, and Cecilia were standing in front of a small piece of paper taped to the glass of the French doors leading into the lounge.

"What's that?" Henry asked.

"It is a dance," Anna said. "For Halloween. They are having a dance here, at the École."

"Halloween? Already?" Rosie asked as Anna, Seydou, and Cecilia went back into the lounge, chatting.

"Well, it *is* October," Henry said.

She looked surprised, and then sort of stricken. Henry wondered what she was thinking about.

"Are you—are you gonna go to the dance?" he blurted out, wanting to keep her there for just a minute longer, even though *he* had been the one to hustle them out of the kitchen.

"Probably." She shrugged. "It might be fun, right? I bet I could make a costume out of something I have here. Be a black cat, maybe. Something easy. Although I don't really have any black clothes, so maybe that's not such a good idea. . . ."

"I have a black hoodie." Henry gestured to it, as he was, in fact, wearing it. "You can borrow it, if you want."

She wouldn't want his hoodie. And even if she did, he was going to have to clean his hoodie thoroughly, to ensure it smelled the best any hoodie had ever smelled since the dawn of time.

"Thanks." Rosie smiled. "I'd love to borrow it. I'll be the coziest cat in town."

Rosie was going to the dance.

And she was wearing his hoodie.

And that, at least, was something.

CHAPTER EIGHTEEN

Rosie

R osie had kind of assumed no one would go to the dance.
She didn't know why, really. Maybe because so many
of the students here were international. Rosie couldn't imagine Anna from pre-calc at a dance back home in Berlin. And
she somehow doubted that Fernando had ever stood under
streamers in a gym in Barcelona. The whole idea of a school
dance just seemed so American.

She couldn't help but think of the last dance she'd been to, back
at home, with Brady. He'd kept her at such a pronounced distance,
Rosie felt like she'd had YOUR FRIEND'S LITTLE SISTER stamped
on her forehead the whole time. Brady had been nice, though.
And he'd taken her to Applebee's after. And kissed her, once,
quickly, when he dropped her off at the end of the night. She'd
wondered if they might date or something, but he never said
anything to her besides a friendly, casual "Hi" in the halls from
that point on. Rosie wondered if she should have been more
disappointed by that.

But she hadn't felt much of anything, really. Not for Brady, and not for anyone else at East Liberty High. She'd sit in the cafeteria and listen to the giggles and whispers around her, watching the girls at her table blush and sneak glances over at guys who blushed right back, but whenever it was Rosie's turn to share who she liked, she always came up blank. But here . . . something was different. *Something.* Rosie chided herself—she knew exactly what was different.

It was Henry. *He* was different.

Rosie tore her eyes away from the door—she had to stop looking for him, she was in danger of being pathetic—and looked around the cafeteria. Whoever had decorated had definitely taken a page from the East Liberty High dance decor playbook. There were orange and black streamers, and what looked like computer print-out pictures of black cats and ghosts taped to the walls. The tables had been pushed to the side of the room with chairs facing inward. Priya was lying down across three chairs, which pretty much indicated the general level of activity. Rosie grabbed another pumpkin cookie from the snack table she'd stationed herself in front of for lack of anywhere better to go. The cookies were good: buttery, nice crumb structure, extremely neat piping on the pumpkin. Rosie wondered who had made them. They looked way too American to have been produced by the École's regular cooking staff. The French made a lot of excellent desserts, but the frosted sugar cookie wasn't exactly in their usual culinary repertoire.

Roland, who had driven the van back on the very first day, was in charge of the DJ station, which was a computer hooked up to a set of speakers. So far he had played a bunch of French techno Rosie had never heard before, and "Monster Mash" three times. Rosie sighed, unsure why she had come. Priya had been the one who had been most excited about it, spending even more time than usual on her makeup and building fairy wings out of cardboard. But now those fairy wings were slowly being crushed by her impromptu nap. As were Priya's hopes and dreams for what this dance could be, most likely. Almost their whole class was there, but no one was actually *doing* anything.

Rosie wiggled her nose, trying to get rid of the itch without smearing the kitty-cat whiskers Priya had drawn on her with eyeliner. She'd expended pretty minimal effort on her costume. Priya had done the cat makeup, and she'd borrowed a pair of Yumi's black yoga pants and Henry's black hoodie, which fell almost to her knees. She'd pulled the hood up over her head and had tried to tape some construction paper ears on, but they definitely weren't standing up the right way. Rosie might have been a lot of things, but crafty wasn't one of them.

Henry's hoodie. It smelled so much like clean laundry, it smelled like a candle Mom had called "Clean Cotton." It was soft, and warm, and Rosie didn't want to give it back.

"This is exactly what I expected," Yumi said from her spot by the snack table. "Total snooze."

Rosie couldn't look right at Yumi or she'd laugh. Yumi had dressed up as a monster. She'd borrowed a T-shirt of Hampus's in a particularly alarming shade of green—it was enormous on her—and had taped large construction paper eyeballs all over it. Whenever Rosie made accidental eye contact with any one of Yumi's eyes, she'd start laughing. And Yumi would protest that she was supposed to be *scary*, which would only make Rosie laugh harder. It was a vicious cycle.

"It's only, um, eight-oh-five," Rosie said, checking the wall clock as she helped herself to another cookie.

"Yeah. Everyone knows things don't really get bumping until eight fifteen," Yumi said witheringly, grabbing two gougères off a round serving plate and popping them both into her mouth simultaneously. "It's Saturday night," she said through a mouthful of cheesy, puffy pastry. "We could have gone *out*."

"We still could."

"No, we're committed to this travesty." Yumi sighed.

And they were, kind of. If they stayed at the dance, they didn't have to be up in their rooms until the shockingly late hour of eleven p.m., but if they left the dance, they weren't allowed back in.

"Maybe it'll get good later," Rosie said hopefully.

"Sure. At the mythical stroke of eight fifteen. Now move, Radeke. I want some cheese."

Rosie stepped aside so Yumi could lift a slice of baguette topped with baked brie and red onion jam off the table. Yumi stuffed it whole in her mouth as she looked toward the door rather forlornly, like she was waiting for someone, too.

"I thought Henry and Marquis were coming," Rosie said, trying to sound casual.

She had spent an exorbitant amount of time imagining a dance with Henry. A slow one, nothing where she'd be required to move with any kind of rhythm, but where they'd be close enough to kiss. Rosie was *still* replaying that night in the kitchen over and over again, reliving the moment Henry had brushed his lips against hers. But then he'd insisted on leaving the kitchen so he could work on an English paper that they'd already turned in, which made absolutely no sense. Did he want to kiss her or not? Rosie couldn't figure him out.

"Maybe the guys decided to bail," Yumi said glumly.

"They wouldn't," Rosie said firmly. "There's no way Hampus is missing this."

He'd been talking about it for weeks, asking Rosie and Henry and Marquis all kinds of questions about American Halloween and American school dances, and Rosie was pretty sure he was going to be devastatingly disappointed, as Hampus had built this evening up to be some kind of prom-as-designed-by-Tim-Burton. Which it most decidedly was not.

And as though his name had conjured him, Hampus burst through the doors. Rosie's jaw dropped a little. He was wearing head-to-toe white, which made him look not totally dissimilar to the Abominable Snowman, but even from across the room, Rosie could see the pink bow tied around his neck, his pink nose, black whiskers, and little white cat ears that were staying on top of his head *much* better than Rosie's were.

"Is he . . . is he the girl cat from *Aristocats*?" Yumi asked. "You know what? Things are looking better already."

"Rosie!" Hampus picked her up, lifting her off the ground in a hug that was surprisingly gentle, given the velocity involved. "We are both the cats!"

"You are both the cats," Yumi agreed. "Let's take a million pictures of this."

"Is Henry coming?" Rosie asked Hampus as they stood with their arms around each other, grinning at Yumi's iPhone.

"Ah, Henry." Hampus sighed, and then chuckled, fondly. "He is coming, but he is being so slow. I could not wait any longer. Marquis is with him, trying to make him hurry."

Rosie felt something within her lift as the DJ started playing, of all things, "Lady in Red." It blasted out of the speakers, somehow louder than the techno had been. Nobody moved toward the dance floor.

"I had no idea a pumpkin could be so fit."

Priya was so loud that Rosie had heard her over the music, but when she followed Priya's gaze, it didn't look like the fit pumpkin had heard her. And the fit pumpkin was, of all people, Bodie Tal, wearing a bright-orange T-shirt with a jack-o'-lantern face on it and bright-orange Beats by Dre headphones, with a little green construction paper stem sticking off the top of them.

"Sweet baby candy corn." Yumi materialized at Rosie's elbow. "Why does *nothing* about Clara's outfit surprise me? Well, maybe the irony of her choice of costume. Although I doubt she's self-aware enough to register it as ironic."

Rosie had been so busy looking at Bodie's pumpkin stem, she'd barely even noticed Clara and Elodie flanking him, dressed like an angel and a devil, but boy, she noticed them now. Clara looked like she was in the Victoria's Secret Fashion Show, in a teeny white dress and full wings made of real feathers spreading out behind her. She was wearing sandals that laced halfway up her long legs, and a little halo stuck out on top of her perfect golden curls. Rosie looked at her and wondered, a little bit, how she and Clara could possibly be the same *species,* never mind the fact that they were both American teenage white girls. She felt like an amoeba looking at a gazelle.

Bodie left Elodie and Clara on the dance floor and went over to talk to Roland. The music cut out abruptly, and Rosie watched Bodie and Roland fiddle with the cords until, with a burst of noise like a sonic boom, Drake started rapping through the speakers. Rosie felt the bass thumping through the floorboards at her feet. She looked to the door, wondering if Madame Besson would come over and tell them to turn it down, but much to her surprise, it looked like Madame Besson was bopping her head in time to the beat.

And Rosie didn't know if Drake was really that popular, or if something in the undeniable charisma of Bodie Tal was at work, but it was like a switch had turned in the room and altered its chemistry. Suddenly, in what seemed like only a matter of moments, *everyone* was on the dance floor. Hampus swinging his arms back and forth as Yumi jumped up and down like she was on springs. Priya twirling gracefully around the two of them. Fernando trying to get Clara to dance as she shuffled, surprisingly self-consciously, from side to side.

"You're not dancing?"

It was Bodie, standing in front of her, shouting.

"I don't want to give up my prime position over here by the cookies," she shouted back.

"Are they good? The cookies?"

"They're great!" This was the loudest conversation Rosie had ever had about cookies. "Really good, tight crumb structure. You can tell the butter is high quality. And each cookie is so consistent. And the piping!" She picked up another one, aware that she'd already eaten way too many of them but was probably about to eat another. "The piping on the front is beautiful, but the frosting still tastes good."

"Thank you." He grinned.

"Did you make these?" Rosie asked, surprised.

"Yeah! I love Halloween."

"*You* love Halloween."

Rosie couldn't believe he'd made all of these. Firstly, they were so identical, they looked like they'd been made by a machine. But what she really couldn't believe was that *Bodie Tal* was exhibiting the same level of Halloween enthusiasm that Owen had abandoned several years ago because he'd decided he was too old for it.

"Halloween is the best holiday ever. Costumes? Sugar? The sick orange-and-black color scheme? What's not to like?"

Rosie laughed as he reached over her to grab a cookie and took a bite. She could smell his aftershave, again. She took half a step back.

"Do you think they're a little too salty?" he asked, chewing.

"No, the salt cuts the butter. You need it to balance the richness. You did it perfectly, actually." Bodie Tal, Halloween enthusiast. Unreal. "Just how much of this did you do? For the dance, I mean," she clarified. "Did you make all this food? Did you do the decorations, too?"

"Oh yeah." He nodded, chewing. "The École had never done anything for Halloween before. But missing it bummed me out too much, so I texted Denis and he made it happen." *Denis*. Chef Laurent. Rosie would never get over it. "I know I'm kind of a baby about Halloween, but it's my favorite episode of *Cake Bomb* every year, with Dad. We always do it together. We've done it since I was a little kid. We usually guest-judge *Halloween Wars*, too. Halloween's kind of our thing. And I thought this might make me miss it . . . him . . . less."

Bodie trailed off awkwardly, and Rosie wondered if he felt he'd shared too much.

"Last year's season of *Halloween Wars* was the best!" Rosie said encouragingly, wanting him to feel less awkward. "I loved that vampire wedding cake. The raspberry 'blood' when you cut into it was awesome."

"Why, Rosie Radeke," Bodie said, and Rosie *instantly* regretted everything that had come out of her mouth. *Why* had she admitted she watched it?! What was she thinking?! "Are you a *fan?*"

"No," Rosie said quickly, unsure why she was denying it now. "It was just. You know. On."

"Sure it was." Bodie smirked. "Dad's gonna be so pleased. He's always trying to break into that heartland demographic."

"No." Rosie shook her head. "I was watching for *you.*"

Was she *high*? Had Bodie laced these cookies with some kind of mind-altering substance?! Rosie was saying—no, *shouting*—things she definitely shouldn't be saying *or* shouting, and *definitely* not saying to Bodie Tal. She'd basically just confessed to being a superfan. Mortifying.

"I can't believe everyone's dancing now," Rosie said, changing the subject.

"DJ Pumpkin never fails."

"DJ Pumpkin?" Rosie nearly sprayed him with cookie crumbs.

"Yeah. DJ Pumpkin." He pointed to the stem on top of his headphones. "It's my Halloween alter ego."

"Your Halloween alter ego. Okay. Sure. Like that's a thing everyone has. Mine's Sad Cat." Rosie reached up to poke ineffectually at her construction-paper ears, which immediately flopped back down.

"Want to dance, Sad Cat?"

"What? I . . . What?"

"Is that a *what* or a *yes*? Because I'm waiting for a *yes*."

He had freckles. Rosie hadn't noticed them before. A very, very faint sprinkling over his nose and across his cheekbones. There were some things, Rosie thought, that even high-def couldn't capture. Only real life.

And when she exhaled, it came out as "Yes."

CHAPTER NINETEEN

Henry

D ude," Marquis said. "What. Are. You. Doing."

Henry knew he was driving Marquis crazy. Honestly, he was driving himself crazy. They were supposed to have left a *long* time ago, but Henry couldn't decide on any of the equally lame costume options he'd assembled at the last minute. Because Henry had *meant* to think of something perfect, something Rosie would love, but between finishing his extra math for Ms. Whitman, writing weekly essays for Mr. Bertram, creating the Napoleonic Wars timeline for Monsieur Reynaud, and the thousands of other things he had to do, Henry hadn't thought of anything good. Never mind the fact that way too much of his brain space had been taken up by the fact that the perfectly roasted chicken he'd attempted for Dish of the Day had *again* been deemed "boring," "safe," and "not *you*, Yi." Whatever that meant.

Groaning, Marquis slumped over on Hampus's bed with

his head in his hands. Henry could just see the top of the name RUSSELL written on the back of his Nets jersey.

"Just wear the jersey, man," Marquis said, his voice muffled through his hands. "Just wear the jersey."

"I'm way too short to be a basketball player. It'll look ridiculous."

"Then *don't* wear the jersey. Wear whatever you want. Wear a red T-shirt and say you're a tomato. *I do not care.* I would just like to get down there before it's November. This is a Halloween dance that a maximum of twenty people are going to. Who cares what you wear?"

"I just . . . I don't want to look stupid."

Henry decided. He whipped off his T-shirt and pulled on Marquis's other Nets jersey.

"*Everyone*'s going to look stupid. I spent almost two hours in the common room this afternoon helping Yumi make fake eyeballs. *Fake eyeballs.* This is the level we're at here."

Henry grunted in response as he pulled open the bottom drawer of his dresser, dug around, and grabbed a pair of gray gym shorts.

"So why the meltdown? Who is this for? Ohhh." Marquis sat up now, lifting his head out of his hands. "*Who* is this *for*?"

"Nobody," Henry muttered, but even he knew that any kind of denial would be a protesting-too-much situation. Methinks. Like in *Hamlet.* See, Mom? Henry thought. After finishing the revisions on his first paper, he was crushing it in English. Sure, he'd had to pull an all-nighter to make sure his last essay was perfect, but he'd gotten a ninety-seven, with a *Well done* written on the top in red pen. The next day he'd fallen asleep doing his homework in the lounge and had woken up to a concerned Rosie shaking him back to consciousness, but it was worth it to prove his mother wrong.

Probably because Henry had poured so much time into his paper, he hadn't studied enough for his science test and now that grade was dipping down into the B range. He couldn't win. As soon as one grade pulled up, another went back down. Henry felt like he was playing GPA whack-a-mole.

"It's Rosie, isn't it?" Marquis was now standing. Crap. Marquis was so much taller than him. Henry was going to look like a little kid in his jersey. Like he was trick-or-treating, and Marquis was his dad. "I know it is. You *always* sit next to her."

"She sits next to me, too, sometimes," Henry muttered.

"She does, man, she does!" Marquis laughed. "Let's go make this happen."

"Marquis," Henry said desperately as they walked into the hallway. "Don't . . . you know . . . *say* anything."

"I won't," Marquis said solemnly, and much to Henry's surprise, he pulled him into a hug, clapping him once, twice, on the back. "I don't *need* to say anything," Marquis continued as they descended the staircase. "Halloween will work its magic. You'll see."

Henry had his doubts. But as they got closer to the cafeteria, and the volume increased, Henry could feel the faint thrum of the bass deep in his bones and saw a flash of colored lights spilling out from under the door.

"I was not expecting this," Marquis mused. "This is like . . . a real party."

Henry nodded, agreeing. Not that Marquis could see him nod, given the lack of light. There was a mass of people jumping on the dance floor, no longer distinguishable as individuals.

It was so *dark* in there. He looked—he couldn't *not* look—for Rosie, wearing his hoodie. *His hoodie.* But he couldn't see her anywhere.

"Hey!" Something small and very green was coming at them, waving. "Hey!" Yumi stopped in front of them, hands on her hips. "You're only, like, a billion years late."

"I had to fix my hair," Marquis said, smoothing a hand over his head and his barely-there hair.

"Hilarious. Cute couple's costume," Yumi said. "You boys are adorable."

"Thanks, girl," Marquis cooed back at her. "Did you forget your pants?"

"Did you forget your . . . ugh, never mind. It's too loud in here to think. Come on. Let's dance."

Yumi grabbed Marquis's arm, and Marquis shot Henry a look that might have said *Help!* or it might have said *Aww yeah* or it might have said *Are you coming?* It was too dark to be sure. But Henry didn't go anywhere.

Because the thumping bass slowed, and John Legend crooned from out of the speakers, and finally, Henry saw her.

Dancing with Bodie Tal.

CHAPTER TWENTY

Rosie

On the one hand, Rosie was glad it was a slow song. All she had to do was sway back and forth. But Bodie was so *close*. His face was right above hers, his lips almost level with her eyes, and when she tilted her head back, even in the dark, she could see his clear gray-blue gaze. Looking at her.

Rosie glanced away, over his shoulder. She still didn't see Henry. She tried to look at the dancing couples around her, wondering if he might have slipped in without her seeing, but it was so hard to tell who everyone was in their costumes, pressed together in the darkness.

Bodie was quiet as he steered her in a slow circle around the room. She was dizzy, almost. Maybe from the heat of the room, or the circular movement, or the scent of Bodie's aftershave. It was so deep in her nose, it was probably working its way into her brain. She found herself leaning on him more than she had been, worried that she might stumble.

The song ended, and Rosie looked back up at Bodie,

wondering *why* he had wanted to dance with her. He hadn't said anything the whole time. It had been nice, but odd, or maybe odd because it was nice. She stood there, realized her arms were still around his neck, then dropped them, hurriedly. Bodie let go, too, and took a step back.

It was loud now, the rhythm frantic, rhymes spit rapidly as the dancing bodies surged and moved around them.

"Hey!" Rosie saw Clara tap Bodie on the shoulder, pouting at him playfully. He turned.

"Thanks," Rosie muttered, because it seemed like the thing to say.

"Rosie—"

Clara grabbed his arm and squeezed his bicep, making a joke about something Rosie couldn't hear. Rosie slipped away while Bodie was distracted, but froze on her way across the dance floor, catching a glimpse of a figure with dark hair slipping into the kitchen. *Henry.* Right? It had to be. Rosie hurried after him, wondering why he was leaving the dance already.

In the kitchen off the cafeteria, something clanged, like two pots colliding, then Rosie heard a giggle and a "Shhh!" Somebody else was in here. Rosie inched closer to the staircase down to the main kitchen, hoping to go unnoticed. But then a flash of neon green caught her eye. Yumi's monster shirt. It had to be. Rosie peeked around the corner, then rapidly stepped back, because it wasn't just Yumi. Yumi and Marquis were kissing—nope, forget kissing, they were making out—and if either of them saw her right now, Rosie would never be able to look them in the face again. Silently, feeling her way in the dark, Rosie crept down the stairs.

The stairs had indeed led her to the big kitchen. None of

the lights were on, but the moon shone through the windows, bathing all the stainless steel in an iridescent silver glow. A full moon on Halloween. Like an illustration in a picture book.

"Henry?" Rosie whispered.

He stepped out of the shadows and into the moonlight.

"What are you doing down here?" she asked, walking toward him.

"Oh. You know. Nothing. Trying not to interrupt you and Bodie."

"What are you talking about?" Rosie stopped in her tracks, stung by his tone. "I was waiting for *you*."

"Really," he said flatly. "That's funny. Usually when I'm waiting for someone, I keep busy by messing around with my phone. Maybe next time I'll try slow dancing."

"It was just a dance. And not that it matters, but I wanted to dance with *you*." This was not how tonight was supposed to go. Rosie was supposed to dance with *Henry*. And they were supposed to be kissing right now, not fighting in a kitchen!

"Yeah, it really looked like you were dying to dance with me," Henry said sarcastically.

"Wow. Okay. Sorry I danced with someone else." Rosie could be sarcastic right back at him. "Sorry I didn't even know if you *wanted* to dance with me because you've been so . . . so . . . grumpy and weird and confusing!"

"Well, maybe *I'm* confused because you clearly like someone else!"

"Seriously?" Rosie took a deep breath. She couldn't even remember the last time she'd been so frustrated. "You obviously don't want to listen to me right now. Let's just—let's just talk about this later, okay?"

Rosie was halfway up the stairs before she remembered she was wearing his hoodie. She unzipped it as she stomped back into the kitchen and dropped it on the counter at the front of the room.

She didn't wait to see if he bothered to pick it up.

CHAPTER TWENTY-ONE

Henry

S he wasn't there.

Every Sunday since they'd arrived at the École, Rosie had been waiting for him across the street from the boulangerie. But the morning after the dance, when Henry stopped on the stairs, right in the middle, and looked across the street to where she'd been every Sunday, she wasn't there.

Henry clutched his bag stuffed full of brioche, his grip tightening around the paper. Although he was probably going to need a lot more than a bag of brioche to make up for last night. He'd acted like a petulant baby who needed a nap. And Henry *did* need a nap—he'd been working so hard, he constantly felt exhausted and grouchy, but that wasn't an excuse. Henry was pretty sure Rosie could stay up for three days straight and she still wouldn't yell at him. He'd apologize to her today.

But every time he tried to think of what to say to Rosie, for some reason all he could think about was Rosie wrapped in Bodie's arms, looking up at Bodie in a way Henry was sure she'd never looked at *him*. The whole thing felt like a punch in the gut. Henry didn't know if he wanted to stuff every last bit of brioche in his face right now or if he never wanted to eat again.

"Pardon!" a woman exclaimed from behind Henry. Right. He was blocking the whole staircase. He ran down the last couple steps and onto the sidewalk, just barely avoiding being sideswiped by a baguette.

"Désolé," Henry mumbled as he nodded at her awkwardly, embarrassed by his bad French. She sniffed, shifted her baguette to her other arm, and passed by him. Henry watched her stalk out of sight, the baguette bobbing as she went.

And when Henry turned back to look across the street, there she was. Standing on the corner, hair piled messily on top of her head, smiling at him. Hope blossomed in his chest.

"Happy Sunday," Rosie called. She held up two glass Coke bottles, one in each hand.

"I didn't think you were coming," he said as he crossed the street.

"New day, fresh start?" She handed him one of the bottles. God, she was nicer than he deserved. She should be yelling at him for being an idiot, not handing him a Coke and a clean slate. "Gosh, I sound like my mom."

She laughed, but her smile didn't quite reach her eyes.

"Here." Henry thrust the bag at her. He wanted to say, *I'm sorry.* He'd meant to say, *I'm sorry*, but what came out was "I got you some brioche."

"My favorite." Rosie took the bag, and Henry hoped his peace offering was enough. "Wanna go sit by the river and eat?"

Henry nodded, and they started walking. Henry couldn't quite tell if they weren't talking about the dance because Rosie wanted a fresh start, or because he was being a chicken. He could feel everything they'd said last night hovering between them like an uninvited guest, but he still couldn't seem to find the words to apologize for how he'd acted.

"Henry?"

"Sorry. I'm sorry." Henry shook his head. "Did you say something?"

"Wow, you're *really* out of it. Let me guess—Hampus found a bunch of deleted scenes from *Bron/Broen* and you guys were up way too late last night?"

"Something like that." Henry forced himself to smile. He'd been up too late obsessing about Bodie and Rosie dancing and the way he'd acted like a sulky little kid. Which was way worse than bingeing Swedish crime procedurals.

"You've seemed tired a lot lately," she said gently. "Like you're having a hard time staying awake in class. And you fell asleep in the common room the other day. Is everything okay?"

"Yeah. Yeah, it's fine. I'm fine. Better than fine. Just. You know. Gotta get everything right."

"Henry, you don't have to get *everything* right. Not if it's keeping you from sleeping. You'll cut your fingers off if you're not careful."

Henry nodded in response and then stifled a yawn. Rosie wrinkled her nose at him, like he was proving her point.

"Wanna cut through the park?" Henry asked her, changing the subject. Even though Rosie looked like she still had something she wanted to say, all she did was nod and start walking.

The branches of the trees were bare and leafless. It was that in-between season, after autumn leaves and before snow, where everything seemed dead and cold and a bit spooky, even in the late-morning sunshine.

Rosie stopped, suddenly, right in the middle of the park. Henry immediately saw why—there was a couple making out on a park bench, directly in front of them. But it wasn't just any couple—it was Yumi and Marquis. Neither Rosie nor Henry said anything, but they found themselves, by unspoken agreement, crossing the street.

"So, um, the thing about brioche," Rosie blurted out, her voice higher than usual, querulous, "is that you want room-temperature eggs and soft butter."

And Rosie kept talking about brioche, but she didn't make eye contact with him until they'd reached the banks of the Seine.

Henry didn't know why they couldn't joke about their friends making out. But as they drank their Cokes and shared their brioche, they never even mentioned Yumi and Marquis. And even though they spent the rest of the afternoon talking, Henry felt like there was too much that went unsaid.

★★★★

Back at school for dinner, Henry still felt awkward as he pushed his coq au vin around on his plate. He was half paying attention to the conversation and mostly concentrating on not accidentally brushing his leg against Rosie's.

"Well, it looks like everybody's finally here," Yumi said, scanning the cafeteria. "It's go-time."

"Go-time? Go-time for what?" Rosie asked, but Yumi was

already climbing on top of her chair, glass and fork in hand. She wobbled once, then steadied herself. "Do you know what she's doing?" Rosie asked Marquis, across the table.

"No, I do not," he said, and Henry felt like he'd started to notice a different tone in Marquis's voice when he talked about Yumi. It wasn't exasperation anymore. It was . . . affection, for lack of a better word.

"Attention. Attention all." Yumi banged her fork against her plastic cup. It didn't produce much noise, but eventually, everyone stopped talking and stared at her. "Thank you so much for your attention, and for allowing me to break into your regularly scheduled Sunday evening activities. As you may or may not know, last night, Marquis and I shared a passionate embrace."

"Oh no," Rosie said softly. "I think I have that thing when you die because you're embarrassed for someone."

"*Fremdschämen*," Hampus said. "It is a German word. Anna taught me when we were watching Henry do his presentation in French class."

"Nice, man. Thanks," Henry said. His French *was* bad. Good thing Madame Huppert graded them on effort rather than ability.

"Shhh!" Yumi glared at them. "As all of you most definitely do not know," she addressed the room, "unless you are *stalking* us, we have decided to make our relationship official. We are both off the market, so single people of the École, better luck next time."

"Did you know she was going to do this?" Henry asked Marquis in a low voice.

"I did not," he replied.

"Again, *shhh*, please!" Yumi hissed at their table. "If you would like to follow our journey on Instagram, you may use our couple name, hashtag-Mumi, or follow us on Snapchat at MumiDoesParis." Yumi smiled brilliantly at the cafeteria. "Thank you so much for your time and consideration."

"You're on board with this?" Henry asked as the cafeteria exploded into a surprisingly robust round of applause, and Yumi, atop her chair, bowed.

"I am on board with this," Marquis said, and Henry wasn't sure if he'd been brainwashed. "Hashtag-Mumi."

"Decided not to go with *Yarquis*?"

"Yumi thinks *Mumi* has better brand recognition."

"What is your *brand*?" Henry asked, dumbfounded.

"You know. Mumi."

"Sure. Mumi," Henry said, and somehow, he was able to say it with a straight face. Maybe it did have better brand recognition than Yarquis.

Yumi made it back down to her seat, and Marquis kissed her, and this wasn't even anywhere near the most intense PDA he'd been forced to witness at close quarters, but Henry found himself looking away, anyway. Not so much because he was embarrassed—not like Rosie, who was concentrating *very* hard on a piece of roasted potato—but because he wanted what they had. With Rosie. He didn't need to be #Renry or @HosieDoesParis—he certainly couldn't imagine Rosie doing anything like that—but watching Yumi and Marquis announce a full-fledged social media campaign made Henry newly aware of how none of their friends even knew he and Rosie had kissed. He couldn't help but wonder if Rosie had kept everything that happened between them on the DL because she was hoping something might happen with Bodie.

Because Henry had replayed their conversation from last night a million times in his mind.

And the thing he couldn't forget was that Rosie had never denied liking Bodie.

CHAPTER TWENTY-TWO

Rosie

So what's coming up this week?" Mom asked, folding her arms and resting them on the kitchen table as she looked out at Rosie from her computer screen.

"Not sure. Chef Martinet still hasn't told us yet." Rosie picked up the laptop and settled it onto her lap, getting comfortable. She'd ducked out of lunch early to Skype with Mom before heading down to the kitchen.

"Here's hoping it's not frogs' legs," Mom teased.

"Henry keeps telling me they're good. Like little meaty chicken lollipops."

"Henry." Mom smiled warmly. "How's he doing?"

Henry. Things had mostly gone back to normal in the week since Halloween. Rosie certainly wasn't as frustrated with him as she had been that night, but she still wanted to know where she stood, and she wanted Henry to know she liked *him*, not Bodie. Rosie knew the rational thing to do would be to just talk to Henry about what, if anything, was going on between them, but his moods had been unpredictable lately, and Rosie was having a hard time mustering up the courage to bring it up. One minute Henry was building snowmen out of dinner rolls and teasing Rosie about getting flour in her hair, and the next he was alternately grouchy and exhausted, falling asleep on top of his math homework or snapping at Hampus for not keeping their table neat enough.

"He seems . . . tired," Rosie said eventually, which was true.

Owen, munching on an Eggo waffle, popped into the frame.

"Bonjour, Rosie!" he announced, affording her a pretty good view of a half-eaten Eggo.

"Don't talk with your mouth full," Mom admonished.

"Bonjour, Owen!" Rosie tilted the screen toward her to get a better view. *"Ça va?"*

"Ça va awesome," he replied. "Crushing this Eggo. Then gonna crush this Monday."

"Is everybody else still asleep?" Rosie asked.

"Don't tell me you're surprised," Mom said wryly.

"Here—wait—Ricky's gonna say hi."

Owen held a cell phone up to the screen and pressed PLAY. Loud, operatic snoring filled the room. Rosie guffawed.

"Owen, is that my phone?" Mom pulled her readers down from their perch on top of her head and squinted through them.

"Um. Maybe."

Mom held out her palm, and sheepishly, Owen handed over the phone.

Looking at the two of them, Rosie's heart ached with the pain of missing her family. Had she even done the right thing, coming here? Her entire experience in the kitchen had been pretty much one big fail, and she'd already missed so much back home. She'd missed the first day of school and home-coming and Halloween and Owen's birthday and next came Thanksgiving, all these calendar days that signified fall in East Liberty, the passing of time the way life had always been. Rosie wondered how it would be to spend Thanksgiving away from them. Maybe she should just pretend it wasn't happening. Like Reed had, the year he'd learned the fate of the vast majority of Native Americans a couple hundred years after that allegedly cheerful first Thanksgiving.

Reed wandered through the back of the frame, still in paja-mas, hair mussed.

"It's aliiiiiiive," Owen whispered dramatically, leaning so close in to the camera that all Rosie could see was his nostril.

"Mom!" Reed yelled from offscreen. "We're out of Eggos!"

"Owen, how many times have I told you? Don't put the empty box back in the freezer." Mom sighed.

"Did you eat the last Eggo?" Reed asked, coming into the frame.

"I ate the last four Eggos." Owen winked at Rosie. "Deal with it."

Reed flicked Owen on the side of the head. Rosie winced sympathetically.

"Ow!" Owen shrieked. Then he shoved Reed so hard he tumbled from view.

"Boys!" Mom said sharply. "Enough!"

But by the sounds of the scuffling, they hadn't had nearly enough.

"I'm sorry, Rosie," Mom said, apologetic, "I've got to—"

"Go." Rosie waved her away. "I have to head down to the kitchen, anyway."

"Love you, Rosie-girl."

"Love you, too."

"Did you just *bite me*?!" Rosie heard Reed say, incredulous.

"I'd do it again!" Owen retorted.

"Boys! Stop!"

Mom hung up, and the image frozen on the screen was of her blurrily standing up, probably about to separate the two of them by physical force. At that moment, Rosie would have given anything to be in the kitchen back home, even if Reed and Owen were biting each other. Although if Rosie were there, she'd have just busted out the waffle maker and no biting would have been necessary. She could picture it now, a huge stack of fluffy pumpkin waffles with maple syrup and spiced cinnamon butter, the perfect breakfast for fall. Something that tasted like crisp, cool air and golden-orange leaves and bundling up in her favorite sweater. Something that tasted like home.

Rosie closed her laptop and stood—time to leave the kitchen in Ohio for the kitchen at the École. Bodie Tal was coming out of the boys' hall just as she left the girls' hall. They hit the stairs at almost the exact same time.

"Hey," he said. Bodie always sounded so relaxed, like he'd just wandered off the beach and decided it might be fun to show up here and cook something.

"Hi," she replied, hoping Bodie couldn't tell how reluctant she was to talk to him. It wasn't *his* fault that she'd had that disastrous conversation with Henry at the dance, but when she looked at Bodie, that was all she could think about.

"Skipping lunch?" Bodie asked.

"No, just left early so I could talk to my mom."

"Funny. I was talking to Dad."

"Isn't that, like, a nine-hour time difference?" Rosie asked. Bodie held the door to the kitchen open for her.

"Yeah. His shooting schedule's crazy, though. He's always up at the weirdest hours."

Rosie nodded and started walking toward her station.

"Hey, Rosie." She stopped, and turned to look at him. "I have a feeling today's gonna be a good day."

And then he winked at her. *Winked.* Rosie could feel herself frowning quizzically as she left him, face probably contorted into a particularly unflattering expression. As she walked over to her station, Priya's eyes were boring into hers like she was trying to mine their depths for state secrets.

"Bodie Tal! Again!" Priya hissed. "And *winking* at you, by the looks of it. What did he *say?*"

"We're getting married," Rosie answered, deadpan.

Priya's mouth opened and closed, like a fish.

"Priya! I'm kidding! Obviously!"

"Étudiants." Before Priya could say anything else, Chef Martinet, up at the front of the room, clapped her hands to get their attention. Standing next to her was a man she hadn't seen in the kitchen before. He was big, maybe not quite as big as Hampus, but almost, with a ruddy beard obscuring much of his face, and a round belly straining the buttons on his chef's coat. He looked familiar, Rosie thought. Maybe it was just because he looked so much like a *chef*, like a cartoon someone would use to sell ready-made meals in the grocery store. "For this week, we shall have a special guest. Please, allow me to introduce Chef Petit." The man waved at them. Rosie couldn't help a little half smile. This one she knew—*petit* meant little, or small. And this chef was anything but. "Chef Petit will be taking over the kitchen this week. We will have pastry week, and then return to cooking afterward. I know you will give him the same respect you give me."

Chef Martinet was still talking, but Rosie wasn't listening anymore. *Pastry week.* It was unbelievable! Finally, finally something she'd be able to do! And she was going to learn pastry here, in France, the capital of pastry. *This* was why she'd come here. This was the moment that was going to make everything worth it, all her failure and frustration.

And then, just like that, Chef Martinet walked out of the kitchen, leaving them alone with Chef Petit. They were learning pastry, *and* Rosie got a week-long break from Chef Martinet? It was an almost-Thanksgiving miracle.

"Bonjour, petits chefs!" Chef Petit said—he earned a few chuckles from the room for that—and Rosie realized where she knew him from. He was the *boulanger,* from the boulangerie she'd gone to almost every Sunday with Henry. And he clearly recognized Henry in the front row, as he tossed Henry a special "Bonjour," and a "Ça va, *mon ami?*"

Rosie was so excited, she found herself bouncing up and down on the tips of her toes. To learn from this man, to be able to make bread the way he did . . . Her mind boggled at all the possibilities. They probably wouldn't start with bread, though. Bread was complicated for something that seemed so deceptively simple, and it took so much time.

In two straight lines they broke their bread. She heard it in Dad's voice. The little girls at the long table, the squiggles on the table that may have been croissants or baguettes or brioche. Rosie breathed, in through her nose, out through her mouth. Focused on Chef Petit.

As Rosie expected, Chef Petit said they were starting with pâtisserie. Specifically, with classic French tarts, and today, with the tart shells. With the three most widely used different kinds of crust.

Finally, something Rosie knew! Her hand shot in the air, and Rosie noticed that the only other person in the room with his hand in the air was Bodie Tal. But Chef Petit must have recognized her, too, because he called on *her*, not Bodie. And she felt like Hermione, rattling off the differences between *pâté brisée*, a standard, unsweetened dough for sweet or savory fillings; *pâté sucrée*, a sugared dough achieved by creaming the butter and sugar; and *pâté sablée*, a crumbly, delicate, almost cookielike dough, sometimes enriched with almond flour. Ten points to Rosie! She felt flush with triumph. Finally, she wasn't an idiot.

"Excellent," Chef Petit said genially, and he began to expound further upon what Rosie said.

"What a bloody showoff," Priya said, teasing. Rosie bumped her with her shoulder.

Chef Petit wrote the ingredients for pâté brisée on the whiteboard, informing them that they'd be making all three doughs today, then setting them in the fridge to chill until tomorrow—all crust, no matter what you did with it, was improved by a good chilling. Tomorrow, they'd do quiche, and tarte au citron, and a fresh fruit tart with crème pâtissière, and they'd move on to puff pastry and tarte tatin, and Rosie could barely restrain the shout of joy that threatened to erupt from her chest. But she restrained it, and moved through the kitchen as sedately as possible, collecting her ingredients and measuring cups.

The mood in the kitchen was different, and Rosie didn't think it was just her. Chef Petit was playing music; a bouncy French tune emanated from the speakers that had gone unused since Chef Martinet had played the welcome video. Rosie laughed as Seydou did a funny little two-step while he moved out of her way, giving her access to the flour. There was levity in the room that had nothing to do with the sunshine streaming in through the windows. Even Clara shot her something that might almost have been a smile as she passed her the flour scoop before heading back to her station. Maybe Rosie wasn't the only one who was stressed out by Chef Martinet.

"I've never seen someone smile like that while scooping flour."

Rosie looked up at Bodie, waiting for the flour, smiling at her.

"Well." She added a final scoop to her prep bowl and stood, sidling out of his way so he could get to the flour. "I'm happy."

Happy didn't even begin to cover it.

"Good," he said. "You're welcome."

"For what?" Rosie asked.

"This." He gestured vaguely around the room, sprinkling his pants with flour in the process. He either didn't notice or didn't care.

"What do you mean, *this*?"

"Our reprieve! A week of pastry with someone who actually knows what he's talking about when it comes to pastry."

"What are you talking about?" Rosie felt a weird, queasy feeling.

"I told Denis we needed a break from butchering animal carcasses."

"What?!"

"Well, specifically, I said I needed a break from Chef Martinet calling me *a literal butcher* because I can't chop up some dead animal to her exacting specifications." Bodie grinned.

Once again, Bodie had texted Chef Laurent, and *poof!* He'd gotten exactly what he'd asked for. Rosie couldn't even imagine. What kind of world did he live in, where he snapped his fingers, and just like that, it was done? Schedules changed and curriculum added and why *not* a Halloween dance, and sure, Bodie, whatever you want?

"You didn't—you didn't do this for *me*, did you?"

"No, no, no. I did it for *me*," he insisted. Obviously. Rosie was embarrassed she'd even asked. Priya's constant insistence that Bodie was flirting with her must have made her jump to crazy conclusions. Bodie wanted to bake—and take a break from butchering—just as badly as she did. "The fact that you've practically got cartoon bluebirds twittering around your head while you scoop flour is just a bonus."

"Well. Um . . . Okay, then," Rosie said, unsure what to say. "Thanks, I guess."

So Rosie did what she did best. She went back to her station and lost herself in the butter and the flour.

"How, exactly, are you doing this?" Priya was holding up her hands as if in surrender. They were covered in pilling, sticky pâte brisée. It looked like there was more pastry on Priya's hands than on her workspace.

"You added too much liquid."

"Not only do I not understand how you're doing this, but I *really* don't understand how you're enjoying this." Priya was attempting to pull the little pastry pills off her hands and add them to the smear of dough on her cutting board. "This is bloody torture."

Rosie thought Priya should probably start over, but they still had two more crusts to make and chill before class ended, so Rosie just grabbed a bench scraper and showed Priya how to use that to get it together. Technically, you weren't supposed to use a bench scraper with pâté brisée—it was for bread dough—but hey, whatever worked.

Rosie wasn't seeing any cartoon birds, but she felt like something in her chest had loosened and floated away. As she started on her pâté sucrée, creaming the butter and sugar together, she had a feeling that felt, like, well . . . felt like *home*. And as she watched Henry working diligently several rows ahead of her, Rosie knew there was only one thing she had left to fix to make everything perfect.

The Eiffel Tower. The idea burst into Rosie's head uninvited, but she knew, instantly, that it was exactly where they should go. It was the most romantic place in the world! Today was too good to end already. Rosie would ask Henry to go to the Eiffel Tower with her, and she knew, she just knew, that once they were there together, they'd get everything back on track.

★★★★

Rosie pushed open the door to the bathroom and slid into a vacant stall. She'd get the flour off her hands, change, and hopefully be on her way to the Eiffel Tower with Henry in no time at all. She was almost buzzing with anticipation. Mere seconds after Rosie had locked the door, she heard two flushes.

"Is everyone going home for Thanksgiving?" Elodie. Rosie was pretty sure. She saw a pair of Adidas Gazelles in rose pink walk toward the sink. Elodie, definitely. "All the Americans, anyway?"

"No. Weirdly." Clara. Of course. Who else would wear boots with heels to dinner? Most people wore sweatpants to dinner. Or pajamas, if they were feeling especially lazy. Hampus had even once had dinner in his bathrobe, before Madame Besson told him that pants were required in the cafeteria. "Henry's staying. Marquis. I had thought Little Miss American Heartland would go home, to whatever Norman Rockwell painting she comes from, but she's staying, too."

Little Miss American Heartland?! They were talking about her. Nobody else came from anywhere in America that could be considered the heartland by any stretch of the imagination. And there Rosie was, trapped in the bathroom stall. How was this happening to her?

"She's probably worried that if she goes home, Martinet won't let her come back," Elodie said.

Hot shame burned at Rosie's cheeks, at the back of her throat.

"Probably. I don't even know how she got *in*. Wasn't it sad today, how happy she was that she finally got something right? If I was that pathetic, I'd just leave on my own."

"If *you* were that pathetic? Please. I can't even imagine it."

They laughed, and Rosie heard the door swing shut behind them and their footsteps retreat down the hall. Rosie felt bile rising in her throat. She closed her eyes tight, determined to keep the hot tears that threatened to spill over at bay.

Honestly, Rosie had barely thought about Clara for weeks. Somehow along the way, she'd stopped being bothered by Clara's perfectly done hair and perfectly cooked food. It really hadn't seemed to matter anymore. Which made hearing Clara talk about her a total surprise, and even more upsetting, somehow. Why would Clara think anything about Rosie? Rosie still wasn't even sure that Clara knew her *name*.

Maybe the best thing to do was to just leave the building. Yes. She'd leave the building. Rosie didn't even bother to stop for her jacket as she power-walked down the stairs and out of the École. The cold hit her like a slap. Rosie didn't have a destination in mind, but she wasn't surprised when her feet led her to the door of the boulangerie. It was still open. The bell tinkled as Rosie pushed open the door and slipped in. The smell of bread and butter enveloped her like a hug, and Rosie breathed in deeply.

"Bonjour!" Chef Petit called from behind the counter. "What is happening at the École this evening? My two best students have come to visit me!"

Bodie Tal was leaning against the wall, eating a croissant from the look of the crumbs on his shirt. Chef Petit did make a dangerously flaky croissant.

"Hey." Bodie nodded at her.

Rosie nodded back, trying not to let the disappointment flood her. She realized she'd been expecting to see Henry here. Rationally, she knew that was stupid. Henry was probably face-first in a bowl of boeuf bourguignon right now, wondering where *she* was. But part of her had been hoping Henry would just be here, somehow, magically. It felt wrong to see Bodie at the boulangerie, like looking at one of those spot-the-difference pictures, where something was glaringly not right. Bodie belonged at the École, not here. The boulangerie was for her and Henry.

"Are you okay?" Bodie pushed off the wall, standing up straight, looking at Rosie with a concern in his eyes that made her cringe with embarrassment. "Your face looks . . . weird."

"I'm fine," Rosie said stiffly. "I should—I should go."

"I have something for you to try!" Chef Petit singsonged from behind the counter, apparently having missed the awkwardness in their exchange.

"I don't— I can't— I shouldn't—"

"On the house!" he called, disappearing into the kitchen. "*Deux minutes!* I need someone to taste!"

Rosie and Bodie were alone in the front of the shop, staring at each other.

"Are you sure you're okay?" he asked.

"I'm fine."

"You don't seem—"

"Just finish your stupid croissant," she said. What was *wrong* with her? Croissants—certainly Chef Petit's croissants—were never stupid!

"Okay then." Bodie raised his eyebrows and popped the last bite into his mouth. "Whatever didn't happen to you must have really been something."

"Étudiants!" Chef Petit returned from the kitchen, a fabric-lined basket in his hands. He paused behind the counter and pulled back the cloth to expose what was inside.

"Cannelés," Rosie said. Little cakes with a dark, caramelized exterior. They had the shininess of a perfectly glazed donut, and even though Rosie had never had one—you had to have a special pan to make them, a cannelé mold—she knew the inside was supposed to be like custard.

"*Exactement!*" Chef Petit said proudly. "You have had before?"

"No," Rosie said, at exactly the same time Bodie said, "Yeah, of course. With Dominique Ansel." Good gravy. *Of course* Bodie was running around eating cannelés with the man who invented the Cronut. His real life was her Instagram feed.

"Please, try." He shook the basket at them. Rosie grabbed one eagerly—it was warm, but not hot. "Cannelés are from Bordeaux, not Paris, but I thought, why not try?"

Rosie bit into hers and felt the slight crispness from the caramelized sugar on the exterior give way to a soft interior that was, yes, almost exactly like custard. She could taste vanilla—*real* vanilla, she had no doubt she'd seen flecks of vanilla bean—and the richness of eggs and milk, and oh, it was just so much better than she'd expected it to be. The contrast between inside and outside was unreal, like a magic trick—a pastry with a secret.

"It is good! I can tell, from your faces," Chef Petit said triumphantly. "Please, finish them. These are for you." He handed the basket to Bodie. Rosie was already reaching inside for her second. "I will be closing the shop for the evening, but take your time."

"These are so good," Rosie half moaned through a mouthful of cannelé.

"Nothing a little sugar can't fix, right?" Bodie said, setting the basket down on the counter.

"Right."

And the sugar *did* make her feel better. Being in a place that smelled like baking always made her feel better. And it made her want to bake. Which was probably why a new idea popped into her head.

"What are you doing for Thanksgiving?" Rosie asked.

"Thanksgiving? Random, but okay." Bodie rubbed his hands together, trying to get some of the stickiness off. "I think I'm going to LA. Kind of depends on my dad's shooting schedule. There's this whole live Food Network thing. They think Alton Brown's hosting, but my dad might be involved? It's not clear right now. And I think my mom might be doing a shoot for some anti-aging skincare line. I'm still not really sure what's going on. Or where anyone's going to be. Or if any of those places are places I can go." His life, as always, remained totally baffling to her. TV shoots and modeling campaigns and all these crazy things. But also she couldn't imagine not being sure where her family would be for Thanksgiving. Not being sure if there was a place for her at their table. "Are you going home?" he asked.

"No," Rosie said. "We should have Thanksgiving *here*. At the École." Once she said it out loud, she was even more sure they should do it. "Except it doesn't have to be turkey and stuffing, unless people want to make that. It should just be everyone making what they like best. The foods they eat with their family, or whatever their nanas taught them to make, you know? The foods that make them feel like *home*."

"Thanksgiving at the École," Bodie mused. "I think I can help you with that."

Rosie was going to make this the best Thanksgiving ever. Even better than it would have been at home.

And she'd even invite Elodie and Clara.

CHAPTER TWENTY-THREE

Henry

Rosie hadn't shown up for dinner.

Nobody else seemed particularly concerned, but by the time Henry finished his second bowl of boeuf bourguignon and his third dinner roll, he started to wonder if something might be wrong.

Maybe he should look for her. Yeah, he thought as he got up to clear his tray. That made sense. He could just take a casual walk, make sure everything was okay. Because if something was wrong . . . like, actually wrong . . . Henry knew exactly where she would go.

He waved at everyone as he headed out of the cafeteria and pushed open the doors to the courtyard. Probably should have brought his jacket. Henry jogged a couple steps across the cobblestones, trying to warm up. Ugh. He could feel all the boeuf bourguignon sloshing around in his belly.

Rosie had crushed it in the kitchen today. Henry couldn't imagine what could have upset her. Probably, he was worrying about nothing, and she was still at the École. Maybe she was up in her room, Skyping her family. Maybe she'd come down to dinner minutes after he'd left. But still . . . there was no harm in checking.

Henry turned the corner and saw the now familiar blue-and-white-striped awnings. She *was* at the boulangerie. The sign on the front door had flipped to FERMÉ, but the lights were still on inside, illuminating Rosie in the big display window. He saw her, leaning against the counter, talking animatedly as she gestured with her hands. Probably talking to Chef Petit about tarts, he thought, grinning. Henry walked toward the door, wondering if he might be able to score some end-of-the-day pastries, wondering if he could share them with Rosie, hoping everything was okay.

But as he got closer to the door, he froze. Because now, from this angle, Henry could see who Rosie was talking to, and it wasn't Chef Petit.

It was Bodie Tal.

What the . . . ? Henry ducked. Should he duck? No, now he was just an almost-adult man crouching on the stairs of a bakery like he was playing some kind of deranged game of hide-and-seek. Slowly, he rose back to standing and flattened himself around the corner, peeping back through the door.

Rosie was still talking. Bodie nodded back at her, enthusiastically. Then he said something, and Rosie laughed, and it hit him like a punch in the gut. Rosie was fine. She was talking and laughing with Bodie, and . . . *eating* something with Bodie. He watched her pull something out of a basket on the counter and pop it in her mouth. They were eating together? No! That was *their* thing! His and Rosie's!

He couldn't believe Rosie had taken Bodie *here,* of all places. To *their* place. The injustice of it all stuck in his throat, lodged there in a lump that made him worry he might start to cry. Or punch a hole straight through the boulangerie door. Well, this explained why Rosie hadn't denied liking Bodie and hadn't wanted to talk about what had happened at the dance. Clearly, she *did* like Bodie. Henry just couldn't believe that she thought so little of *him* that she'd brought Bodie to their place. This was the worst kind of betrayal: when the person who'd hurt you didn't even realize they'd hurt you. Or maybe didn't even care.

Henry watched Rosie rise up onto her tiptoes to hug Bodie—a quick squeeze, and then she released him. Henry felt newly aware of the two bowls of boeuf bourguignon he'd devoured. Watching Rosie and Bodie hug on a full stomach was even worse than jogging across the courtyard on a full stomach.

★★★★

Friday morning, Henry woke up with his worst Swedish TV hangover yet and poorly done homework. When they met before class, Ms. Whitman seemed disappointed by what he'd done, and Henry dreaded what she might say when she e-mailed his mom. Then he realized he'd forgotten to do the reading in English, bombed a pop quiz in history, and accidentally used the feminine while describing himself during all of French class. By the time he made it down to the kitchen and Chef Petit announced that for Dish of the Day they could create any dessert they wanted, all Henry wanted to do was go back to sleep and start the day over again.

Henry blinked, but he wasn't hallucinating—Chef Martinet

had appeared in the kitchen. Henry swore he could feel something almost imperceptible change in the atmosphere. He was pretty sure that there would be no peppy French jazz bopping out of the speakers as they baked today.

"Ah, *oui*! Chef Martinet!" Chef Petit waved Chef Martinet over to the front of the room with him enthusiastically. "Have you come today to taste our desserts?"

"Yes," Chef Martinet said, her voice clipped. "Bonjour, étudiants. I hope you have enjoyed your week of baking with Chef Petit. I am anxious to taste your dishes today and see what you have learned with him."

Anxious. Henry wondered if that was a weird translation thing, or if she was, in fact, anxious. He was feeling anxious. Henry *still* hadn't successfully produced a Dish of the Day that Chef Martinet felt told her who he was. At this point, Henry wasn't even sure he knew who he was anymore.

"I also wish to speak with you about your final exam for this semester." At this new piece of information, a low buzz filled the room. Chef Martinet stared them down until the buzz was no more. "Your final exam will be simple. Please prepare a three-course meal that best represents who you are as a chef. Hopefully, you have learned well this week with Chef Petit, for your third course must be dessert."

A three-course meal. Anything they wanted! No more chopping, no more chickens, no more eggs—total freedom. Henry *should* have been ecstatic. But all he could think about was the fact that his Dishes of the Day—the only times they'd had any freedom—had been complete fails. Would his final meal be a fail, too?

"And there is one final announcement." More? There was

more? "I will not be tasting your dishes alone. Chef Laurent will be available to join me for your presentation."

Now the buzz was more of an explosion. Everyone was talking so loudly and so excitedly, Henry couldn't even make out any words, except for, over and over again, "Chef Laurent!" Hampus was shaking Henry's arm with excitement. Henry worried it might pop right out of its socket.

Chef Laurent. Here. At the École. Eating his food. *Eating his food!* Dad was gonna *freak*. Henry couldn't believe he'd actually get to meet Chef Laurent. And not just, like, in line at a cookbook signing or something, but in the kitchen, where Chef Laurent would be *eating his food*. Chef Laurent. Eating. His. Food. Finally, Henry could think about something other than Rosie laughing it up at the boulangerie with Bodie.

These three dishes had to be *perfect*. This wouldn't be like Dish of the Day. It couldn't be. Henry had to show Chef Laurent exactly who he was. Exactly what he could do. And how much Chef Laurent had inspired him.

"That is all!" Henry could finally hear Chef Martinet over the noise in the kitchen, which had slowed to an excited babble. "Thank you. Perhaps you may consider today's Dish of the Day as a test run for the third course of your final meal. Chef Petit, please proceed."

Now? They were supposed to make something now, after all that? Once again, when it was time for Dish of the Day, Henry felt like his brain had been completely wiped clean. Think, Henry. He knew he wasn't a great pastry chef. And he certainly wasn't functioning at his best today. He needed something simple he couldn't screw up.

Bread pudding? Henry had seen hundreds of bread puddings

on the third round of *Chopped*. Bread pudding it was. Maybe he'd get dinged for using a baguette somebody else made, but he wasn't in this one to win it. This was Rosie's Dish of the Day—Henry had no doubt in his mind that she was going to crush it. He was still annoyed at her for bringing Bodie to their place, but not so annoyed that he wanted her to fail.

Henry cubed the slightly stale baguette he found in the back of the room, remembering how Rosie had smelled his bread the first time he'd bought one at the boulangerie. Argh! No! He didn't want to think about her. He whisked his eggs so forcefully they sloshed over the side of his bowl, like if he only whisked hard enough he could drive her from his mind. But he couldn't, of course. He thought of the way Rosie's eyelashes had lowered before she'd kissed him by the Seine, of the sugar on her lips as they'd met his, and the way her arms had wound their way around his neck. He'd thought she really liked him. She'd kissed him like she had. And Henry couldn't—wouldn't—believe that she'd kissed Bodie like that, too. From the moment he'd seen her on the plane, there hadn't been anyone else for him. And he thought she'd felt the same way. Or maybe he'd just wanted so badly for her to feel the same way, he started to believe in something that wasn't actually there.

Before Henry knew it, he realized he'd assembled the entire bread pudding without putting any sugar in.

He could barely muster up the energy to care as Chefs Petit and Martinet took bites of his dessert, their faces contorting with confusion. While Chef Martinet derided bread pudding as yet another safe choice, Chef Petit kindly assumed Henry had attempted some sort of failed play on sweet and savory, and Henry let him think that—it was less embarrassing than admitting he'd forgotten the sugar because he was obsessed with the fact that he'd once kissed someone who was clearly into another guy.

Until Chef Martinet arrived at Bodie's station, Henry hadn't paid attention to any of her critiques. But he couldn't help but hear that she thought Bodie's creation was "marvelous." Privately, Henry thought a "black sesame sponge cake with poached longan, popcorn brittle, and a miso-butterscotch gastrique" sounded unbearably pretentious, not to mention that miso-butterscotch was so played out.

When the Chefs made it to Rosie's station, Henry could feel his pulse speeding up. Chef Martinet poked Priya's cake with her spoon, and Henry swore he could hear the spoon knocking against something hard from all the way up at the front of the room. Chef Martinet deemed it "inedible" and wouldn't even try it. Chef Petit gamely took a bite but seemed to be having an incredibly hard time chewing. Eventually, after expending what looked like superhuman effort, he swallowed it. And then it was Rosie's turn. And even with all the confusion swirling between his brain and his heart, Henry couldn't wait to see her blow them away.

Only . . . she didn't. Henry could tell something was wrong before they even tried her dish. He saw Chef Petit place his hand on Rosie's shoulder, and he murmured something, low enough that Henry couldn't hear it, but he could see the concern etched on Chef Petit's brow. Rosie shook her head, then looked away, like she couldn't meet his eyes. Her face was red as Chef Martinet took a bite of what looked like cheesecake, pursed her lips, and then sighed. Chef Petit squeezed Rosie's shoulder and said something else to her as Chef Martinet walked back up to the front of the room. Rosie nodded.

As Chef Martinet started talking about next week, Henry wasn't even paying attention. What had happened? He knew Rosie could make cheesecake. He was sure of it. She could bake *anything*.

Chef Martinet announced Bodie Tal had won Dish of the Day, and Henry felt an unfamiliar urge to punch the smile right off his smug face. That was Rosie's spot. Bodie had done fine during pastry week, but *Rosie* had been the one who had crushed it, day after day. *She* deserved the win, not that miso-butterscotch poser.

After writing Bodie's name on the whiteboard, Chef Martinet dismissed class, and everyone massed toward the doors, scurrying upstairs to change out of their chef's whites before dinner, the major topic of conversation, of course, being the final exam and Chef Laurent's impending visit. Henry hung back in the hall after they'd climbed the stairs from the basement, bobbing and weaving his way back to Rosie, not sure if he was even ready to talk to her, but drawn to her side anyway, knowing she'd be upset.

"I was worried poor Chef Petit was about to crack a tooth," Henry heard Priya say. "I honestly haven't the foggiest idea what happened with that bake."

"I don't know what happened, either." Henry hated how despondent Rosie sounded. "I've made hundreds of cheese-cakes, and they've *never* had a crack like that. Maybe I shouldn't have attempted something so complicated," she added glumly. "Chèvre cheesecake with honey-rosemary poached pears and pistachio sablé crust. Who do I think I am? I'm not chèvre and rosemary. I'm chocolate chip cookies. I'm butterscotch pudding. I'm brownies. I'm *basic*."

"Excuse me." Bodie Tal squeezed past Henry, flashing him a smile that had definitely been professionally whitened. But it was a *sincere* professionally whitened smile, which just made everything worse. There was a part of Henry that still kind of wanted to punch Bodie, but now he felt bad about it. Henry slipped past Rosie and Bodie and made his way back upstairs to his room before he said—or did—something he'd regret.

By the time Henry and Hampus changed, walked down to the cafeteria, and grabbed a plate of whatever fish-and-vegetable thing was being served for dinner, Rosie, Priya, Marquis, and Yumi were already sitting at their table, chatting away, and Rosie didn't look upset at all anymore. Probably because Bodie had cheered her up somehow, Henry thought morosely.

"Do you celebrate Thanksgiving in Tokyo?" Rosie asked Yumi. "With your mom?"

"Sure. But she *hates* cooking. And she says turkey is overrated. So we've never done the big turkey and gravy thing. Mom says the most important part of Thanksgiving is feeling uncomfortably full. So every year we head to Ginza and eat yakitori until we're about to explode."

"Yakitori?" Rosie asked.

"Chicken on a stick. But trust me, that description does *not* do it justice."

"Do you think you could do it here?"

"What? At the École?" Yumi asked, confused.

"Yes, at the École," Rosie said. "I want to have Thanksgiving here."

"A real American Thanksgiving!" Hampus said eagerly.

"Yup. A real American Thanksgiving. With Japanese chicken," Yumi said.

"Or with whatever anyone wants to make!" Rosie said. "It doesn't have to be American. I want people to cook their favorite dishes. The foods that make them feel like home. I mean . . . we talk about all these foods that I've never even tried. We never get to taste each other's food, you know? So that's what we should do for Thanksgiving."

"Oh, man. I *love* Thanksgiving," Marquis said. "Every year at my grandma's place, we've got tables full of trays of mac and cheese as far as the eye can see. The good kind, that gets all crispy on top, but is all gooey and cheesy inside."

"That sounds ace," Priya said dreamily.

"You know you have to make that now, right?" Yumi asked him. "Like, you *have* to make it for Fakesgiving, or I'm going to murder you."

"It's not *Fake*sgiving. It's a very Realsgiving. What about you, Henry?" Rosie asked him. "What do you do for Thanksgiving?"

Be normal, Henry admonished himself. Rosie didn't even know he'd seen her with Bodie at the boulangerie. And she might not even think it was a big deal. The last thing he wanted was for her to pity him because she'd hurt his feelings. Even thinking about it made him feel like a giant baby.

"My dad loves to cook," he said, still unable to quite meet Rosie's eyes. "So on Thanksgiving, it's all about the two of us. We don't usually do turkey—we do duck a lot, actually—but I do have one Thanksgiving obsession: mashed potatoes."

Rosie burst out laughing, and finally, Henry looked at her. She mouthed "Potato maniac" at him, and he felt the bundle of hurt and anger he'd been carrying around with him start to dissipate.

"Oh, I *love* the mashed potatoes." Hampus put his chin in his hand and sighed. "Have you had them with meatballs? And gravy? And lingonberry jam?"

"Um . . . at the Ikea in Schaumburg. Once."

Hampus recoiled like Henry had just slapped him.

"I do not know where Schaumburg is, but of this, I do not approve." Hampus shook his head at Henry, and then turned to Rosie. "For your Thanksgiving, Rosie, I will make the meatballs. And the gravy. And the jam. If I can find the lingonberries."

"That sounds perfect," Rosie said. "And Priya's already promised me samosa."

"And you'll actually be able to chew them, I assure you," Priya said. "Unlike the Victoria Sandwich I foolishly attempted for Dish of the Day."

"Samosa. Another great potato dish," Henry said.

"You're obsessed. I really think you have a problem." Rosie shook her head at him.

"Potatoes are never a problem," Henry replied.

"So is this a 'just us' thing, or are you inviting all the randos?" Yumi gestured to everyone else sitting in the cafeteria.

"They're not *randos*, Yumi. They're our classmates. Of course they're invited. So I should probably . . . invite them," Rosie said. "I hadn't really thought about how to do that."

"Stand up and ask them!" Priya suggested. "Now! Go on!"

"Now?" Rosie looked around the cafeteria. "Here?"

"Yeah," Henry agreed, warming to the idea. "Why not? Go for it, Rosie."

Henry started banging his knife against his cup, much like Yumi had before she announced the birth of @MumiDoesParis, as Rosie stood up, looking around the room. Eventually, the cafeteria quieted, and all eyes were on their table.

"Hi. Um . . . Hi," Rosie said squeakily. "Sorry. Public speaking is not my thing. But. Well, I have an exciting announcement. Hopefully exciting, anyway." She cleared her throat. "This year, we'll be having Thanksgiving at the École for the first time *ever*. And," she added warmly, "it's all thanks to Bodie."

As everyone applauded, Bodie rose to his feet and *bowed*, like a total clown. Henry looked around his table, hoping someone would share his look of disbelief at what a doofus Bodie was, but everyone was blandly smiling and clapping away. Even Yumi, who Henry was so sure he could count on to look disgusted, was typing something into her phone with a perfectly pleasant expression. But the worst part of it all was when Henry caught sight of Rosie's face. She was looking across the cafeteria at Bodie like they were the only two people in the room, like romantic music might magically fill the air and they'd float into each other's arms. Watching everyone treat Bodie like homecoming king wasn't great. But watching Rosie look at Bodie like he was the answer to some unspoken question was horrible. For crying out loud, the guy made *miso-butterscotch*. Why couldn't everyone else see what a hipster hack he was? Why couldn't *Rosie*? Unable to take even a minute more, Henry stormed out of the cafeteria, abandoning his tray.

Rosie probably wouldn't even notice he was gone.

CHAPTER TWENTY-FOUR
Rosie

S o can you see?" Rosie held her notebook up to the computer screen. "There's each person's name, and then what
they're making."

"I can see." Mom leaned in closer to the camera, giving Rosie
a good view of her hairline and not much else. "My goodness.
I don't know what half of these things are. What's . . . what is
that . . . Leberknödelsuppe?"

"I'm not totally sure," Rosie admitted. "Anna's making it.
She's from Germany. I think it's some kind of dumpling soup?"

"Probably not chicken and Bisquick dumplings, I'm
guessing."

"Probably not."

"Now *that's* been a staple at pretty much every potluck I've
been to. Not that I ever get to make it. Because when your
last name starts with R—"

"You always have to bring dessert," Rosie finished for her.
Mom laughed.

"Thank goodness you came along to save the women of East Liberty from my terrible desserts."

"Everybody likes that trifle you make."

"Rosie. Sweetheart. It's boxed brownie mix, Jell-O instant pudding, Kit Kats, M&M'S, and Cool Whip. I don't think anybody over the age of five *actually* likes it."

"It's Ricky's favorite food."

"Your brother does not have your refined palate," Mom teased. "You know, Ro," she continued, suddenly serious. "I think what you've done is pretty amazing. Pulling together this whole Thanksgiving for your classmates is really something—I'm proud of you."

Rosie decided to take the compliment and soak it in, instead of shrugging it off. It *was* going to be pretty amazing. The list of dishes people had signed up to make was killer. Rosie was going to be able to taste all kinds of foods she'd never had before. Her mouth was practically watering already at the thought of it all.

"What pies are you making, hon?"

"Dutch apple. Chocolate pecan. Maybe one more if I get ambitious. But I'm going to skip pumpkin—I'm not sure I can find it here. What are you guys doing for Thanksgiving?" Rosie asked, even though she was pretty sure the answer was going to be Cracker Barrel.

"No judgment, please—"

"I'm not judging!" Rosie protested.

"But we're gonna do the take-home from Cracker Barrel." Rosie tried to keep her face as nonjudgmental as possible. And she didn't even feel judgmental! When it came to food, Mom always assumed judgment when there was none. "There's just too many hungry people for me to cook for. Plus, Cole is bringing home his roommate *and* his girlfriend, so even though we'll be missing you, we'll have more than usual."

"Girlfriend?" Rosie asked. She heard from Cole very rarely, but this seemed like a pretty big development to have missed. She kept forgetting that life back home in Ohio continued on without her, that they weren't frozen in time, waiting for her to come back.

"Brooke. She seems very sweet. She plays soccer, too," Mom said, then looked out of frame, distracted. "Rosie, honey, I'm sorry, I've gotta go. Your brother is doing something weird."

Rosie was pretty sure Mom said, "Love you!" and then she definitely said, "OWEN!" before the screen went black. Rosie smiled as she shut her laptop. She missed Mom, but in a good way, in a way that made her happy to talk to her, not in a way that was, like, crippling-homesickness-that-made-her-hide-under-her-covers.

"Sorry! So sorry!" Priya announced as she kicked the door open so forcefully it banged against the wall, causing Rosie to jump. "I couldn't use my hands." She gestured to the bulging white shopping bags swinging from her arms. "Come down to the kitchen with me? You can make your pie crusts, and I want to fill my samosa today so they're ready to fry fresh for Thanksgiving tomorrow. Want to learn how to make samosa?"

"Obviously." Rosie grabbed one of the bags from Priya, staggering slightly at its unexpected weight. "What's in there?" she asked as they left the dorm.

"Well, *maida*. That's a bit like cake flour. Ghee—clarified butter. Carom seeds. Ginger. Cumin seeds. Asafoetida. A green cardamom. Fennel. Coriander. Dry pomegranate seeds.

Probably other things I'm forgetting. I wasn't sure exactly what we had here for spices—I may have gotten more than I need."

"Where did you find all of that?"

"Little India!" Priya answered as they made their way down the stairs. "There's an Indian-slash-Pakistani neighborhood only a bit north of us. Not a far walk at all. I found a grocery store with everything I needed."

"That's so cool." Paris was so much bigger and more complex than Rosie knew. At this rate, she'd never see all of it. She'd barely seen any of it.

They clearly hadn't been the only ones who'd wanted to get a jump start on cooking for Thanksgiving. Even though there was no class, the kitchen was buzzing with activity. Rosie did a quick scan of the room—no Clara, no Elodie. A rush of relief. True, Rosie had invited them, although that was a bit of an empty gesture, since she knew they'd be on their way back to their respective coasts. Which was more than fine by Rosie. She didn't even feel jealous that they got to go home; she just felt happy she didn't have to see their faces. Every time she passed them in the kitchen or spotted them in the cafeteria, she could hear their laughter and felt a pit in her stomach. She couldn't even look directly at them without feeling an uncomfortable prickle in the back of her throat.

Hampus looked up from the pot he was stirring on the stovetop to wave at them. No Henry. Rosie fought to keep the disappointment off her face. He'd definitely been avoiding her. And when they ended up in the same place by necessity, he was unmistakably cold. Did Henry just hate her now? Obviously that would have been bad no matter what, but the worst part of it all was that Rosie didn't even know *why* he hated her. What had she done wrong?

From the back of the room, Bodie caught her eye and waved. Was that what Henry was mad about? Bodie? Because he'd danced with her, and then he'd helped her out with Thanksgiving? If so, Henry was being ridiculous. Rosie literally would have been unable to do Thanksgiving without Bodie. Which she would have been happy to explain to Henry, if only he'd *talk to her.*

"No Henry? No Mumi?" Priya asked as they stopped at Henry and Hampus's table.

"I do not know where Henry is. Mumi is out 'doing Paris.'" Hampus air-quoted.

"As Mumi does," Priya said.

They'd definitely been seeing less of Marquis and Yumi since they turned into Mumi. Of course, they never missed a meal, and they'd still hang out on the weekends in the city or in the common room after class, but Yumi hadn't been spending as much time in Priya and Rosie's room as she used to. Rosie missed her but didn't begrudge Yumi the time she spent with Marquis. She was falling in love in *Paris*, for Pete's sake. Rosie understood why she wanted to spend time with her boyfriend. Alone.

"Carry on, then," Priya said. "Come on, Rosie. Let's get started."

They walked back, and Rosie saw Cecilia making pasta and Anna working on her dumplings, and at almost every station there were students laughing and cooking, and Rosie loved how it felt in there. Even better than when Chef Petit had been teaching. It was kind of amazing how much free rein they'd been given in the kitchen. For all of the strict rules about the dorm floor, the rest of the École was basically unsupervised. Rosie wondered, for a moment, whether people had been disappearing into the nooks and crannies of the École to do things that didn't involve food at all.

"I heard you're making samosa."

Rosie and Priya looked up to see Bodie Tal walking toward their table. He leaned in conspiratorially and peeked into Priya's shopping bag, arching an eyebrow, like there was something in there that was far more scintillating than maida flour.

"Oooo," Priya said. "Ahh. Err. Yes."

Rosie shot her a look. But she also didn't totally blame Priya. Rosie didn't understand how Bodie made jeans and a white T-shirt look so good. It was the blandest outfit on planet Earth. Of course, Priya would probably say it had nothing to do with the outfit, but more with what was underneath. . . .

"Shouldn't you be on a plane to LA right now?" Rosie asked hurriedly, like Bodie could tell what she was thinking.

"Tonight. This is just such an awesome idea, I wanted to be part of it any way I could."

"You *are* part of it, Bodie. You're the biggest part of it. It wouldn't have happened without you."

"No way. This is all you, Rosie," he insisted. "I'm just here to help with prep."

"Should we start making samosa, then?" Priya blurted out of nowhere.

Luckily, Priya calmed down a bit as she started telling them what to do. Bodie got everything out of the bag as Priya directed Rosie around the kitchen to grab mixing bowls and staple ingredients. Before long, they'd assembled their own small mountain of ingredients.

"Will you two make the dough for me?" Priya asked Rosie and Bodie. "I'm cursed with pastry—yours will be lighter by miles. I'll tell you what to put in."

"Sure," Bodie said at the same time Rosie said, "If you're sure," not wanting to step on Priya's toes. It was *her* dish, after all.

"'Course I'm sure."

And so Rosie dumped maida flour into the bowl while Bodie measured the carom seeds and salt, and added those in, too. He stirred, then Rosie rubbed the ghee into the dry ingredients.

"What's funny?" Bodie asked.

"Huh?"

"You're smiling. What's funny?"

"Here. Rub some of this together." Bodie put his hands into the bowl, too, and Rosie hadn't counted on how close they'd be, how their knuckles would accidentally graze each other. "Does this remind you of anything?"

"Biscuits," he said, a smile on his lips.

"Exactly what I was thinking!" Rosie exclaimed. "It's just like making biscuit dough. That's what's sort of funny about it."

"How two things that seem so different have so much in common?"

"Exactly."

"Yes, yes, baking is a universal language," Priya said. Rosie had almost forgotten she was there. "Will the two of you stop fingering my bloody dough and finish up with it?"

Well, Priya certainly didn't seem starstruck by Bodie Tal

anymore. Embarrassed, Rosie looked away as Bodie pulled his hands out of the bowl casually, like he wasn't in the least bit concerned that Priya had just called them out. Whistling, he poured water into the bowl, and Rosie kneaded the dough until it came together into a beautifully smooth ball. Then they covered the bowl with a towel and set it aside to rest.

As Priya continued toasting and grinding spices, she sent Bodie off to run around the kitchen and get everything else they needed for the filling. Rosie leaned against the counter, resting her elbows there for a minute and looking around the kitchen. She couldn't help but smile as she watched everyone working side by side. She'd made this happen. And Bodie . . . he'd made it happen, too. How cool of him to come and help out, even when he wouldn't be there for the actual Thanksgiving dinner. From across the kitchen, Bodie held up three potatoes and attempted to juggle them. Badly. Rosie laughed as a potato narrowly missed dropping into whatever was simmering on Seydou's back burner.

This was *exactly* the point of Thanksgiving. Everyone laughing and having fun and sharing their food.

And Rosie hoped that tomorrow, Henry would be part of it, too.

CHAPTER TWENTY-FIVE

Henry

The gravy was warming up on the stove, the potatoes had been boiled, and Hampus was rolling meatballs by hand. It was Thanksgiving at the École, and the kitchen was a riot of tantalizing smells, all disparate but somehow delicious as they came together. Right now, the lamb tagine Seydou was working on smelled particularly irresistible. But even with all this delicious food, Henry swore he could smell the faint vanilla scent of Rosie's skin everywhere he went. He heard laughter and knew it was her from all the way across the room. Every time he turned around, his eyes couldn't help but follow her as she moved through the kitchen, talking and tasting.

He had to get her alone today. No more sulking, no more storming out, no more avoiding conversations because he was too afraid of what she might say. Maybe she liked Bodie. Maybe she didn't. But Henry had to find out one way or the other, once and for all. At least Bodie wasn't here right now to screw things up for him.

He knew Bodie had been in the kitchen all day yesterday. Henry had hidden at a coffee shop and worked on his history paper instead of doing Thanksgiving prep with everyone, and that sucked. But he hadn't had much choice. After consistently bombing his way through every pop quiz on the nineteenth century, he needed a flawless paper to bring his grade back up into the A range. As they got closer and closer to finals, Henry was starting to seriously worry that he might not be able to pull this off. All of his grades were hovering in the danger zone. If he had to leave the École because of some stupid multiple-choice questions . . . It was too painful to even think about. So he wouldn't think about it. Today was about food and about finally hashing things out with Rosie. The minute Henry got the butter into these potatoes, he was going to talk to her.

Before he lost his nerve.

"Bodie!" Henry heard Rosie cry.

No way, Henry thought. You've got to be kidding me.

But there Bodie was, standing on the stairs, an expensive-looking leather duffel bag slung over his shoulder. It looked like it had been distressed on purpose and like it probably cost more than all of Henry's clothes put together. Fantastic, Henry thought. Just fantastic.

"I thought you were going to LA!" Rosie said.

Yeah. That's what Henry had thought, too.

"I was going to go to LA," Bodie replied. "But this felt more like home, you know?"

"I know," Rosie said.

Barf. Henry was going to barf right into the mashed

potatoes and ruin the dish he and Hampus had spent all week conceptualizing.

"It'll definitely beat sitting around the soundstage, waiting for Dad to have five seconds free."

Right. Because Bodie *could* have spent Thanksgiving with his dad and Alton friggin' Brown, filming a Food Network special. But instead, he was here. Henry shot potatoes through the ricer with such force that they sprayed Hampus.

"This is why I prefer the food mill to the ricer." Hampus sighed, brushing potato bits off his apron.

"A food mill works the starch too much," Henry muttered.

"I've gotta admit, this is a lot cooler than I expected," Yumi called to Rosie and Bodie from over at her station, where she was busy turning chicken skewers with tongs. "You guys did it. This is legit."

"I think they make a very good team," Anna said as she passed by Rosie and Bodie with a bunch of fresh parsley. Bodie put his arm around Rosie and squeezed.

"They are cute together, no?" Cecilia murmured sotto voce as she paused near Henry on her way to the walk-in. "Perhaps love is in the air."

"It's Thanksgiving, not Valentine's Day!" Henry barked. Cecilia's eyebrows practically disappeared into her hairline. Awesome. Now she'd probably tell everyone he was unhinged. And even worse, Bodie's arm was *still* around Rosie as more and more people came up to them, thanking them, congratulating them, talking about how cool this was. They certainly *looked* like a couple. Argh. Henry was sick of torturing himself. He just needed to talk to her about what was going on. As soon as he could get her alone. He wasn't quite desperate enough to shout *DO YOU LIKE ME?* in front of their whole class.

"We are ready to fry the meatballs!" Hampus announced, and sure enough, he'd assembled a veritable army of tiny meatballs. Henry dragged his gaze away from Rosie and Bodie. He put the oil on for the meatballs and started browning the butter for his mashed potatoes in a separate pan, losing himself in the foaming butter. At least here he could cook whatever he wanted and not have to worry that Chef Martinet was about to tell him his seared hanger steak was "executed with perfection and no imagination," like she had on his last Dish of the Day. God. Would he *ever* get it right?

"Happy Thanksgiving." Rosie was standing next to him. He hadn't even heard her walk up. "I got you something."

She placed a small glass bottle of Coke on his station.

"It's not Sunday," he said, a smile tugging at his lips.

"I know. But I'm thankful for every Sunday I've spent with you."

She was gone before Henry could even thank her for the Coke, hurrying back to her station. He knocked the bottle cap off on the counter's edge and took a swig, and hope fizzed in his chest just like the bubbles in the soda. She was *thankful* for their Sundays?! This Coke was a *sign*. A sign that things between them were far from over. Henry was going to do whatever it took to make Rosie see that they belonged together.

Now he just needed to think of something *awesome* to do for Rosie. Something that showed her exactly how much she meant to him.

By the time Henry finished his Coke, everyone was ready to carry their dishes out of the kitchen. Someone had pushed a bunch of the cafeteria tables together so they formed one long table, and pretty soon, almost every inch of the surface was covered in food.

Priya's samosa. Seydou's tagine. Cecilia's cacio e pepe. Marquis's mac and cheese. Yumi's yakitori. Anna's Leberknödelsuppe. Fernando's fideuà, fat prawns and shiny mussels nestled among the noodles. All *three* of Rosie's pies. Henry didn't even know where to look, let alone what to eat first.

The chatter around the table died down, and Henry could see everyone looking around expectantly, almost like they weren't sure what to do. Or maybe nobody wanted to be the first one to start eating.

"Speech, Rosie!" Hampus said. "Yes! Speech."

Rosie shushed him, shaking her head, but by that point, Yumi was chanting, "Speech! Speech! Speech!" and pounding her fists on the table. And soon, she wasn't the only one. So Rosie stood from her spot at the head of the table.

"Um . . . Hi, everyone," she said. "Thank you for being part of the École's very first Thanksgiving." A couple people clapped. "Especially a big thank-you to those of you who are celebrating *your* first Thanksgiving."

"Like the pilgrims!" Hampus said, then whispered, so only Henry could hear him, "I have googled Thanksgiving."

"Yes. Like the pilgrims. Except, for me, Thanksgiving was never about pilgrims. For me, it's always been about the food." That got a loud round of applause. Henry grinned at Marquis clapping with his hands above his head, and Yumi, next to him, whistling her approval as she filmed Rosie with her phone. "My favorite part of Thanksgiving is spending all day in the kitchen. And then sitting down with my mom and my brothers and my nana, all of us sharing our favorite dishes, the dishes we make every year."

Henry realized, for the first time, that Rosie had never mentioned her dad. Ever.

"And when I realized I'd miss Thanksgiving, of course I knew I'd miss my family, but almost more than that, I'd miss cooking, sharing the food I love, and sharing the food other people love. And I'm so glad that today, I get to share my food with you, and you get to share yours with me."

"Did you write this ahead of time?" Yumi asked from her seat down by Rosie's elbow, watching Rosie through her phone screen. "This is pretty good."

"I didn't— Yumi! Put your phone away!" Rosie scolded her.

"I'm making a memory!"

"No phones at the dinner table!"

"Sorry, *Mom*." Yumi rolled her eyes. But she put her phone away.

"Anyway." Rosie cleared her throat. "I promise I'm not going to make everyone go around the table and say what they're thankful for, like my mom does." At this, most of the Americans laughed. "But right now, I'm really thankful for this meal. And for all of you. And all that you've shared with me, and with each other. So, um, happy Thanksgiving?"

"And here's to Rosie." Bodie stood, and Henry realized then that Bodie and Rosie were sitting at opposite ends of the table, like they were everyone's mom and dad.

"Oh, no, it's okay . . ." Rosie protested, coloring, as Bodie toasted her with his glass.

"Rosie, none of this would have happened without you," Bodie continued. "It's incredible. Thank you for thinking of this, for inviting us all to share it with you, for making it happen."

"Well, really, *you* made it happen."

"I didn't do anything."

"You did."

Henry was dying. He was literally dying, watching them ping-pong back and forth, and by the time they stopped complimenting each other, there would be only a skeleton wearing a green sweater sitting in his chair.

"Hurry it up!" Yumi bellowed, and Henry had never appreciated her more. "I'm starving!"

"Right." Rosie laughed awkwardly. "Let's eat, then," she said as she took her seat. "Meatballs, please."

She crooked her finger at Hampus, and he passed the plate over to her. Rosie started telling them about her nana's crockpot meatballs, and that no offense to her nana, but they did *not* compare to these. And then she was so complimentary about the mashed potatoes, both Priya and Yumi started eating them off her plate, and then Marquis leaned over Yumi to try to get some, and then Yumi stabbed him in the hand with her fork, and Henry was laughing, and eating, and before he knew it, he could almost forget Bodie Tal was even there. Almost.

Coming out of the fog of his food coma, Henry realized he'd forgotten something. He couldn't believe he'd forgotten it, but in his defense, he had made it a while ago. Suddenly, he pushed back his chair and darted out of the room, back to the kitchens.

Down the stairs and into the walk-in, Henry pushed aside some produce until he found what he'd made back when Rosie had first mentioned wanting to try it, all the way back on their first night out in Paris. He grabbed the Tupperware and peeled off the plastic lid. The familiar sour smell hit him right away, and there were still bubbles of fermentation on the surface. This was a little fresher than he usually liked his kimchi, but it would still be good. Hopefully.

"Henry?" Rosie stood in the front of the walk-in, half a samosa in her hand. "Are you okay?"

"I'm fine. I just forgot something I'd made. For you."

"For me?"

"Yeah. Because . . . because I'm thankful for you."

If she could be brave and say it, so could he. The smile that lit up her face was better than any amount of mashed potatoes.

"It's—kimchi, right?" she said hesitantly, like she was afraid of saying it wrong, as she peered into the Tupperware.

"Right. Kimchi. It's like a fermented . . . cabbage . . . thing. . . ."

Definitely not the best description, but kimchi was so much its own thing, he was struggling to describe it. Henry wondered what she'd think of it. Kimchi could be a bit of an acquired taste if you hadn't grown up eating it.

"Let's get a fork," she said, then, "Good gravy, my hands are already full of food. Want a half-eaten samosa?"

"Absolutely," he said, and finished it in a couple bites as they left the walk-in, grabbed forks, and met back up at the counter, where Henry put the kimchi down. From upstairs, they heard a loud laugh. Rosie looked up toward the noise, and then back down at him.

"Thanksgiving is definitely a success," he said.

"I think so, too." She smiled. "So do I just, like, tear off a bit of cabbage, or . . ."

"Here—I'll get you a good bite." He speared some cabbage, a bit of daikon, and some carrot onto his fork. Awkwardly, they exchanged forks, and Rosie popped the bite into her mouth. Her eyes opened wide, then she wrinkled her nose, then frowned, then chewed. Then she went back in for another bite. "Do you—do you like it?" he asked.

"I *do*," she said. "It's so . . . different than anything I've had before."

"Yeah. The flavor profile—the fermentation—not common American tastes."

"Mmm." She was still eating it, ferreting out bits of daikon. "Spicy. I like it."

Henry had thought it was pretty mild, and was grateful he hadn't added any more *gochugaru*. He was mostly grateful he'd been able to find gochugaru at all. He'd found it at a grocery store in the 13th arrondissement, in a neighborhood called Petite Asie. It was mostly Vietnamese and Chinese, but he'd found some Korean stuff.

"This is good, Henry," Rosie said. "*Really* good."

Henry smiled, but this was just one small step. Rosie deserved even better than *really good*.

And that was exactly what he was going to give her.

CHAPTER TWENTY-SIX
Rosie

Getting back to real life after Thanksgiving was hard. It reminded Rosie of when she'd been little and had looked around her living room on Christmas after all the presents had been opened. There were new toys, yes, but tomorrow it would just be winter, not Christmas anymore. She had that crumpled-wrapping-paper kind of sadness.

At least things with Henry were better. Something had shifted on Thanksgiving. True, he hadn't declared his undying love or tried to kiss her or anything, but at least things between them were easy again, like they had been before the whole Bodie debacle. He still seemed tired all the time, and occasionally grumpy, but at least he no longer seemed grumpy with *her,* specifically. Rosie wished she'd given him a pop earlier, if a bottle of Coke was all it took to fix whatever had gone wrong.

Rosie poked her shrimp with a fork. Fish and shellfish week had not been a great success. Rosie hadn't managed to fillet a single denizen of the deep correctly, and she'd nearly amputated her hand when she tried to shuck an oyster. And it had all been overcooked. And these shrimp, from the look of it, were going to be no exception. And they certainly weren't going to win her Dish of the Day. Rosie couldn't even win Dish of the Day on pastry week. As much as she tried to pretend it didn't bother her, she was still embarrassed about that. Tripped up by a cheesecake. Mortifying.

So Rosie wasn't surprised when Chef Martinet said her shrimp were overcooked and underseasoned. And she wasn't surprised when Yumi won Dish of the Day for her play on a Nicoise salad in a beautiful bite-size portion. But Rosie *was* surprised when, at the end of class, Chef Martinet stopped her on her way out of the kitchen.

"Rosie, a word, please."

Chef Martinet had never called Rosie by her first name before. Ever. And even though *Rosie* sounded beautiful in her accent, Rosie couldn't help but feel that this portended something ominous. Priya agreed, clearly, if the sympathetic look she shot Rosie was any indication.

"Come right up when she's done with you," Priya whispered as they made their way up to the front of the kitchen. "Make sure you're in our room as quickly as possible. Promise?"

"Promise," Rosie whispered back. "But why—"

"Never you mind." Priya smiled. "Just be there."

Rosie would have given anything to be filing out of the kitchen with her classmates, on her way upstairs to shuck her whites, shower the shrimp smell out of her hair, and find out what Priya was being so mysterious about. But instead, Rosie stopped in front of Chef Martinet, and said, "Yes, Chef?"

"We are near to the end of the semester, as you know."

Rosie nodded.

"And I am sure it will not surprise you to hear that I have seen no real improvement."

No real improvement. It *didn't* surprise Rosie, but that didn't make it any easier to hear. Rosie reached down to her pocket, wanting to hold on to her plastic pilot's wings for luck, but as she patted around in vain, she realized they weren't in there. And now that she thought about it, she couldn't remember the last time she'd put them in her pocket before heading to class. She could picture them, on her desk, waiting for her. But she hadn't reached for them in so long.

"Chef Petit speaks very highly of you, but I did not, for myself, see anything spectacular with your pastry."

"No, Chef," Rosie said, almost in a whisper. Because there had been nothing spectacular about that cheesecake.

"It is not— As you know, one is not required to stay the entire academic year at the École."

No. *No.* This couldn't be happening. This was so, so much worse than anything Rosie imagined Chef Martinet might possibly say. Rosie knew, of course, that being asked to leave was a possibility, but hearing Chef Martinet actually say it out loud was so much worse than Rosie had ever imagined.

"In fact, many students do not return for the spring semester. It is quite common. From what I have seen, I believe you should not return after the holidays," Chef Martinet said. "Perhaps it would be best."

Her voice, as she said that, was almost *kind.* And that was maybe the worst part of all of it. Because anytime Rosie had allowed herself to worry about being asked to leave, or listened to Priya's fears about getting "chucked out," Rosie had imagined Chef Martinet kicking her out with a stern voice and a sour face. Not asking her to leave *nicely*. Like it was for her own good.

There was so much Rosie wanted to say. That she wanted to be here. That she belonged here, even if Chef Martinet didn't think so. That she would prove it, somehow. But it all stuck in her throat, and Rosie couldn't even get a word out.

"Think on it, yes?" Chef Martinet said, and then patted her on the shoulder. It was a bit mechanical, like maybe Chef Martinet was an alien who had learned how to comfort people by reading a book about human social responses, but it was a pat of comfort nonetheless. And it was downright terrifying.

Chef Martinet walked out of the back of the room—not up the stairs into the cafeteria, the way they always went, Rosie didn't even *know* where that back door went—and Rosie felt all the air rush out of her in a single *whoosh*, like when Ricky had kicked a soccer ball into her stomach accidentally when they were little. Rosie clutched the cool stainless steel counter for support.

How was this possible? Rosie knew she was struggling. It wasn't a secret. But she hadn't thought she was struggling *that* badly, badly enough that Chef Martinet thought she should leave. She couldn't leave! The last thing she could do was head back to East Liberty halfway through the year with her tail between her legs. The thought of Priya spending the rest of the year staring at an empty bed turned Rosie's stomach. Or even worse, that bed filled with some other girl, some other girl who'd take Rosie's place. Some other girl who would sit next to Henry at lunch. She couldn't do it. She just couldn't.

The final meal! Rosie gripped the counter harder, a shot of adrenaline coursing through her veins. *Of course.* The final meal. It was her last shot—literally—to prove herself. And if she could impress Chef Martinet, and even more importantly, Chef Laurent, they'd have to let her stay. They'd have to. All she needed to do was cook a final meal that was so perfect it guaranteed her a spot in the spring semester.

Easier said than done. But at least it was something. A chance. A lifeline.

When Rosie entered the stairwell to leave the kitchen, she almost jumped as she realized she wasn't alone.

"Hey." Bodie reached out and touched her arm. "Are you okay?"

"Were you—were you eavesdropping?!" What was he *doing* there, in the hallway, listening to her private conversation? Rosie was furious. *Furious.* She couldn't remember ever being so mad. She wasn't even sure *who* she was mad at, she just knew that she was *mad.*

"I wanted to make sure you were okay."

"You could have done that without listening in on a *private conversation!*" She felt like a cartoon, red-faced, arms wheeling, steam shooting out of her ears. She wished she could explode Bodie Tal with a stick of dynamite, like he was Wile E. Coyote, and shoot him far, far away from her. Where was good Rosie, quiet Rosie, responsible Rosie now? That Rosie felt a million miles away.

"I didn't think you'd tell me what she said."

"You're right. I wouldn't have. Because I didn't want anyone to know. Especially not you!" She smacked him in the chest with both hands, then stepped back, horrified at herself. "Sorry—I'm sorry."

"It's okay—"

"I don't—I don't hit people—it's not a thing I *do*—"

"It's okay, you're right, I shouldn't have listened in—"

"You shouldn't have. But I shouldn't have hit you. Gosh." Rosie laughed shakily. "I'm sorry. That was uncalled for. Even if your mother should have told you that it's not polite to eavesdrop."

"Trust me. That gem was not on Mom's list of unconventional advice. She's got some great tips on how to prevent sun damage, though," he said wryly. "Come on. Let's get out of here."

"Where are we going?"

"Someplace where things make sense."

"Someplace else? Without showering? I smell like shrimp," Rosie said.

"That makes two of us. But I'm betting you'd rather not head upstairs to change and face any questions from your posse."

"I don't have a posse."

"Are you kidding? You have *the* posse," Bodie said. "You, Priya, Yumi, Marquis, Hampus, Henry. It's more than a posse. It's a clique. The height of exclusivity at the École. Nobody else could ever sit at that lunch table. I'm surprised you guys don't wear pink on Wednesdays."

"You like *Mean Girls*?" Rosie asked, trying to process what he'd said. What, had Bodie Tal *wanted* to sit with them? He'd always seemed perfectly happy at his table full of beautiful people. It's not like he'd ever complained about sitting with Clara before.

Clara. What would *she* think, if she knew what Chef Martinet had said? Well, obviously, she'd think that Rosie had it coming. She probably wouldn't believe it had taken Rosie so long to get kicked out. Rosie could hear her and Elodie laughing about it already.

"*Mean Girls* is a great movie," Bodie said. "Come on."

Rosie figured out where they were going before they got there, but that didn't make her any less happy to see Chef Petit's boulangerie. Away from Chef Martinet, away from the École, away from her *failure*. Away from all of it. She could feel the tension in her chest easing as they pushed open the door, bell jingling. She breathed in the intoxicating aroma of butter and sugar, and thought, for the first time, that things might really be okay.

"Bonjour, étudiants!" Chef Petit called from behind the counter. "Ah, Bodie, is it time already?"

"Like you would not believe," Bodie said. "Cool if we head back?"

"Of course, of course." Chef Petit waved them on as Bodie stepped behind the counter as confidently as if he'd been working there every weekend since school started. "Call for me if you need anything!"

"Thanks, man," Bodie said as he disappeared into the kitchen. Within, there were tall stacked rolling racks filled with baguettes and boules and croissants. There was an industrial stand mixer so big it was almost up to Rosie's shoulder, several enormous ovens, and all the counter space was crowded almost to the point of clutter. It smelled even better back here than it did in the front.

"When I have a crap day," Bodie said, "there are two things I do."

"Enlighten me."

"One: bake something. Something *easy*." He opened the freezer, rummaged around in it, and pulled out a rectangular Tupperware. "Two: eat ice cream. Preferably with hot fudge."

"Is that ice cream? Did you make that?" she asked, trying to see into the Tupperware, but all she could see was opaque white. Probably vanilla.

"Yeah. I made it at the École, then brought it over here— they have an ice cream maker and Chef Petit doesn't." He popped off the lid, and Rosie peered in. Definitely vanilla. "I'm just happier in the kitchen here than at the École. All those *rules*. Chef Martinet criticizing everything. Telling me I cook like I don't care about it. News flash: I don't care about cooking. I care about *baking*. Sometimes I feel like I can't breathe there, you know?"

"Believe me, I know." Rosie hated the way her voice sounded. All whiny and desperate and *sad*. "So what are we making?" she asked briskly. "Ice cream, hot fudge, baking . . . a brownie sundae?"

"Brownie sundae? Please. This is *France*. We're not in Bald Eagle, Ohio, anymore."

"East Liberty," Rosie corrected automatically.

"I knew it was something patriotic." He shrugged. "We're making profiteroles."

Profiteroles. Little cream puffs filled with vanilla ice cream and drowned in thick chocolate sauce.

"Ha! I knew it!" he said triumphantly. "You already look

ten times better. There is *nothing* as satisfying as making choux pastry."

It was exactly what she'd been thinking. Choux pastry was literally one of her favorite things to make in the whole world. But she didn't tell him that. Instead, she grabbed an apron from a hook on the wall and tied it on.

Together, they melted the butter with water in a saucepan, then added the flour, stirring with a wooden spoon until it pulled away from the sides and formed a ball—that was Rosie's favorite part, the way it came together like that. There was something so *satisfying* about it. Then they scooped the choux into bags and piped them into little circles on a baking sheet, competing to see who could do it better—Bodie was faster, but Rosie was neater. As the pastry baked, they made the chocolate sauce on the stovetop, and by the time they'd assembled a huge plate of profiteroles, Rosie hadn't thought about Chef Martinet for quite some time. Until, of course, she took a bite, and it was *good*—really good—and she wished Chef Martinet could taste this dish. Rosie sighed and put her spoon down.

"What's wrong?" Bodie asked. "I know it's not the prof-iteroles, because they're perfect. What are you thinking about? Imagining what Chef Martinet would say?"

"Don't do that."

"What?"

"Read my mind," Rosie said. "I don't like it."

He chuckled, but then he looked at her, *really* looked, and Rosie had to look away. He cleared his throat, then said, "You know you're not going anywhere, right?"

"I'm not—I *won't*." She wasn't. She *couldn't*. "I'm going to cook the most incredible meal that . . . that . . . *trout* has ever eaten." Rosie struggled to think of something to call Chef Martinet, but *trout* felt right. "I'll show her I belong here. I will."

"Of course you will. And your dishes will be amazing, I'm sure. But even if they're, um, not . . . you'll be okay. You can stay here."

"Okay?" Clearly, Rosie wasn't getting what he was trying to say.

"Chef Martinet's not in charge." Bodie set his jaw, like someone was challenging him. "She doesn't make the final decisions. About anything. Denis does."

A chill passed through Rosie's whole body. An ice-cold chill of dread that no amount of profiteroles could fix.

"Bodie." Rosie needed to be as serious as she possibly could. She needed him to understand. "Do not talk to Chef Laurent about me. *Do not.*"

"I already *have*—"

"No!" Her voice sounded anguished, even to her. "Don't. Please. I don't want your charity! Your *pity,*" she spat.

"Not like that! Not like that," he said hurriedly. "Not about this. Not about Chef Martinet. Just about . . . you."

"Explain. Now. What did you tell him about me?"

"How much you love baking, too. How great it felt not to be the only one."

"Oh." That was fine, then. Rosie relaxed a little.

"The only thing I didn't tell him was how beautiful you are."

And just like that, Rosie was decidedly un-relaxed. She blinked at Bodie, half expecting he'd be a fish or something when she opened her eyes again, because this had to be a dream. But no matter how much she blinked at Bodie Tal, he was still a hot guy in chef's whites, and not a fish. A hot guy who was staring at her like she was, in fact, beautiful.

This was insane. Rosie had never even had a real boyfriend, and now Bodie Tal, professional hot guy, former boyfriend of many professional hot girls, thought she was *beautiful*? Had every guy in East Liberty just been missing something for the past sixteen years? He was crazy. *This* was crazy. This was not the kind of thing that happened to her.

Rosie realized, suddenly, that he was standing close. Very close. She hadn't noticed him stepping nearer, but he was near now, very near, his chest almost pressed against hers, his face close enough that she could see the freckles dancing across his nose, the freckles she hadn't noticed until Halloween.

"Rosie, can I—can I kiss you?" he asked. He brought his hand up, and it hovered near her ear, like he'd maybe been about to tuck her hair behind her ear, or cup her head in his hands, but then stopped himself, as if he'd thought better of it.

She could have kissed Bodie, and maybe it would have meant nothing, or maybe it would have meant something, but she knew, with an ache that thrummed through her, both painful and powerful, that it wasn't Bodie she wanted to kiss.

"Bodie, I—"

"That would be a no, then." His hand dropped.

"You don't really know me, Bodie," she said gently.

"I'd like to," he said, and for the first time, she saw the cracks in his confident facade. Rosie wanted to reach out and touch his arm, but she wasn't sure how he'd receive it, if he would read it as more than she meant it.

"I'd like to know you, too. Just. Um . . . You know. As friends."

Rosie winced at the awkward string of words that had tumbled out of her mouth. She was not prepared for this. Letting down hot famous guys was not a skill she had previously needed.

"Sure," Bodie said, half-heartedly. "Friends."

Rosie didn't really know what to say after that. But what she *did* know was exactly who she wanted to kiss.

And she wasn't going to wait anymore.

CHAPTER TWENTY-SEVEN

Henry

D ad, you are a literal lifesaver," Henry said into the computer screen propped up on his bed. "For this, I'll do all the math you and Mom want."

"Do you have any math for me to do?" Marquis asked from behind Henry, trying to lean into the frame. "Because I'd *love* to have dinner in the kitchen at Les Oies."

"You are here for ties. Not to third-wheel," Henry said.

"Then pick a tie!" Marquis gestured to the ties lying over his arm. Henry had never thought he'd be grateful Mom had made him pack a suit. But he was even more grateful that Marquis was letting him borrow a tie so Henry didn't have to wear a novelty tie with hot dogs printed on it—the only one he'd packed.

"Not the bow tie," Hampus said from where he sat cross-legged on his bed. "Henry cannot pull off the bow tie."

"And you're gonna do something with your hair, right?" Marquis asked.

"Can I get a little less input, please?" Henry ran his hands through his apparently not-good-enough hair, frustrated. Dad, onscreen, laughed.

"So what's the plan?" Dad asked him for the millionth time.

"Dad. I got it. Les Oies. 42 Rue des Ails. Seven p.m. Don't be late. Ask for Michel. Table for two set up in the kitchen."

"Cue the panty drop," Marquis said.

"Dude! My *dad* is here."

"I went selectively deaf, momentarily," Dad said, straight-faced. "Seriously, Henry. Don't be late. They don't set up the table in the kitchen for just anybody. Michel's doing me a big favor."

"I still can't believe your dad knows the chef de cuisine at Les Oies," Marquis marveled. "That is so cool."

"They were at culinary school together."

"It is the oldest restaurant in Paris, yes?" Hampus asked.

"Yup," Henry and Dad answered, almost simultaneously. Les Oies had been serving dinner since the 1580s, to kings and queens, famous revolutionaries, Napoleon Bonaparte, Victor Hugo, Coco Chanel, and Ernest Hemingway, to name a few. And now, they'd be serving dinner to Henry and Rosie. With their table set up in the kitchen, they'd get to watch each course coming together, and best of all, when it came time for Les Oies's signature dessert—soufflé au chocolat—Henry and Rosie would get to help the pastry chef make it, at the very same restaurant that claimed to have invented the soufflé back in the 1700s. Hopefully, it would be a meal just as spectacular as Rosie.

Or almost as spectacular, anyway.

And finally, Henry would tell her how he felt.

"Where's the victim?" Alice elbowed her way onto the screen.

"Hi, Alice." Henry tried not to sound too exasperated, and failed.

"Where's the girl you tricked into going out with you? I don't see any girls." Alice scowled into the computer. "See, Dad? I told you she didn't exist."

"She exists very much!" Hampus insisted, insulted on Henry's behalf.

"Hmmm." Alice narrowed her eyes. "I'll believe it when I see it on the Insta."

"Not everyone puts their entire lives on Instagram," Henry muttered.

Marquis shot him a look. Henry shrugged—he hadn't meant that as a burn on #Mumi.

"Well, I'll let you go," Dad said. "Have fun. Enjoy every bite. And don't be late!"

"I won't, Dad," Henry said. "I promise."

Alice hung up when Dad was mid-wave good-bye.

"I still do not see what is wrong with the hot dog tie," Hampus said. "Hot dogs are very good."

"There isn't enough time for me to explain what's wrong with the hot dog tie. Here—this one." Marquis held out a dark blue tie covered in a pattern of tiny white stars.

Looking at his reflection in the mirror, Henry tied it on. It looked pretty good with the gray suit. He ran his hands through his hair again, trying to make it do something, but not sure what, exactly, he wanted it to do. He could feel himself starting to sweat through his shirt already. God, he hoped Rosie liked the restaurant. He hoped she liked *him*.

"You're ready, man." Marquis clapped him on the shoulder. "Ready as you'll ever be."

"Do not forget the flowers!" Hampus sprung to his feet and grabbed the bouquet off Henry's desk, crumpling it only slightly as he handed it to Henry. Roses. Cliché, maybe, and kind of a stupid joke about her name, but Henry didn't know crap about flowers. These ones were pretty, though, a mix of reds and pinks.

Henry walked to the door, Hampus and Marquis right behind him.

"Don't come with me, guys," Henry warned them as they followed him down the hall. "You're making it weird."

But they came with him anyway. And they were making it weird. But as they got closer and closer to the staircase that delineated the boys' hall from the girls' hall, Henry was so nervous that he probably wouldn't have noticed if he'd been accompanied by a marching band and a full police escort.

This was it. Henry felt like his heart had leaped up his esophagus and was lodged in his throat. They turned the corner, but when they got to the end of the hall, only Priya and Yumi were standing there.

No Rosie.

Behind him, Marquis and Hampus stopped talking. Henry hadn't even noticed they'd been talking before, but now the lack of voices felt ominous. They crossed the last couple feet to the staircase in silence.

"I don't know where she is, Henry," Priya said, her eyes full of something horribly like pity.

"She's not in the building," Yumi said bluntly. "I looked

everywhere. And I think her phone's dead. She hasn't answered any of my calls. Or responded to my texts."

"I'm sure she'll be here any minute," Priya said. Her voice sounded reassuring, but like she was trying too hard to be reassuring, like a flight attendant on a plane going down. "Any minute now. She promised."

But she wasn't there. And she didn't come. And she didn't answer her phone when Henry called, either.

First, Yumi marched Marquis off to dinner. And then Hampus promised Henry he'd be right back, but he had to get some food. And then there was just Henry and Priya. Henry sat on the top step, feeling his suit wrinkle with each passing minute.

"Cafeteria closes in five minutes, Henry," Priya said gently, rising to her feet. "Shall we go, then?"

"No thanks." Henry couldn't imagine eating anything.

"D'you want me to fix you a plate?" she asked.

"No thanks."

"Well—that's all right, then."

Priya smiling at Henry only made him feel worse. He looked away as she went back down the stairs, his eyes alighting on the bouquet that had looked so good a couple hours ago. Now, it was all wilted and weird, like it was decomposing in front of his eyes.

The clock in the foyer struck nine. Henry counted each bong as it chimed—one, two, three, four, five, six, seven, eight, nine. They'd definitely missed their reservation. Henry groaned and buried his head in his hands, thinking of all the trouble Dad had gone to, imagining what he'd say when Henry told him they hadn't shown up.

The front door of the École swung open with its typical creak. Henry lifted up his head, and from his perch on the top of the stairs, he could see two figures in chef's whites walk through the door.

And there was Rosie.

With Bodie Tal.

Henry willed them away, off to the cafeteria, into the lounge, back out onto the street, but no, they continued their inexorable progress toward him. Should he hide? Where would he even hide? Lie down flat, pretend he was a stair, and hope they stepped right over him? There would have been a really solid metaphor in that maneuver, but Henry couldn't muster up the will to move, either for a stair-disguise situation, or to flee back to the relative safety of his room, where maybe Hampus would be waiting with *Söderblandning* tea and sympathy.

"Hey, man." Bodie nodded at Henry, then sped past him toward the guys' dorms, as if he didn't want to be on that staircase any more than Henry did.

"You look nice," Rosie said as she met him at the top of the stairs, something sweet and hopeful in her voice that made it hard for Henry to stay mad at her. Was he mad at her? Or maybe he was just mad at himself? Henry didn't know how he felt other than really, really embarrassed. "Are you going somewhere?"

"Not anymore."

Henry stood up. He'd forgotten about the flowers, and the movement as he stood jostled them. The bouquet rolled onto the next step, and then bounced from stair to stair, all the way down, until it finally came to a stop at the bottom of the staircase, where it lay, looking all sad and bedraggled. I get it, universe, Henry thought. You don't need to drive the point home any more.

"Those looked . . . nice," Rosie said. "Um . . . Yes. Also nice."

She was looking up at him, like she was waiting for *him* to explain about the flowers and the suit. But he wanted *her* to explain why she smelled like shrimp and chocolate. And what she'd been doing with Bodie.

Voices trickled out from down at the bottom of the stairs. Henry and Rosie both turned toward the noise. Yumi, Marquis, Hampus, and Priya stopped, stared at the two of them, and then quickly turned around, hustling back into the cafeteria and out of sight.

"Henry. What is happening?" Rosie asked, bewildered. "Why are they avoiding us?"

"They're for you," he blurted out.

"Huh?"

"The flowers. They're for you. Or they were, I guess."

"Oh," she said softly. "Are, um . . . are *we* going somewhere?"

"We had a reservation at Les Oies."

"Les Oies," Rosie repeated. "Les Oies. Are you kidding me?"

"Nope." Henry was having a hard time looking at her. "We were going to sit in the kitchen."

"The *kitchen*? At Les Oies? Oh, Henry." She reached out for his hand. He jammed both of them into his pockets. "Why didn't you *tell* me?"

"It was supposed to be a surprise."

"I wish I'd known. I wouldn't have— I never would have—"

"Gone out with Bodie instead?"

"Not like that," she said sharply. "It wasn't like that."

"Then what *was* it like, Rosie?" he asked, surprised by how angry, how hard his voice sounded. "Because every time I turn around, I see the two of you together. Talking. Laughing. Hugging."

"Are you even listening to yourself right now?" she asked, incredulous. "You're upset that we're *hugging*? I hugged Priya at lunch. Is that a problem, too?"

"That's not the same."

"Me and Bodie? We're *friends*, Henry. That's it."

"You sure about that? Because I don't think that's what he wants."

Rosie opened her mouth, then closed it suddenly, like she was reconsidering what she was going to say. Something flitted across her face, making Henry think that maybe something *had* happened between her and Bodie.

"He *is* my friend," Rosie insisted eventually. "And I'm sorry if you have a problem with that, but he's been there for me when you haven't."

"I haven't *been there for you*?" That stung. That stung so much that Henry found himself taking a couple steps back, like he was absorbing a blow.

"You're always disappearing! And moody! And I can never figure out where I stand with you, what you think about me—"

"I've had a lot going on—"

"Then why don't you tell me what's going on?!" she interrupted. "Talk to me, Henry. Why won't you just talk to me?"

"It's just been—it's just been all this stuff, okay?" Henry felt like he was exploding. Like if he didn't tell her everything immediately, the weight of it would crush his chest. "My mom made me do all this extra work. And she said she'd pull me out of the École if I didn't keep my grades up, which has just been this endless cycle of up and down and up and down, desperately trying to balance out a failed quiz with a perfect paper or whatever. Desperately trying to get everything right so I can stay here—stay with you."

"How was I supposed to know that?" she said, matching his volume. "We kiss *once* and then anytime we almost kiss again, you run away. We *never* talk about it. What was I supposed to think? I thought you were embarrassed by me or something."

She thought *he* was *embarrassed* by her? Henry was so shocked he couldn't even come up with the words to refute it. "You could have told me all of this, you know. I would have understood. I know something about struggling here," she added bitterly. "Chef Martinet asked me to leave the École."

That stopped Henry in his tracks. As did the fact that her eyes were welling up with tears.

"What?" he asked. "That's not— When did she—"

"Right after class. That's why I left so fast."

Crap.

"I'm really sorry I missed dinner," she said. "I would have loved to go to Les Oies with you—I'd love to go anywhere with you—but you don't have to worry about me or Bodie or any of it anymore. Because I probably won't be here for much longer."

She walked down the stairs. Where was she going? Back out of the building? Nope. She stopped at the bottom of the stairs and picked up the roses.

This was a disaster. Henry had to save the night. But how?

She was coming back up the stairs now, faster and faster, taking them two at a time. He had to do *something*.

"I'm sorry, Henry," she whispered as she fled past him, clutching the bouquet. Crying. Her tears hit him in the chest, each one a small stab of pain.

"Rosie, wait," he said. "Please!"

But she had already turned the corner, running down the girls' hall.

Screw the rules. Henry was going after her. He'd apologize. He'd fix it.

"Going somewhere, Yi?"

Madame Besson stood in the doorway of her room between the boys' and girls' halls, filing her nails.

"I was just—uh—"

Henry watched Rosie disappear into her room, the door slam shut behind her.

"Can you tell Rosie I need to talk to her? It's kind of an emergency."

"No. I cannot," Madame Besson replied. "It seems clear to me that she would like some privacy."

"Right. Sure."

Henry considered sprinting past her. Considered vaulting straight past Madame Besson and pounding on Rosie's door, begging her to talk to him, begging her to give him a chance.

But instead, he dropped his gaze away from Madame Besson's stern glare, and walked back to his room.

Alone.

CHAPTER TWENTY-EIGHT
Rosie

There was one thing Rosie didn't love so much about baking: it was very, very hard to fix a mistake.

There were some minor mistakes you could cover up with frosting or whipped cream, but for the most part, you were better off starting over from scratch. Forget an ingredient, add in too little or too much of another, and you were basically screwed. One wrong move, and everything was ruined.

Exactly like last night.

If she had just gone upstairs to change. If she had just *waited* five minutes instead of running off with Bodie, everything would have been different.

Rosie could see it so clearly in her mind's eye. Henry, handsome in his suit. The roses fresh, instead of crumpled and decaying. Rosie in the one nice dress she had brought with her, the dress that had been waiting for her on her bed when she'd fled back to her dorm room, carefully laid out by Priya and Yumi. Henry and Rosie tucked away at their own private table amidst the hustle and bustle of the kitchen at Les Oies. Les Oies! Rosie still couldn't believe it. She groaned and slumped against Priya as they walked, hiding her face from the sting of the wind.

"None of that groan, please," Priya said as she hustled Rosie down the street. "I know exactly what that groan means."

"Can the two of you hurry it up?" Yumi said. "I'm freezing my taste buds off."

Priya was half carrying Rosie as they followed Yumi's retreating back down one road and across another, each step taking them farther and farther away from the École. Rosie had sleepwalked her way through class today, and when Priya and Yumi had insisted on taking her out for dinner, Rosie didn't have the energy to resist.

"Oh, Yumi," Priya said disapprovingly as they crossed the street to see a long line winding its way out of a restaurant with a bright red awning. "You can't honestly expect us to wait in line at Le Relais de l'Entrecôte. It's bloody freezing, and if Rosie leans on me much longer, my shoulder will lose all feeling."

"Sorry," Rosie muttered. She tried to lift her head, but the effort was too much. Priya patted her gently.

"The line is not for us," Yumi scoffed. "A little credit here, please."

Yumi led them past the line, pushed open the doors, and paused in front of the hostess stand. Warm air and the tantalizing aroma of meat hit Rosie all in one comforting blast. She lifted her head and sniffed the air.

"Ah, Yumi!" The hostess bent down to kiss Yumi's cheeks, her dark glossy hair swinging as she did so. "We are three today?"

"Needed some girl time. Usual booth free?"

"For you? Always."

"Absolutely nothing about this is surprising," Priya muttered as they followed the hostess into the restaurant, squeezing through the narrow spaces between tiny tables topped with red tablecloths and bright yellow napkins. "Of course she's a VIP at the most famous steak-frites place in Paris."

Rosie slid into the booth the hostess indicated, Priya right beside her, as Yumi took the seat across from them.

"*Bisous* to Marquis!" the hostess called as she left their table. Yumi threw her a thumbs-up as she went.

"So this is where you've been disappearing off to with Marquis all these months," Priya mused as she looked around the room, squinting at the Vermouth posters on the walls.

"Yup. Where did you think we were going?" Yumi asked.

"I thought you were shagging on the roof."

"Priya!" Yumi looked delightedly scandalized.

"You know about the roof?" Rosie asked. She hadn't been back since that first night with Henry, when they'd joked about potatoes and he'd made her feel better about her terrible omelet.

"Duh." Yumi rolled her eyes. "*Everyone* knows about the roof."

"For shagging," Priya said. "Bit cold for that now, though."

"Yumi!" Their waitress appeared, and repeated the whole delighted-double-cheek-kiss ritual. "Where is Marquis?"

"He's doing some recipe testing at school," Yumi answered. "Can we get the usual?"

"No salad, all the bread, steak *saignant*," the waitress confirmed. "Of course."

"No salad? Have you eaten a single vegetable all semester?" Priya asked as the waitress left. "I'm surprised you haven't contracted scurvy."

"Worry about my vitamin intake later," Yumi said. "This is a *meat* conversation. Little Miss Zombie." Yumi turned to Rosie, her voice gentle. "You wanna tell us what happened?"

And so Rosie told them. She told them everything. As Yumi demolished the never-ending bread basket and Priya listened with her chin in her hands, Rosie talked about meeting Henry on the plane, talking to him on the roof, kissing him by the Seine. The waitress dropped off thinly sliced steaks and mountains of fries drenched in a velvety sauce, and Rosie told them about Henry getting so stressed-out about his grades and Bodie actually liking her and Chef Martinet asking her to leave, and before Rosie knew it, she was scraping the bottom of her empty plate, suddenly starving. Probably because she hadn't eaten all day. For the first time in her life, Rosie had forgotten to eat.

"You could have told us some of this earlier," Priya chided her gently.

"I know." Rosie watched the waitress return and fill everyone's plates back up with more steak and more fries. This place was magic. "I was embarrassed. I kissed Henry, and then things got weird, and I thought he didn't like me—"

"I'm gonna stop you right there." Yumi used her steak knife

to point at Rosie. "Let's deal with the big issue first. Food is more important than love."

"Food *is* love," Priya interjected. "And I don't mean that in a ghastly, Bridget-Jones-sobbing-into-her-ice-cream way."

"Spare me the culinary metaphors. I'm talking about Chef Martinet." Yumi cut an impressive bite of steak and popped it into her mouth. "You're not going home, Rosie. None of us are. And I am personally going to guarantee that your final meal is a superlative symphony of dining that blows that oni away."

"How?" Rosie asked.

"I'm gonna taste it for you. Like you're gonna taste mine. Marquis is down in the École kitchen right now tea-smoking ducks until he's got them *perfected*. And that's what we're all gonna do with our final meals until we get them right. Practice. Taste them. Help each other. Because we're *friends*, and that's what friends do. So I don't want to hear any *I can't break down a chicken* or *I can't bake* from either of you."

"This isn't about *me!*" Priya protested.

"Figured you were here so I might as well mention it." Yumi polished off her steak, and the waitress returned with more. "You're only supposed to get two rounds of steak-frites, but in case you didn't notice, I'm kind of a big deal here. Okay. Moving on to the other thing."

"Henry," Priya said. Even hearing his *name* made Rosie feel all shaky and unsettled. She swiped a couple fries through her sauce and stuffed them into her mouth. "He's mad for you, Rosie. Don't you think you should just talk to him?"

"I *should* talk to him," Rosie admitted. "Of course I should.

And I've tried to talk to him before. But the way he talked to me last night . . . the way he *looked* at me . . . if he *did* like me, I don't think he does anymore."

"Yeah, how dare you commit the unspeakable crime of leaving the building," Yumi said sarcastically. "You didn't do anything wrong, you know."

"Of course you didn't," Priya agreed. "But I *do* think it's rather up to *you* to do something about it now."

"I know." Rosie couldn't stop eating the fries. Gosh, they were good. So crispy and golden-brown and perfectly potatoey. Henry would love them.

"So what do you wanna do about it, Radeke? Ball's in your court. Ugh." Yumi blanched. "I can't believe I just used a sports metaphor. Gross. Maybe I *have* been spending too much time with Marquis."

"I'm going to talk to him," Rosie said firmly. "That's what we needed to do this whole semester. *Talk*. I can't believe he didn't tell me he was struggling so much with his classes. If he'd just *told* me, everything would have been different."

"He was probably self-conscious," Priya said.

"I should have known," Rosie said. "I mean, he kept falling asleep. I should have figured it out."

"Again, not your fault," Yumi said. "We could unpack a lot here about how the culture of toxic masculinity doesn't teach boys how to ask for help, but maybe that's a discussion for another dinner."

"I'm going to help him," Rosie said. "Like you guys are gonna help me with my dishes. I'll make sure his grades are good enough to stay."

"We can all help," Priya said.

"I'll check my schedule and let you know," Yumi said, but Rosie knew she'd help.

"And then . . . and then I'll make sure he knows exactly how much I like him."

Rosie watched Priya nodding at her with concern and Yumi waving the waitress over to make sure Rosie got more fries. Part of Rosie wished she could stay here forever, swallowed up in the warmth and the light of the restaurant, safe with her friends. Part of Rosie wished she could turn back the clock, so she could have gone out with Henry instead of running off with Bodie. And another part of Rosie wished she was just back home in Ohio, reading in bed, where maybe not much of anything happened, but at least everything was familiar. Safe.

No. Rosie was done with *safe*. But she wasn't done with fries.

And just like that, with yet another deep-fried, starchy bite, Rosie knew *exactly* what she was going to do for Henry.

CHAPTER TWENTY-NINE

Henry

Rosie was avoiding him. This past week, she'd skipped every meal in the cafeteria, been completely absent from the lounge, and slipped in and out of class like a ghost. He hadn't even had time to say hi to her, let alone to explain himself, to apologize. And as Henry watched her sprint out of the kitchen, it looked like today wasn't going to be any different. Maybe he'd get to talk to her at dinner. She had to eat eventually, right?

But as Henry scanned the cafeteria that evening, he didn't see a single one of his friends. Maybe they were *all* avoiding him now. Henry loaded up his tray with some kind of meaty brown stew that didn't look even remotely appetizing and took a seat as his usual table. Alone.

"Eh-hem."

Henry looked up to see Hampus standing over him, clearing his throat.

"Dude, aren't you gonna sit?" Henry asked. "Where is everybody?"

"You have alternate dining arrangements this evening, my friend."

"What are you talking about?"

"This way, please."

Henry followed as Hampus grabbed his tray and headed back down into the kitchen, dumping the stew as they went.

They were all there. Priya, wiping her hands on an apron. Marquis, with his arm around Yumi. And right in the middle, there was Rosie. She looked exactly like he'd seen her on the very first day they'd met, in her jeans and gray hoodie and V-neck tee, her braid resting on one shoulder. She looked hopeful, and nervous, and that's when Henry noticed what was on the station behind her. The whole thing was covered in dishes. Plates and bowls and platters on every available surface.

"What is all this?" Henry asked, looking from plate to plate. "Are those . . . are those potatoes?"

"Um . . . Yes." Rosie laughed. "Baked potato. Mashed potatoes. French fries. Potato salad. Hash browns. Potatoes au gratin. Twice-baked potatoes. Potato skins. Potato chips. Hasselback potatoes. Rosti potatoes."

"The rosti potatoes, they were my idea," Hampus said proudly.

"We had to reheat most of them, so the texture might be a bit dodgy, but the flavor's bang-on," Priya said.

"Potatoes," Henry said again.

"I thought you'd like it better than chocolate," Rosie said. "Or flowers."

"How did . . . how did you even do all this?" Henry marveled.

"She stayed up all night making this stuff, and then stored it in the walk-in," Yumi said. "Literally all night. So you better be worth it."

"I'm trying to be," Henry said seriously, looking right at Rosie. She smiled, and it lit up her whole face, just like it had back on the plane when she'd seen his magazine.

"Well, you're welcome. Just FYI, so the two of you know, we have lives," Yumi said. "We can't just sit around facilitating your grand gestures all day. You're both officially cut off from grand gestures."

"But if you ever need a small gesture," Marquis said, "like, I dunno, man, maybe some help with your homework? We're here for you."

"Marquis has a lot of opinions about where the commas are supposed to go," Yumi said.

"They're not opinions. They're facts about grammar."

"Thank you," Henry said, before Marquis and Yumi really got into it. "I'll ask for help. I promise."

"Sounds great. But before finals? I'm proofreading your English paper whether you want me to or not," Marquis said.

"And I'm here to listen to your French project," Priya said. "Well, Seydou said he'd help me listen to your French project."

"And I have made flash cards for history!" Hampus added.

"And I know you're probably sick of math packets," Rosie said, "but I *did* make us a review packet for the final."

Henry didn't know someone talking about a math packet could sound so wonderful—or look so beautiful.

"I think that's our cue to leave," Marquis said, gently pulling Yumi toward the stairs.

"What, we don't even get to see her big declaration?" Yumi asked. "After all that?"

"You microwaved a potato. It was hardly a Herculean effort," Priya said as she, Marquis, Yumi, and Hampus disappeared up the stairs.

Now it was just the two of them, alone, in the kitchen. Rosie stepped forward, closing the distance between them.

"Hold out your hand," she said.

He did, and she pressed something small and plastic into his hand. Henry uncurled his palm and looked at it: a set of pilot's wings.

"You kept these?" he asked.

"I kept them." Rosie took a deep breath. "I like you, Henry. I always have. Always. From the minute I saw you on the plane, reading through that magazine. I knew. I couldn't stop looking at your hands, all scarred and beaten up, just like mine. And the hairs on the back of your neck. And your forearms—I didn't know a person could have hot forearms, but you do. Everything about you. I couldn't look away." He shifted, angling his body toward hers, almost unable to believe what he was hearing. Rosie thought he had *hot forearms*?! "So I—I wanted to start over. And give *you* wings. And this time, I want to tell you I like you right away."

"I don't want to start over," Henry said, and he watched a little bit of the light in her eyes dim. Crap. Not what he meant. "I just mean that everything we've done together this semester? I wouldn't start over because I wouldn't want to lose that. I wouldn't trade that for anything. Not even for the tasting menu at Alinea."

"I don't know, Henry. I've heard that's a lot of courses," she teased.

"I mean it. You've been part of everything for me this

semester—no, you've *been* everything for me this semester," he clarified. "I couldn't imagine Paris without you. I wouldn't want to. There's no one else I'd rather eat with."

And maybe that was sort of a weird thing to say. Maybe he should have complimented her hair or told her she was beautiful or commented on her *fine eyes*, like in that movie Priya was always watching on her iPad in the lounge. But Rosie must have known what he meant, because she closed her eyes—which were, actually, very fine—and she leaned toward him. Henry barely had time to close his eyes, too, before they were kissing. Her lips were soft and warm, and she tasted like powdered sugar. Henry could smell the vanilla scent he always thought of as hers, and something else, something warm and buttery. He felt her hands snake around his neck, shivered as the calluses on her fingers brushed his sensitive skin back there. Rosie fit into his arms as perfectly as she had the first time they'd kissed. Henry could have kissed her forever, but he had something he wanted to say first.

Reluctantly, he pulled away.

"I like you, too, Rosie," Henry said, still cradling her face in his hand.

"Well, good." Rosie leaned into his palm. "Otherwise that would have been really awkward."

Henry stroked her cheek with his thumb and felt something wet. Tears? Nope. Butter. He was pretty sure it was melted butter.

"Rosie," he said. "You have butter on your face."

Henry started laughing. And Rosie laughed, too, and they couldn't stop laughing, like Rosie having butter on her face was the funniest thing that had ever happened. They were laughing so hard they were clutching each other, so hard that Henry saw tears spring to Rosie's eyes. This, he knew, was his favorite sound in the whole word. Rosie's laugh. Better than even the sizzle of butter as it hit a hot pan. And as much as he liked kissing her—and he really, *really* liked it—he might have liked laughing with her even more.

"Butter." Rosie hopped up to sit on the station behind them, the one that wasn't covered in potatoes. Henry joined her. "Really elegant, huh?"

"I like that you have butter on your cheek," Henry said. "Just like I like the way you always end up covered in flour. The way it settles on the tip of your nose, on your eyelashes, in your hair." He brushed her hair back, out of her face, smoothing it into her braid. "And I like the way you look when you taste something you love. The way your nose wrinkles when whatever you've bitten into isn't what you were expecting. The way your whole face lit up every single day we were in the kitchen with Chef Petit. The way it lights up every time I've seen you turn on a stand mixer. Or pick up some brioche. Or look at a cake in a magazine." Her face was lit up just like that, right now. Looking at him. "I like everything about you, Rosie Radeke."

"I like everything about you, too, Henry Yi." She reached out for his hands and squeezed. "I like how you always order way too much food and you're impressively committed to finishing it, but you always insist I get the first bite. I like how you'll try anything, even some strange weed Hampus plucked out of a crack in the sidewalk. I like how easily you laugh, like you expect the best from everyone. I like how you make *me* laugh, more than I've laughed in a long time. I like how focused you are in the kitchen, how you execute even the smallest steps with incredible precision. Except with salt. You throw salt into your food like a crazy person. But I like that about you, too." She smiled. "I even like your weird potato obsession."

"What are you talking about? Potatoes are incredible! It's not weird—"

"It's a little weird. But it's okay. I like it." Rosie squeezed his hands again. "Guess we should have *really* talked about all of this a long time ago, huh?"

"We should have. I'm sorry."

"You don't have to apologize—"

"I *do* have to apologize. About last week. I was a jerk," Henry said. "I was upset we missed the reservation, and jealous of Bodie, and stressed about all the stuff with my mom, like I have been all semester. I took it out on you, and I shouldn't have. I'm really, really sorry."

"I'm sorry I missed dinner."

"That was *not* your fault. And we can probably go back, anyway." Maybe. Henry hadn't responded to any of Dad's e-mails blaring *WHAT HAPPENED?!?!* and *WHERE ARE YOU?!?!* He hadn't answered any of Dad's calls either. Henry should probably let Dad know he wasn't dead in a ditch somewhere. And that he was really, really sorry about Les Oies.

"I don't care about Les Oies," Rosie said. "I don't even care about chocolate soufflé. I care about *you*."

And Henry kissed her again. He wanted to lose himself in her, in her vanilla smell, in the softness of her lips. Something metallic fell to the floor and reverberated with a clang so loud, adrenaline shot through Henry like he'd fallen off the precipice of something. As if there wasn't enough adrenaline coursing through his body already.

"Sorry. Oh man. Sorry. That was me. My foot. I kicked over a knife block," Rosie apologized. Her hair mussed, escaping from her braid, her lips pink and swollen. "I don't even know how my foot got up here," she added, confused.

Henry laughed, and Rosie laughed, too. What had they been waiting for all these months?

As their laughter died down, Rosie looked at him, seriously now, like she was considering him. "I want to tell you something." She took a deep breath. "My, um, my dad died a couple years ago."

That was not what he'd expected her to say.

"Rosie," he said, "I'm so—"

"It's okay," she said, cutting him off. "Thank you. But it's— it's okay. It was more than a couple years ago at this point, honestly. But it felt like . . . like something broke inside me, when that happened. And that since then, I haven't been able to get back to being me. That I'd be places, with people, but I was never really *there*, you know? Always just looking at it from the outside. Doing things that I knew should make me happy, that used to make me happy, but I couldn't *feel* happy, not the way I used to. Except when I was in the kitchen. Baking. Where things make sense."

He nodded. He couldn't know how she felt, not really. Henry had never known loss, not on that level, not of that magnitude. He'd barely known loss at all. But he knew, at least, what it meant to be in the kitchen. Where things made sense.

"And I'm not saying this to, like, make you feel bad, or

anything—I don't even know *why* I started talking about it."
She sighed. "I guess—I finally started to feel like myself again
here. The Rosie I was before. The Rosie who hangs out with
her friends and laughs and actually *is* where she is. The Rosie
who is present. The Rosie who can have crushes." Rosie smiled
at him, shyly.

Henry wanted to say the right thing, but wasn't sure what it
would be. He took her hand and ran his fingers over the faded
scars on her thumb.

"Did your dad—did he like to cook?" Henry asked.
Maybe it wasn't the right thing to say. But it was what he'd
thought of.

"No. No, definitely not. But he *loved* to eat." She grinned.
"Didn't matter what I made, even if it was a disaster, an experiment gone wrong, he'd finish it. He was also great at helping
with cleanup, washing dishes, that kind of thing. He was in the
military, and he'd done KP duty, back when he was younger,
when he'd first enlisted. Dad was like a *machine* in the kitchen.
No matter the mess I made, in under ten minutes, you'd never
be able to know someone had been cooking in there."

"It sounds like you guys were a good team."

"Yeah. We were." She closed her eyes, squeezing them, and
Henry hoped he hadn't said the wrong thing. "He actually—he
only ever cooked one thing."

"What was it?"

"Burgers. On the grill. Every Fourth of July. Practically the
whole block would come over to get one, that's how good
they were. I was thinking . . . about maybe doing a burger.
For my final meal."

"I think you should."

"I know it's not very chef-y, or that the idea of a chef-y burger is overdone, I guess, but I just . . . I just want to cook something that feels like *me*. Like home. Like family. Like . . . love."

"Like potatoes?"

"Potatoes," Rosie repeated.

"Potatoes are nature's most romantic starch." From his perch on the counter, Henry leaned over to the other station and picked up the nearest plate—it had a stack of thick steak fries on it. "Wasn't that the whole point of all this?"

"The whole point of all this is that I like you. And you like potatoes." Rosie grabbed a fry.

"I like you more than potatoes." Henry grabbed one, too.

"Now that would make a great Valentine's Day card."

"I'll keep that in mind," Henry said. Valentine's Day. With Rosie. It was only a couple months away. Maybe Dad *could* get them back into Les Oies. At this moment, Henry felt like anything was possible.

"Can you reach the mashed potatoes?" Rosie asked.

"Think so." Henry reached over and slid the bowl closer. "This really is an overwhelming amount of potatoes. It might be too much even for me to finish them."

"Should we get everybody to help us eat them?" Rosie asked. "Honestly, I'm sure they're right outside. Yumi's probably hiding on the staircase, eavesdropping."

"We'll get them in a minute," Henry said. "They can wait."

Henry pushed aside the mashed potatoes and kissed her again. He'd waited long enough.

★★★★

"Open up."

Henry's lips closed around the spoon Rosie held up to his mouth. Oh God. He'd been wrong about everything. Maybe chocolate *was* better than potatoes. He *mmm*ed involuntarily as his eyes closed.

"Is it good?" she asked anxiously.

"Better than good. It's delicious."

But *delicious* was inadequate. The only way Henry could think of to tell her how good it was, was to lean down and kiss her, slowly. The kiss felt like tempering chocolate, something solid melting to form something new.

"Henry!" Rosie chided him as she pulled away. "Focus. Does it need anything? More salt?"

"Give me more. I'm not sure."

It didn't need more salt. But he needed more chocolate whatever-it-was. Rosie fed him another bite, and Henry *mmm*ed in response.

"Can you please stop being gross?" Yumi complained, interrupting Henry's chocolate reverie.

"I'm not being gross!" Henry protested. "I'm *tasting the food.*"

"I don't think you're gross." Rosie put down the tasting spoon to squeeze his hand. "You're very decidedly un-gross," she whispered as she rose up to kiss him again.

"Stop it! The both of you! No more kissing! No more *mmm*ing! It's repulsive and you know it." Yumi looked around the kitchen, where she, Marquis, Hampus, Priya, Rosie, and Henry were clustered around Priya and Rosie's table. "I hope everyone is noticing how hashtag-Mumi over here has *never* tortured you with PDA. Or *mmm*ing sounds. This is why we're the École's best couple."

"The École's best couple is Hampus and that sandwich," Marquis said, pointing to the stool where Hampus sat, busily demolishing his snack.

"I am sorry!" Hampus said between bites. "I was hungry!"

"Must be nice to be relaxed enough to take a snack break," Priya said wryly. "The advantages of already knowing you've been guaranteed a spot here in the spring."

"Everyone is coming back and I will tolerate zero negativity in my kitchen!" Yumi barked. Henry wasn't sure when it had become Yumi's kitchen, but she was running it like a boss. "Priya, if you serve Chef Laurent that same rack of lamb you just served me, he'll be *begging* you to stay!"

Henry watched Priya stand up a bit straighter. The lamb had been cooked perfectly. So had *everything* they'd tried. He was really glad Yumi and Marquis had made them all practice their dishes together. Henry was excited to cook for Chef Laurent, obviously, but there was still that low thrum of anxiety that he hadn't earned his spot here next semester yet. Never mind the fact that all he'd heard all semester long was that he couldn't put himself on the plate, which was exactly what he was supposed to do now. Henry was happy with the dishes he'd come up with, and his friends seemed to like them, but was that enough? Was *he* enough?

And what if he *did* pull it off, but Mom made him leave the École anyway? Henry had no idea how he'd done on his finals. It was entirely possible he'd sink into the B range.

Henry needed more chocolate.

"You guys have to try this dessert Rosie made," Henry said. "It is ridiculous."

"Really? It's good?" Rosie whispered to him as everyone crowded toward the small glass dish, tasting spoons at the ready.

"It's better than good, Rosie." Henry squeezed her hand, and suddenly things didn't seem so bad. "It's perfect."

"Mmmmmm."

Yumi was *mmm*ing loudly, her eyes closed. Henry burst out laughing.

"What?" Yumi said defensively. "Some things are just that good, okay?"

Henry looked down at Rosie smiling up at him.

Some things *were* just that good.

CHAPTER THIRTY
Rosie

He was here.

Chef Laurent was here, physically here, in the building. Rosie wiped her hands on her chef's pants for what felt like the millionth time. She was sweating out of places she didn't even know she could sweat. What would happen when she actually *saw* Chef Laurent? Her body couldn't produce any more sweat than this. Or at least she hoped it couldn't.

Rosie kept an eye on the clock at the front of the classroom as she plated her biscuit. The time limit wasn't insanely tight— they'd even been able to do some prep work yesterday—but she still had to be ready to go when Madame Besson called her name. They were going in alphabetical order, which meant Rosie was near the end. But poor Henry—Yi—was absolutely last. Which would have made Rosie feel *more nervous*, but Henry, working alone at his station at the front of the room, seemed completely relaxed. Hampus—last name Andersson— had gone first, and most of the kitchen had cleared out as they'd worked their way through the alphabet. Priya was gone, and Yumi, and Marquis. Bodie was still working a couple rows behind her, but Rosie wasn't looking at him. She couldn't. She couldn't afford any kind of distraction.

Which was unfair, because this had basically been the most distracting week of her life.

"Parker-Green and Radeke." Madame Besson stuck her head into the kitchen. "Please bring whatever you need to finish plating up to the prep kitchen. You will be next."

Next. Rosie looked from her incomplete appetizer plate to the total chaos of dishes and bowls surrounding her.

"Here." Henry was at her side, already picking up everything she needed. "Let me help," he said. "I've got time."

"Henry," Rosie chided him. "You should be finishing your meal. I can do this—"

"I know you can," he said firmly. "But let me help."

Rosie smiled, grabbed her dessert from out of the fridge, and followed him up the stairs to the kitchen that led out to the cafeteria. Clara was already up there, arranging her plates on a counter along one wall. Rosie and Henry set her stuff up on another counter, away from Clara. Rosie scanned her plates with her eyes—yup, it was all here. Everything she needed. She wiped her hands on her pants. Why couldn't she stop *sweating*?

"I've gotta go downstairs before my sauce reduces too much," Henry said, "but I just want to say good luck. Not that you need it, because you don't." He smiled at her, and she was tempted to grab on to his hand and refuse to let him leave the kitchen. "This meal is fantastic. It's *you*, Rosie."

And he said it like being *Rosie* was the best possible thing something could be.

Henry leaned down and brushed his lips against hers. Rosie answered his kiss with one of her own, and if she hadn't known Henry had to go check on his sauce, she might have just kissed him forever and forgotten about the whole Chef Laurent thing. But she didn't forget the sauce, so she stopped kissing Henry, and he disappeared back down the stairs, and Rosie found that she missed him already.

"That's a new development."

Clara. Rosie had forgotten she was in the kitchen, too. In fact, Rosie was having a hard time remembering the last time she'd even thought about Clara.

"Um . . . Yes. Yes, it is," Rosie said awkwardly. "A new development. It was a long time coming, though."

"Oh. I thought you and Bodie had, like, a thing."

"Nope." Rosie shook her head. "We're just friends."

"Well." Clara fiddled with her earring. "He talks about you a lot. And he's always over at your station. I see him there *all the time.*"

"Like I said. We're friends."

Clara had been jealous of *Rosie and Bodie*? Perfect Clara, with her gorgeous hair and her flawless skin and her effortless ease in the kitchen, had been jealous of *Rosie*? The whole idea of it was so absurd Rosie almost burst out laughing, but it explained a lot. As Clara stood there, still fiddling with her earring, Rosie felt nothing but empathy for her. Rosie certainly understood how hard it was to find the words to tell someone you liked them.

"Parker-Green." Madame Besson appeared in the doorway. "You are next."

Clara drew in a shaky breath before she rolled her shoulders back, picked up her dishes—how she managed to balance all three effortlessly, Rosie didn't know—and glided into the cafeteria, as serene and flawless as she'd always been.

Now Rosie was alone in the prep kitchen. She finished plating her dishes, spooning sauces, and adjusting her food, and in what felt like no time at all, Madame Besson was back in the kitchen.

Clara never came back. She must have gone out the front.

"Radeke!" Madame Besson called from the front of the room. "You are next!"

Rosie went to pick up her dishes, but found, much to her dismay, that her hands were shaking uncontrollably. She tried to pick up her appetizer, but the plate rattled noisily against the stainless steel countertop.

"Please." Madame Besson was now next to Rosie, and stilled her shaking hand by placing one of her own perfectly manicured hands on top of it. "Please. Let me. I will carry your plates. Take only your dessert."

This small gesture of kindness almost undid Rosie, but as Madame Besson whisked her appetizer and entrée out of the room, Rosie didn't have the luxury of coming undone at the moment. She had to follow. And gripping the glasses that contained her dessert like her life depended on it, she did.

The cafeteria was empty except for one table, where Chef Laurent and Chef Martinet sat, across from each other. *Chef Laurent.* There he was, chatting with Chef Martinet— her face was pinched as ever, but his! The corners of his eyes crinkled exactly the way they did on the cover of his cookbooks, and then he ran his hands through his hair—graying, but still thick—just like Rosie had seen him do so many times on his Food Network show. Except this wasn't TV. This was real life, and Chef Laurent was *here*, in front of her, and he was about to taste her food.

"Rosie Radeke," Chef Martinet announced as Rosie stood at the head of the table, in between them.

"Rosie? This is Rosie?" Chef Laurent said, and he turned and looked at her. Rosie was hyperventilating. This was the end. She was going to keel over right here and die, her face planted in one of her carefully plated dishes.

"Yes," Chef Martinet said, almost suspicious. "This is Rosie."

"I have heard so many wonderful things about you," Chef Laurent said warmly, and he reached out his hand. Oh no, not her hand, her sweaty, sweaty hand. As Rosie shook the hand of one of the world's most famous chefs—the hand that had *invented* new dishes and *revolutionized* classics and created things that Rosie could only begin to dream of—Chef Martinet just looked . . . confused.

Of course she was confused. Why on earth would Chef Laurent have heard of Rosie? Chef Martinet didn't know about the whole Bodie Tal situation. Well, she probably knew that Chef Laurent was Bodie's godson, but she didn't know that Rosie was . . . whatever she was . . . to Bodie Tal.

But now was not the time to worry about Bodie, or what he may or may not have said about her to Chef Laurent. Because Chef Laurent was about to take his first bite of her food. His first bite of a meal that meant *everything* to Rosie and to her future at the École.

It was good. It had to be good.

Rosie couldn't bear to contemplate the alternative.

"Tell us about your meal, Rosie," Chef Laurent said, casually, like he was inviting her to tell a story at a backyard barbecue he was hosting. Like this wasn't about to be the most important ten minutes of her entire life.

"Well. Um . . . Okay." Why did her voice sound so *high*? Did her voice always sound like that? If so, it was annoying. "For this meal, I was really inspired by my family. And the idea of home."

"Where is home, Rosie?" Chef Laurent asked.

Where is home? Good question. Home was where Mom and Cole and Ricky and Reed and Owen were. Home was here, at the École, in her room with Priya and at the lunch table with her friends and hand-in-hand with Henry. Home was in the kitchen, no matter where that kitchen was. Home was all of these things, and these places, and these people, and these feelings. But all she said was "East Liberty, Ohio."

"Ah!" Much to Rosie's surprise, his eyes lit up with delight. "I had a very nice sausage in Ohio once, with Tony. For his show."

Tony. His show. Rosie was pretty sure he was talking about Anthony Bourdain. Which was not helping her sweating.

"Sausage. Well. Um . . . Funny you should mention it. Ha."

What was wrong with her?! Rosie needed to calm down. *Now.* And she needed to stop looking at Chef Martinet's confused frown. Rosie took a deep breath.

"It's funny, I mean, because there's sausage in my first course." Chef Laurent nodded at Rosie like that had been a totally normal segue and not an insane sequence of words. If he hadn't been her favorite chef before this very moment, he certainly was now. "For our first course, we have a play on biscuits and gravy, a classic Southern dish that's also popular in the Midwest."

Chef Laurent picked up his fork and cut into the biscuit. "Here, we have a miniature biscuit topped with a boudin blanc sawmill gravy and a poached quail egg."

Chef Martinet poked at the quail egg until the yolk burst. Probably looking for egg flaws. Rosie decided to just keep talking. If she kept talking, she wouldn't be thinking about what they were eating.

"I first had biscuits and gravy at the restaurant where my mom works."

"Your mother, she is a chef?" Chef Laurent asked. He was going back in for another bite. That had to be a good sign.

"No. She, um, manages the store . . . at the restaurant . . . where she works." No matter how much time Chef Laurent may have spent in Ohio, Rosie was pretty sure he hadn't experienced a Cracker Barrel. But he nodded like a combined restaurant and gift store was nothing out of the ordinary. "I put my own spin on sawmill gravy by using boudin blanc instead of breakfast sausage to incorporate some of the flavors I've discovered living here, and I kept the biscuit small and used a quail egg to keep the portion appropriate for a first course."

"The biscuit is excellent," Chef Laurent said. "Fluffy, light, buttery—it is everything a biscuit should be. I should tell Marcus that this is exactly the kind of appetizer he should serve."

He must have meant Marcus Samuelsson. Rosie felt her hopes start to rise.

"For our next course, we have a burger topped with Gruyère and caramelized onions on a brioche bun." Chef Martinet was making a face at the burger. It was too simple. Rosie knew it. She should have done something more complex. But it was too late now, and she just had to keep talking. "The burger is inspired by my dad, who grilled burgers for our whole neighborhood every Fourth of July. It was the only thing he ever cooked."

Dad. She couldn't believe how much she'd talked about him, with Henry. It was the most she'd talked about him since she could remember. Since he'd passed. She tried not to think about Dad too much, and talked about him *never*, because she was afraid of missing him. Afraid that talking about him would open up something inside her that she wouldn't know how to close again. But talking about him with Henry, and even more than that, making this burger . . . it had made her miss him, yes, but not in a way that hurt. Or not in a way that hurt like it used to.

She hoped Dad would have liked this burger.

No, she *knew* he would have.

Even if he would have raised an eyebrow at her choice of cheese.

American cheese was specifically engineered to melt, Ro, he used to say. Rosie grinned at the memory, remembering how it felt to stand barefoot in the grass in their backyard, hands on her hips, asking her father to use some other kind of cheese as he manned the grill. And maybe American cheese did melt really well. But she'd never been a Kraft Singles kind of girl. And she knew that Dad had loved that about her, too. Just like he'd loved everything about her.

"And then I wanted to use Gruyère for the cheese," Rosie continued, "because that was the first French word I recognized on a menu here in France. When I went out for crêpes, with my friends."

Like Chef Martinet cared what Rosie did with her friends.

But that was part of the story of this burger, too, so Rosie told them. Chef Martinet was busy cutting the burger in half with surgical precision. The meat, at least, seemed to be cooked correctly—the pink of medium rare was what Rosie had wanted.

"Did you make this brioche yourself?" Chef Laurent asked.

"Of course, Chef," Rosie answered. She'd done the dough yesterday so it could rest in the fridge overnight, and had gotten up early today to let it rise for three hours before baking. It had literally been a two-day process, but the nod of approval Chef Laurent gave her made it all worth it.

They had only taken a couple bites of each dish, but Rosie didn't read anything into that. By this point, they must have tasted, what, seventeen three-course meals? It wasn't possible to take more than a bite or two of each. Okay. Time for dessert. This was where Rosie would really prove herself. Hopefully.

"My mom hates to cook," Rosie said. "But every time she's had to go to a potluck, she brings one thing. A trifle she makes, with brownies and pudding and candy and whipped cream." Rosie had plated her dessert into two glasses—she was pretty sure they were champagne coupes—and the two chefs poised their spoons at the rim of the glasses. "This is my version of my mom's trifle. Made with moelleux au chocolat, choco-late mousse, vanilla whipped cream, and chocolate *feuilletine* between each layer."

Rosie loved moelleux au chocolat. The internet seemed to translate it as *molten chocolate cake*, but every moelleux au chocolat Rosie had had in Paris wasn't like a molten chocolate cake at all, but like the richest, fudgiest brownie on the planet. Which made it the perfect base for her trifle. And then the feuilletine, Rosie thought, would give the same crunch as a Kit Kat. The M&M'S were the only thing she'd discarded. There really was no substitute for an M&M.

"My goodness!" Chef Laurent covered his mouth with his hand and giggled. Actually giggled. A fifty-something chef with enough James Beard awards to fill up the whole cafeteria *giggled*. "This dish . . . it makes me feel like a boy again."

Rosie's heart soared. She'd done it. She'd taken home and love and childhood and Mom and Dad and herself and put it all on the plate, and they could taste it. This dessert, especially—it was pure Rosie. And it wasn't that Rosie *couldn't* do fancy things, or complicated things—yes, she was still embarrassed about her fail with the cheesecake for Dish of the Day, but she felt confident that given another opportunity, she could knock that out of the park—but she wanted to bake things that felt more like her. Simple, maybe, but comforting. And so delicious you'd want to lick the plate.

Chef Martinet put her spoon down with such force, it banged on the table and Rosie jumped, startled. Rosie had seen Chef Martinet disappointed before—many times. She'd seen her exasperated. But she had never seen her look so *angry*.

"Where have you *been* all semester?" Chef Martinet asked.

Rosie didn't know what to say. She wasn't even sure what, exactly, Chef Martinet was asking.

"The girl who cooked this meal—that girl has *not* been in my kitchen for the last four months."

Rosie stared at her, dumbfounded. She liked it, then. She must have liked it. Rosie didn't know why, exactly, that was making her so mad, but she liked it.

"Your bread and pastry is excellent," Chef Laurent said. "The biscuit, the brioche, the dessert—all very impressive. I think you can challenge yourself a bit more with your savory elements. I look forward to tasting your next meal in the spring." He held out his hand again, like he had at the beginning of the meal, and as Rosie shook it, she was so proud of herself she felt like the buttons on her chef's coat might pop right off. And she knew Mom would be proud of her—Rosie couldn't wait to call her tonight and tell her all about her meal. And she knew Dad would have been proud of her, too.

Your next meal in the spring. Chef Laurent thought she belonged here. That *of course* she would be here at the end of the year. And he'd be tasting her food once again.

"You still cannot poach an egg precisely," Chef Martinet said. Rosie deflated a little. "The meat was underseasoned and overcooked, and that dessert was . . . fine. I admit: I like your dessert." Was that a *smile*?! Was Chef Martinet *smiling*?! Rosie couldn't have been more shocked if Chef Martinet had bounced out of the room on a pogo stick. "You have much to learn, but I think it will be good for you to learn here."

Rosie beamed. Maybe Chef Martinet hadn't said, *Rosie, you have earned your place here*, in so many words, but Rosie heard it, nevertheless.

"Now that I know you can cook so much better than I'd thought, I will be much harder on you." Chef Martinet sniffed. Harder on her? Rosie couldn't even imagine what that was going to be like.

But she didn't have to imagine.

Because she'd be here, in the kitchen, next semester.

"Rosie Radeke," Chef Laurent said, like he'd just remembered something. "I know why else I know your name, now. I remember your application."

First of all, Rosie couldn't believe that Chef Laurent himself had actually read their applications. And she definitely couldn't believe he remembered hers.

"The way you wrote about cooking," he continued. "It was . . . extraordinary." *Extraordinary?* Rosie had always considered herself to be profoundly ordinary. But she was starting to think that in order to do extraordinary things, you had to believe that *you* were extraordinary, too. "I can taste all of that in your food. You cook with your heart, and that is a very a good thing."

That was exactly what Rosie had done. She had cooked with her heart, her whole heart, every bit of herself.

And it was a *very* good thing.

CHAPTER THIRTY-ONE

Henry

Henry had hoped his last few moments in the kitchen before serving his meal to Chef Laurent would be tranquil. Calm. Maybe even reflective, as he put the finishing touches on his meal. But no, they were none of those things. They were awkward.

It was the alphabet's fault, really. And whoever had decided they were going to serve their meals in alphabetical order. It was that person's fault, too. Because Bodie Tal came right before Henry Yi, and as they worked silently in the prep kitchen upstairs, Henry felt like the two of them were singlehandedly redefining the concept of an awkward silence.

Henry still didn't know if Bodie actually ever had feelings for Rosie, or if it had all been in his head. But if it was all in his head, then why was this silence so awkward? Or was *Henry* making it awkward? Or imagining that it was awkward? Maybe Bodie was standing over there cool as a cucumber, and Henry was projecting awkwardness onto him.

"Henry!"

Rosie burst through the swinging doors of the kitchen, her braid flying behind her like the tail of a kite. He barely had time to put down his spoon before she launched herself into his arms, and she was hugging him, and laughing, and kissing his face all over, and then she let out some kind of weird snorting sound that was maybe crying, but not *sad* crying, because she was so clearly *happy*.

"Eh-hem." Madame Besson coughed delicately from the doorway. "Bodie Tal, you are next."

Rosie and Henry sprang apart, but she grabbed his hand so they were still connected. He snuck a quick look over at her, and she was blushing, but grinning from ear to ear.

"Yup. Right. Yeah," Bodie said, but didn't move toward the doorway. "So, this is a thing." Bodie gestured vaguely at Henry and Rosie.

"Yeah, it's a thing. A new thing." Rosie was blushing maybe even more than she had been before. She was clearly struggling, as if she couldn't figure out what it was she wanted to say. Then she looked down at the dish in Bodie's hands, and her face softened. "Are those cannelés?"

"Yeah. Yeah, they are." With his free arm, Bodie scratched behind his ear—self-consciously, Henry thought. "Cannelés with cinnamon ice cream and salted caramel sauce. Kind of like a profiterole meets a cannelé."

"That sounds really good," Henry said.

"Oh. Uh, thanks." Bodie looked as surprised as Henry felt by what he'd just blurted out. "Thanks, man."

"They do sound really good, Bodie," Rosie said, so gently that Henry felt like it couldn't just be about cannelés.

Definitely wasn't just about cannelés. Henry looked back and forth from Bodie to Rosie, and he thought he saw something soften in Bodie's face, too. Maybe Bodie *had* really liked her. Maybe Rosie had even liked him, too. But Henry found he was no longer jealous of Bodie Tal. Rosie was holding *his* hand, not Bodie's. And that was all that mattered.

"Bodie Tal," Madame Besson said again, from the door. She helped Bodie carry his plates out, and then they were gone.

"So they liked it?" Henry asked.

"Yes," Rosie said, and Henry didn't think he'd ever heard a more triumphant *yes* in his whole life. "They more than liked it. I think. Well, they liked it enough, and that's all that matters. Because I'll be here. Next semester. For sure. So we—"

"Rosie." Madame Besson was back in the kitchen. "You need to leave the kitchen. Now."

"Tell me about it later." Henry squeezed Rosie's hand. She was safe. She'd be here next semester, and Henry was so happy for her, happy for her in a way he didn't know that it was possible to be happy for another person. She rose onto her tiptoes and gave him a quick kiss on the cheek.

"For good luck," she said. "Not that you need it."

"Rosie," Madame Besson warned.

And then Rosie disappeared, too, and Henry was alone in the kitchen. The last meal of the day. Chef Laurent and Chef Martinet had tasted their way through nineteen three-course meals today, and now, it was his turn. Henry tried not to let the weight of that settle on him. Or the weight of Chef Martinet telling him how perfect he'd been all semester, minus his Dish of the Day flops. Or the weight of Dad's expectations. And his need to prove Mom wrong. And the fact that he had to show Chef Martinet that he could cook something that was really *him*.

All semester, Henry had never seriously worried about being asked to leave the École because of his food. He'd been worried about *Mom* making him leave, and he was still worried—some of his grades were hovering close enough to the B mark that waiting to get the grades back from his final exams was going to make Christmas break agonizing—but he'd never worried about Chef Martinet kicking him out. Until now. What if he'd produced another set of bland dishes, like all of his Dishes of the Day, and she decided she'd had enough?

"Henry Yi," Madame Besson said, startling Henry when she appeared in the doorway. "They are ready."

They were ready. So he had to be ready. Madame Besson picked up his appetizer and entrée, and he carried his dessert out of the kitchen and into the cafeteria.

"I have all your cookbooks," Henry blurted out when he first saw Chef Laurent. "I've seen all your shows. I just—I love you, man."

Did I just tell Chef Laurent I love him?!

He could have said, *I respect you.* He could have said, *I admire you.* He could have said, *Sir, you have had a profound impact on my life in the kitchen and on my desire to become a chef.* But instead, Henry had said, *I love you.*

"Henry is one of our most promising students," Chef Martinet said, saving him. "His work all semester has been excellent."

"We have saved the best for last, perhaps?" Chef Laurent said, smiling.

And Henry smiled back. But that was exactly the mentality he had feared most walking into this room. How could he *not* be disappointing, if that's what they were thinking? There was no way he could measure up.

You already made the food, Henry.

Dad. Henry could hear Dad's voice in his head, as clearly as if he had spoken aloud. Wildly, Henry looked up at the ceiling, wondering if he would see a cartoon of Dad's face up there, made out of stars, like when Mufasa sent Simba some encouragement from the beyond in *The Lion King*.

Dad—imaginary Dad—was right. Henry had already made the food. There was nothing else he could do now.

"For our first course, we have Italian beef mandu," Henry said, gesturing to the plate with the two little dumplings and the dipping sauce. Boy, now he really felt like was on *Top Chef*, explaining his menu to a panel of judges. He half expected to look past Chef Laurent to see Tom and Padma. "Mandu is a traditional Korean dumpling. I wanted to make a dish that reflected my Korean heritage and the place I'm from—Chicago."

"Chicago!" Chef Laurent exclaimed. "Excellent food city. You get your deep-dish at Lou Malnati's, I hope?"

"Yes, Chef," Henry said. Obviously. "I incorporated the traditional flavors of an Italian beef sandwich into the meat in the dumpling filling and made a giardiniera dipping sauce. Giardiniera is a Chicago thing—pickled vegetables," he said quickly, answering Chef Martinet's confused expression.

"Giardiniera is good on everything," Chef Laurent said. "And this is no exception." His mandu had disappeared already. "This dumpling is fantastic. Familiar and wholly new at the same time. I understand why even Chef Martinet has praised you," he added, chuckling.

Chef Laurent liked his food. Holy crap. He couldn't believe it. Chef Laurent liked his food. Dad was going to *freak*.

"Very nice." Chef Martinet nodded at him, approvingly.

He could do this. He *was* doing this. Buoyed by confidence, Henry gestured to his entrée.

"Up next," Henry said, "we have a play on steak-frites. Steak-frites was the first French food I ever had, at a restaurant down the block from ours, back home in Chicago. My dad took me there." Henry remembered the first time he'd been there, squeezing into the tiny tables, the rare steak and the crisp fries, the smell of garlic and butter, the sense that food could transport you far from Damen Avenue. "I've put my own spin on it by using a bulgogi marinade and kimchi butter on the steak, and instead of fries, those are deep-fried batons of garlic mashed potatoes."

This was one of his favorite kinds of dishes. From the outside, it looked like a traditional steak-frites, with its melting pat of butter on top, and fries that were thicker than usual but still shaped like fries. But then you started eating, and the flavors were different, and the fries were a totally different texture than what you were expecting.

"Aha!" Chef Laurent said after he bit into his potatoes. "How clever this is!"

"The steak is perfect." Chef Martinet held up a bite on her fork—Henry could see the exact shade of pink he'd hoped for. "The potato batons are inspired. And I like your butter very much."

Henry wondered if Chef Martinet had ever had kimchi before. She went back in for two bites of steak with butter—something she did so rarely—so she must have liked it enough.

Dessert. It was the simplest thing he'd done. Hopefully not too simple.

"My sister, Alice, is a really picky eater," Henry said. "But there's only one food she really loves—the hot fudge at Margie's, this ice cream shop in our neighborhood. So I made this dessert for Alice. Banana ice cream with hot fudge sauce and peanut butter brittle."

"Your heart is not in this, the way it was in your other dishes," Chef Laurent said. "But it is very well executed."

"The ice cream is smooth, the hot fudge is very well balanced, and the crunch of the brittle is a nice touch." Chef Martinet put her spoon down and dabbed her napkin delicately at her mouth. "Well done."

"I think we have indeed saved the best for last," Chef Laurent said, and it took everything Henry had in him not to blurt out *I love you* again.

"You have surprised me today, Henry," Chef Martinet said. "Nearly all of your dishes this semester have been perfect, but these are the first that have shown me who *you* truly are." She smiled. Henry couldn't believe it. It actually took him a minute to register that that was what she was doing. At first, he'd thought her face was itchy, or something. "I look forward to seeing more of you next semester."

"Excellent work." Chef Laurent stood up and extended his hand, and then Henry was *shaking Chef Laurent's hand.* "I believe this was my favorite meal I have ever eaten at the École."

Forget freaking out. Dad was going to have a heart attack when Henry told him what Chef Laurent had just said. Henry would have to make sure Dad was sitting down.

And Mom . . . Henry wondered if she would have rather he'd failed. If she'd been hoping Chef Laurent wouldn't like his food, and that Henry would come home to Chicago ready to apply to all the colleges on Mom's list, abandoning his plan to attend culinary school. He'd like to think she wouldn't actively hope he'd fail, but if he was really honest with himself, he wasn't sure. But he hadn't failed. He'd triumphed.

"Um, Chef Laurent?" Henry said. "Would you mind talking to my mom real quick?"

If Chef Laurent thought this was a weird request, he didn't show it. As Henry pulled his cell phone out of his pocket and dialed, he thought Chef Martinet might have raised an eyebrow, but she didn't say anything.

"Allo?" Chef Laurent said into the phone. "Ah, yes, Madame Yi! This is Chef Laurent. I am here with your son! No, he is not in trouble." Chef Laurent chuckled. *Of course* that was Mom's first thought. "Henry has just served my favorite meal I have ever eaten at the École. I'm sorry? Yes, *favorite*. I said *favorite*," he enunciated carefully. "Your son is exceptionally talented. You must be very proud." Henry couldn't even imagine the stunned silence that must have met that remark. "I believe he has a very exciting career ahead of him. Perhaps a stage at one of my restaurants this summer, no?"

A stage at one of Chef Laurent's restaurants?!? Henry's heart stopped. To work in a professional kitchen, alongside Chef Laurent . . . it was more than Henry had even dared to hope for.

"She wants to talk to you." Chef Laurent was holding out the phone toward Henry. He took it.

"A stage, huh?" Mom asked. Henry was surprised by the softness in her voice. "It sounds like you've done very well, Henry."

"This is what I want, Mom," Henry said, and he couldn't believe how calm he felt. "This is where I belong. In the kitchen."

"Maybe it is," she acquiesced. Henry almost dropped the phone. "It sounds like you're doing incredible things over there. But I just want you to *think* about college, okay? Just tell me you'll think about it. I just . . . I don't want you to feel like you have to grow up right away. Like you have to run into the kitchen." Her voice cracked. "There's no need to rush."

Henry didn't feel like he was rushing. He felt like he was exactly where he was supposed to be, doing exactly what he was supposed to do. And it didn't feel like college was part of that, but now that Mom was actually acknowledging what he wanted instead of haranguing him about his grades, the idea of considering college felt a lot less distasteful.

"Maybe we could tour some schools when you're home from the École this summer? When you're not busy with your stage?" Mom asked. That simple question made it seem like she was cool with him staying for the full school year *and* doing a stage with Chef Laurent. If that was true, Henry would tour a sewer with her if that's what she wanted.

"I'll do some tours with you," Henry said. "If that means I can definitely come back to the École? Even if I got a B in history?"

"I hope you *didn't* get a B. But yes, you can go back next semester. Even with a B. I know how hard you've been working."

Henry had to stop himself from fist-pumping.

"I'm proud of you, Henry," Mom said. Henry felt a lump forming in his throat. "I always have been. And I always will be."

"Is that Henry?" he heard Dad shout joyously from the background.

"Tell Dad I'll call him back," Henry said quickly before he hung up, suddenly cognizant of the fact that Chef Martinet and Chef Laurent were still sitting there, watching him.

"Thank you, Chef Laurent," Henry said as he returned his phone to his pocket.

"My pleasure." Chef Laurent shook his hand one last time. "I will see you in the spring."

Springtime in Paris. Henry couldn't wait.

He walked out of the cafeteria and into the hallway, where he was greeted by a rousing chorus of cheers, and all of his friends bundled up in winter coats.

"They have saved the best for last, I am sure!" Hampus said.

"Did it go all right, then?" Priya asked.

"Of course it did." Marquis held out his fist for a pound, and Henry obliged. "He crushed it."

"Perfect Boy strikes again." Yumi winked.

"It was good, Henry?" Rosie asked. She was holding up his jacket.

"It was good." In fact, everything was good. "Well, I did tell Chef Laurent I loved him. So that wasn't great."

Everyone laughed and teased him, and Henry didn't even mind that they were laughing at him. Because he'd done it. He'd proved to himself and to Mom and to Chef Martinet that this was what he was meant to do. And now he was here, with his friends, and in the middle of them all, there was Rosie.

With her chocolate-brown eyes and her braid resting on one shoulder. Somehow just the same and wholly different from the first time he'd seen her on the plane. So much more than he'd known she could be. Than he'd known anyone could be.

The door to the cafeteria opened behind Henry, swinging square into his shoulder blades. He stumbled forward a few steps, nearly falling on top of Rosie.

"Sorry," Bodie said as he stepped through the door. "Sorry—I didn't know anyone was standing there."

"It's okay." Henry stepped out of the way, next to Rosie, letting Bodie into the hallway.

"What is this?" Bodie looked around him at everyone standing in their coats. "You guys going somewhere? A posse field trip?"

"We're not a posse," Rosie said firmly.

"Sure we are," Yumi said. "Let's get matching jackets for next semester."

"With our nicknames on the back in rhinestones?" Marquis asked sarcastically.

"Mine will be *The Puma*," Hampus said seriously.

"I'm not wearing a bloody rhinestone jacket," Priya said. "If we're getting jackets, let's at least get nice jackets."

"Heard you crushed it, man," Bodie said to Henry as the others discussed jackets. "Denis was really impressed."

Bodie held out his hand, and Henry found himself in the middle of yet another poorly executed bro handshake.

"Denis *did* say my dessert was better than yours, though," Bodie told Rosie.

"No, he didn't." Rosie nearly gasped with surprise.

"You're right." Bodie grinned. "He didn't."

Rosie reached over and shoved him, playfully, and they laughed.

"Have fun, you crazy kids," Bodie said as he turned to walk up the stairs. "Wherever it is you're going."

Henry probably should have asked Bodie to come with them. But he wasn't that evolved *yet*.

It was something he could work on for next semester.

"Where, exactly, are we going?" Henry asked Rosie.

"Put on your jacket, Henry," she murmured. "We're going to the Eiffel Tower."

CHAPTER THIRTY-TWO

Rosie

Rosie held on tight to Henry's hand as the six of them tumbled out of the metro stop and raced toward the Eiffel Tower. They were running—Rosie didn't even know *why* they were running, but she found, for the first time in her life, she actually *could* run. She could run as far and as fast as she wanted to. Or that was what it felt like, anyway. That once she'd started, she could just keep going. Forever. The sidewalks disappeared beneath their feet as they got closer and closer, the golden glowing legs of the tower growing larger and larger as they approached.

"Come on, then!" Priya called. "The queue's just up there."

Rosie looked up from beneath the tower, stunned by the metallic structure climbing above her. It was almost as amazing as the feeling of Henry's hand in hers. And as if he knew exactly what she was thinking—maybe he did—he leaned down and gave her a quick kiss, before everyone saw and started oohing at them.

Honestly. You'd think they'd never seen two people dance around each other for four months and finally decide they should be a couple.

"I'm buying us all tickets to the top," Yumi declared as they joined the ticket line, "because Chef Laurent said my takoyaki were a 'revelation' and I feel like a *baller* right now!"

And they all protested, of course, that Yumi didn't have to buy them all, but she marched up to the counter and slapped down a credit card. And promised that she would defeat them by physical force if necessary, if they attempted to intervene with her purchase. So they let Yumi buy the tickets, and they barely had to wait at all to get in line for the elevator. They rode up to the second floor, switched elevators, and rode up, up, up, all the way to the top.

When Rosie stepped out, she lost her breath. It felt like the air had changed, like they had entered an atmosphere composed of something different. They'd all been chatting and laughing in the elevator, but once the doors opened and they stepped out, everyone hushed. Even Yumi.

Rosie was mesmerized by the lights spread out before her. They seemed to extend infinitely, pinpricks of golden glow as far as the eye could see. Farther. She could see the bright lights lining the banks of the Seine, and the straight lines of lights that marked each bridge, and the hundreds—no, thousands; millions, maybe—of lights in each building, each window. Each one seemed to flicker softly at Rosie, beckoning her to discover, to explore. This was Paris. Light. Promise. Possibility.

She leaned against the railing and closed her eyes for a moment. She felt the prickle of tears, but, for once, she didn't try to stop them, or hold them at bay.

In an old house in Paris . . . she thought. Thanks, Dad. She knew, she knew it down to her core, that she never would have come here if it hadn't been for her father and those early memories of him reading to her about Paris—a place where girls were fearless. And Rosie also knew that she would never have come here if it hadn't been for Mom, who had printed out the application and dropped it on her bed, coaxing Rosie out of her comfort zone, away from everything that was safe and familiar and into something that was *better* than safe and familiar.

Rosie opened her eyes and let herself cry a little as she looked over the city, blown away by this extraordinary place and the people she'd met here. And by the person she'd become.

"There's still so much I haven't seen," she said softly, not even sure who she was talking to.

"*We* haven't seen." Henry stood next to her, looking out over the city, his eyes shining in the darkness, two more spots of light in Paris. "We've got lots to see, Rosie."

And Rosie knew they could never see it all. That Paris would never stop unfurling itself, revealing more and more to discover. But Rosie would see all that she could. With Henry.

She turned away from the city to face him, and now he was looking at her, and they melted into a kiss. This time, it wasn't a quick one in an attempt to avoid a chorus of *Ooo*. This time, it was his hands on her waist and her hands in his hair, and Rosie felt the *rightness* of it all thrum through her like a deep vibration.

Henry was Paris, for her. And she wanted to discover all of him.

"Bloody unbelievable." Priya sighed. Guiltily, Rosie stopped kissing Henry. And she looked over to see Marquis and Yumi disentangling themselves from a similar embrace. "Everyone's snogging in the City of Love and it's so cliché I want to wallop all of you with a baguette. What do we do now, Hampus?" Priya asked. "Are we supposed to fall in love, then?"

"I am gay, Priya," Hampus said gently.

"I'm not seriously propositioning you, Hampus! Honestly." Priya rolled her eyes. "Come give us a hug, then. Forever alone, the two of us."

"Next semester, we will find love," Hampus said, and it sounded like a promise, and Rosie had no doubt they would. But for now, Hampus folded Priya into his enormous arms.

"*I* love you, Priya!" Rosie cried, and let go of Henry's hand so she could hug Priya from behind.

"Well, that's all well and good, but I'm not going to snog *you*," Priya said.

"I love you, too, man," Henry said, and then he was hugging Hampus right next to Rosie, his arms around her, too, while her arms were around Priya.

"This is the lamest thing I've ever seen in my life," Yumi said.

"The group hug is happening, Yumi," Marquis said as he folded himself in next to Henry. "Get on board."

"I'm finding new friends next semester," Yumi said, but Rosie knew she didn't mean it, because she came over and hugged them all, anyway. And if the other tourists thought they were nuts, thought that six teenagers in a group hug was the last thing they ever expected to see at the Eiffel Tower, Rosie couldn't have cared less.

"All right, that's enough, then," Priya said briskly. "If you hug me much longer, I'll start to feel pathetic."

"Come on. Let's go look at the view," Yumi said. "Also, someone in that hug needs to reapply their deodorant."

"Yumi!" Marquis exclaimed.

"It was definitely you, then."

And they bickered as they made their way to the railing, and then Priya stood next to Yumi, and then Rosie next to Priya, and then Henry on her other side, and Hampus next to him, and the six of them looked out over the city.

"'If you are lucky enough to have lived in Paris as a young man,'" Henry said, "'then wherever you go for the rest of your life, it stays with you, for Paris is a moveable feast.'"

A moveable feast. Rosie had heard that before.

"Women can go to Paris, too, Hemingway," Yumi said.

"Hemingway?" Hampus asked.

"It's one of my dad's favorite quotes," Henry explained. "It's from a memoir by Ernest Hemingway."

Rosie loved that idea, of a moveable feast. Of something you could enjoy whenever you wanted, something that went with you no matter where you happened to go. Like home. Home was a place you carried in your heart. And Paris, she knew, would be a place that she carried in her heart, forever. Her own moveable feast. With pastries in pink boxes from Chef Petit's boulangerie and kimchi in Tupperware and crêpes sparkling with sugar. And with Henry. Always, always Henry.

She wouldn't say this out loud, not even if they were alone, because it was just too cheesy to exist anywhere outside of her head, but Henry had been her moveable feast. Literally, sometimes, when he'd bought more pastries than he could carry or ordered more crêpes than he could eat. But mostly, she didn't mean it literally. Because that was the thing about food:

for Rosie—and Henry and Priya and Yumi and Marquis and Hampus and everyone at the École, probably—food was never just food. It wasn't literal. It couldn't be. It was never just the bites you took, or even the tastes that lingered. Food was the people you cooked with, the people you cooked for, the people you ate with, and the people you thought of as you ate. The people who made the meal what it was. The most important thing about cooking wasn't even how everything tasted. The important thing was the way it made you feel.

Eventually, Rosie knew, they'd have to leave the Eiffel Tower and head back to the École before curfew. And in a few days, she'd go home to Ohio for Christmas. And a few months after that, she'd leave the École forever.

But she would never leave Paris. Not really.

Because she knew that it would all stay with her.

Wherever she went.

For the rest of her life.

Acknowledgments

As you probably guessed from this book, I love my bread, and I love my butter, but most of all, I love the following people:

Every first thank-you goes to my incomparable agent, Molly Ker Hawn. Somehow, you magically make everything happen. Kind of like yeast. I have no idea how yeast makes bread rise, and I don't know how you do all the billion things you do, but I am so grateful for you. Thank you for responding to all of my e-mails (even my most neurotic ones) so quickly, for poking the people I'm afraid to poke, and for being my best and fiercest advocate.

Kieran Viola, I gave you a lump of flour and water and you somehow turned it into a beautiful loaf of bread. I can never thank you enough for all of your patience and your mind-bogglingly brilliant insight through these many, many rounds of rewrites. Thank you for always having an eye on what was best for Rosie and Henry and their story, and for loving Hampus as much as I do.

Thank you to Mary Mudd for keeping everything running smoothly, and for somehow not laughing at me when I didn't know what # meant. (If you laughed at me when I wasn't there, I do not blame you.) Thank you to copy editor extraordinaire Jody Corbett for your extraordinary attention to detail, to Bonnie Dain and the design team for making this book so beautiful, and to everyone at Hyperion for all the love and care you're put into this book. Thank you to superstar publicist Amy Goppert for sending me and this book out into the world, and especially for sending me places with Crystal Cestari. #TeamSprinkles.

Thank you to Lily Choi for your thoughtful read and to Jaewon Oh for your incredible notes—I am so grateful for your work in making this book better. Thank you for asking all the right questions about Henry's parents, for pointing out the obvious things I missed, and for saving me from making a terrible bibimbap mistake. Your help has been invaluable.

Thank you to Lauren Emily Whalen for your beta read at a time when I needed it most, for knowing that fancy ice cream can be overrated, and for having the hard conversations about loss and how it never really leaves. Southport Grocery biscuits on me.

Thank you to Kathie Miller for the trifle that inspired Rosie's mom's, except yours was way more delicious than I could ever have described, and to Megan for a friendship that has spanned decades and continents. Thank you to Evie, whose own junior year at SYA inspired some of the École, and to Caitlin, who was remarkably forgiving when I slept through the majority of our Paris trip. Jet lag is very real. Thank you to Becky for helping me survive a terribly awkward Chandeleur party and for being the best thing about Poitiers. Rosie would definitely have approved of our extreme chocolate Easter egg experiment.

Thank you to the members of the Chicago Korean Restaurant club and to San Soo Gab San, Da Rae Jung, Chicago Kalbi, Han Bat, Cho Sun Ok, Ban Po Chung, and Joong Boo for all the fun and delicious times, and to En Hakkore and Parachute for providing inspiration for Henry's family restaurant and his own cooking style. There's always room for japchae. Or baked potato bing bread. One order is never enough.

I was somehow born into a family of tiny appetites, but despite the fact that they never want dessert, I love them anyway. Thanks to my baby sister, for always gossiping with me while I'm cooking, mocking my terrible cookie decorating, and texting me instant feedback on my books. You can't get the meat sweats from cheese pizza. Thank you to Mom, who hates the kitchen, but was always willing to bake Ma's Heart Cakes from *The Little House Cookbook* with me, and who let me take over the Thanksgiving pies at an absurdly early age. To Dad, who thinks salad and a handful of raw almonds is the pinnacle of culinary excellence, but somehow produced a deep-fried, butter-soaked, frosting-loving daughter. The family vacation we took to France when everyone else had a stomach virus and missed out on all the restaurants was when I first really fell in love with food—I can still taste my first steak-frites. So in a way, it's all your fault.

Max, I don't know what else I can say except that you're my favorite person to eat with. Thank you for always encouraging me to try more, whether that's in writing or banchan. I wish I were as brilliant and talented as I you think I am, but I love you so much for thinking it. Also, thank you for not divorcing me because of my terrible knife cuts, particularly my unique approach to "mincing" garlic.

Thank you to the readers, bloggers, librarians, teachers, bookstagrammers, authors, and booksellers (especially the Book Cellar! Hi, friends!) who have tweeted at me, said hi at events, taken beautiful pictures, written wonderful posts, supported me, and most importantly, read my books. (Kolbe, I see you and your preorders, and I appreciate you!) I am so grateful to each and every one of you.

Finally, when I wrote this book, I never imagined Anthony Bourdain would be gone by the time it was published. Thank you, Chef, for showing me the first bite is always an adventure, for taking me to places I may never be able to visit, and for proving that nothing brings people together like a good meal. I promise I'll enjoy the ride.